WHEN THE LIGHT WENT OUT

ALSO BY BRIDGET MORRISSEY

What You Left Me

when

the light

went out

BRIDGET MORRISSEY

sourcebooks
fire

Published by Sourcebooks Fire, an imprint of Sourcebooks
P.O. Box 4410, Naperville, Illinois 60567-4410
(630) 961-3900
sourcebooks.com

Library of Congress Cataloging-in-Publication Data

Names: Morrissey, Bridget, author.
Title: When the light went out / Bridget Morrissey.
Description: Naperville, Illinois : Sourcebooks Fire, [2019] | Summary: Seven
    friends reunite five years after their friend's accidental shooting death
    when a box of letters from her are found.
Identifiers: LCCN 2018057113 | (trade pbk. : alk. paper)
Subjects: | CYAC: Death--Fiction. | Friendship--Fiction. | Memory--Fiction. |
    Letters--Fiction.
Classification: LCC PZ7.1.M675 Wj 2019 | DDC [Fic]--dc23
LC record available at https://lccn.loc.gov/2018057113

Printed and bound in the United States of America.
VP 10 9 8 7 6 5 4 3 2 1

In loving memory of Elizabeth Eileen O'Connor.
(January 1990–January 2018)

It's you I see in the stars.

part one

PLIABLE TRUTHS

1

SOMEBODY SOMEWHERE DECIDED THAT EVERY FIVE YEARS, tragedies must be made extra important again.

For the first *celebration of life*, the Marley Bricket Memorial Committee printed Marley's freshman year photo onto one of those durable foam boards designed for real estate agents to stick in lawns. At every subsequent event, the committee would prop foam Marley up on a tripod next to the food. The dust that coated her told the truth of the dank storage room where they tucked her away for 364 days of rest and irrelevance. Her glossy, level eyes said there was a better place for her to be, but she'd been forced into this. If she could smile through it, so could I.

Each July 11, long before the townspeople wandered out of their houses and over to City Hall for the annual memorial, I woke up drowning in Marley. I let myself drift to the bottom, then waited until I was buoyed up by the profound responsibility of everyone else's belief that I was fine. Mom and Dad and my older sister, Aidy, were always sitting in the kitchen with a full breakfast spread on the table and apprehensive smiles plastered on their faces.

Reading any room became like looking at the weather forecast. Other people wanted me to be solemn but accessible. Sad but not unreachable.

Other people wanted me to be okay.

After Marley died, she showed me how pliable the truth could be. How it molded itself to serve the situation at hand. My family, my classmates, even the people paid to help me cope—they all tried to trick me into thinking her death didn't affect me because it happened before I'd worn a bra or gotten my period. "It's a good thing you were just a kid," they would say sometimes, like my resiliency was all but guaranteed thanks to my age. I would also hear, "She was just a kid," whispered in serious tones, meant to serve as the perfect excuse for any unseemly behavior from me. As these truths bent, so did I, until I was nothing more than a contortionist, squeezing myself into the box of a life Marley left behind.

I spent hours getting ready for each memorial. Washing my hair and letting it air-dry, covering my head in every product I could find until every brown strand glistened like sugar being caramelized. Pale pink blush tinged my cheeks, and a careful sweep of eyeliner widened my tired eyes. Moisturizer slicked my pale skin, scenting me like cotton candy. I smiled at myself in the mirror until my face hurt, then drove with my family over to City Hall, ready to drink from the punch bowl and eat the sweets left over from the Fourth of July.

To the other residents of Cadence, California, Marley was nothing but an event. A flower to drop outside Mr. Bricket's front door. An extra thank-you to give to God once a year. A lesson.

To me, she was everything.

I always showed up to the memorial wearing one of her old baby-doll dresses, waving like a pageant queen at the same collection of faces I saw every year, greeting them with exuberant hellos and tight-squeezing hugs. It was incredible how much they all started to like me when I learned to do this for them. They loved knowing that the dress I wore was Marley's, and how honored I was to have it. I would always say some variation of: "Wow, I know, I can't believe I'm almost as old as Marley was," which would make them pat me on the cheek with a tender hand. Adults were always obsessed with my age, my growth, my transition into *womanhood*. With every passing year, I'd get to change how I phrased my signature line, until finally, year five, I was preparing to say things like, "I can't believe I'm *older* than Marley was," which should've made them sad, but would only make them amazed, I knew. It was as if all of us didn't age in the year that passed. Only me. And that finally growing older than my dead friend was something worth smiling about. For good measure, I'd planned to throw in a "Yes, I do hope Nick Cline turns his life around, you know, to pay respect to Marley. *He's lucky he was just a kid.*"

There were tales of the real Marley right under my tongue, dissolving into my spit until they disappeared. It was a pill I choked down every time I went out in public. These were the unwanted truths. They carried too much weight. I tried once, at the start of the first memorial, to share them, and I was met with nothing more than teary stares and sympathetic pats on the back. The weather called for year-round sunshine in Cadence. So I never made mention of the things I held closest, like the time Marley put melatonin pills in the heart-shaped sugar cookies she baked for her homecoming dance.

"I don't know what this will do, but it seems appropriate," she'd said.

"For what?" I asked.

"Don't worry about it." She kissed my nose, dusting me with flour. When we put the cookies in the oven, we danced while we waited for them to bake. She twirled around me as I waltzed across the kitchen, the two of us pretending to be different people with different lives, trying on accents and attitudes and memories that didn't belong to us.

I didn't make a peep about how we'd crashed the old Cadillac that used to be permanently parked in Ruby's driveway. Marley liked to hide inside it when she didn't feel like being social. I liked to do whatever Marley did. She only let me hang out alone with her when she didn't want to be around anyone else. I never passed up the opportunity. That particular day, she was telling me about how earthworms could survive being sliced in half.

"They just wiggle off in two different directions," she said.

"Gross," I replied, my feet atop the dashboard. I picked at a small scab covering my knee.

"It's kind of amazing, actually." As she spoke, she shifted the car's gears. The engine wasn't running, but the old boat of a car caught the downward slant of the driveway, rolling across the street and into the mailbox on the other side.

Marley and I leapt out of the car without a second thought, sprinting so fast we had to ice our shins afterward. We were back in my yard before anyone in Ruby's house could get outside to see what happened. We pressed our hands into each other's chests to feel our rapid heartbeats. The crash became an unsolved mystery in the Marquez family. Blamed on a ghost, faulty mechanics, or an earthquake, depending on who you asked.

I barely dared to even *think* of all the times Marley and I stood side by side in her mother's closet, combing through racks of old, bedazzled gowns. Relics from her mom's pageant girl days. We'd drape ourselves in satin and sparkles and more tulle than anyone could ever need. We'd rummage through drawers stuffed with feather boas and glitter hats. We'd step into high-heeled shoes that didn't quite fit, stomping around until we found a hard surface. Carpet only dulled the satisfying thunderclap of the heel, and all we wanted was to make noise. Mostly Marley liked to dress me up like her mother would dress her. She'd pinch and poke and prod until my cheeks blushed red and my body shimmered like fish scales in sunlight. She'd ask me questions about the state of the world and hold a hairbrush microphone to my mouth while I made up the most ridiculous answers I could imagine.

These were the only times Marley ever accepted me without any caveats. I wasn't Aidy's annoying little sister in those moments. I wasn't five years younger and more immature.

I was her friend.

Sometimes I even convinced myself I was her favorite.

These memories would only serve to prove that Marley was a complicated person, not a pure, everlasting symbol of our almost-forgotten desert town. As far as Cadence was concerned, those tales died right alongside Marley. Nothing was to get in the way of the girl they'd chosen to represent us—our greatest tragedy and only noteworthy occurrence. *We're a town that cares about things! Look at us! We had a girl die! She was blond and white and pretty! We matter!*

But somebody somewhere decided that every five years, tragedies must be made extra important again.

A giant tent in the center of the City Hall courtyard enveloped the view of the barren land in the distance. The memorial committee swapped the usual punch bowl for mixed drinks, made by an attendant forced to stand behind a folding table all night. Store-bought patriotic cookies were exchanged for an entire spread catered by the local bakery. There was even music, complete with a DJ who said things like, "Rest in peace, Marley. You're our angel now," as he hit the space bar on his laptop. A second, enormous replica of Marley's portrait, done in oil by the high school art teacher, was also on display, soon to be hung in the halls of Cadence High School. And the local news crew came to get their rudimentary story. City Hall Holds Fifth Annual Memorial for Local Girl Killed in Accidental Shooting.

Yes, five years to the day after a single bullet blew up Marley

Bricket's heart, Cadence held the nighttime spectacle of the summer. It was all designed for everyone to smile bigger. Laugh louder. Love her more.

Our sweet Marley.

I glided into the memorial like my pale pink ballet flats had wheels. "I know, I can't believe I'm older than Marley now," I practiced saying, working to strike the precise balance between somber and casual. As if those two should ever be balanced. The delicate daisy fabric of Marley's old dress landed several inches above my knees and held around my rib cage like a tightened noose. Small breaths for short conversations. Each person I passed looked traced over, penciled-in changes to account for the 364 days between events. And still, like me, they wore old clothes that didn't fit and old smiles that didn't light up.

All was as I expected, until I scanned the crowd once more. My heart sprung up to my throat.

A large orb of a light hung above him at the peak of the ridiculous tent we stood under. And though he cowered, hoping body language alone could cloak him, he still carried the mark of a boy you couldn't help but notice. A boy you discussed as soon as he left the room, if only to say, "Who was *that*?"

I once overheard my mom saying, "If Harrison would learn to look people in the eye, he'd be such a pleasant boy," and, "If Aidy would spend more time on her schoolwork, she'd be doing so well in school." She went on like this for most of our friends, except for Nick. Nick Cline was a When. "When that Nicky Cline grows up, he's going to be something."

Success wrote itself into his genetics. Mama's boy smile, jolly upturned nose, bashful cheeks, and cheerful eyes, he'd once looked the part of a young white hero waiting for time to catch up to him. There he stood, eyes no longer cheerful but a face as handsome as ever. He'd never dared attend Marley's memorial before. He was the one person who lived on the flip side of every Marley news piece. CADENCE NATIVE NICHOLAS CLINE, 11, FIRED THE GUN. Underdressed in a white tee and dark jeans, he kept his steady gaze on the dessert display in front of me. He started moving closer.

To me?

To me.

"Hi," I said, before I could stop myself.

The word fireworked in the air, surprising us both.

Nick froze. "Really?" he asked, like *Are you sure you mean me?* and I nodded. His eyes flickered across my face and he said, "Hi," and I said, "Hi," again, because where do you go from there? He scuffed his shoe on the floor. I cleared my throat like *Don't be a fool or I will crack my olive branch in half and bury it under every bit of unresolved anger I have toward you,* and he said, "Thanks," and I said, "You're welcome," because I gave a cruise-control response before realizing how strange it would sound. I tried again with "Yes," in a very definite way, like I, the official spokesperson for the Tragedy of Marley Bricket™ was confirming that it was indeed very nice of me to speak to him.

Then came the lull we both needed: a chance to catch our breath and climb out of the tangled web of random pleasantries we'd stumbled into, and he said "Want to," to which I finished with "Get out of here? No. I'm giving a speech later."

He let out a small laugh, which made things worse, because everyone in Cadence was always saying that Nick Cline could've been something, but he'd done a terrible thing. By accident, of course. But terrible. So terrible. *He's lucky he was just a kid.* I'd spent years committing myself to that truth. Yet there I was blushing, forgetting to boycott him, being neither somber nor casual.

"To talk somewhere quieter," Nick said. "I can barely hear myself think over the music."

"It's not even that loud," I argued.

It was so loud. Everywhere. My heart had a beat that countered the music. The syncopation made for chaos inside and out.

"You want to talk right here?" he asked.

An unwanted truth exploded out from under my careful compression. "I'm not sure I want to talk at all."

After the police found Nick hiding behind the dumpster of an apartment complex nearby, they brought him into the station for questioning. I was already there, bloodstained and exhausted, sitting on a bench with Aidy's arm wrapped around me. Our parents like bookends, terrified of the weight they were expected to support, on either side of us. Nick looked right at me, his eyes even wilder than when he left me lying on the floor of the shed near the scene of the crime. He didn't say a word. That's pretty much how it went the day after that. And the next. And the next. And so on.

Until year five.

I'd long since decided it was his job to open the lines of

communication again. But something about the extra energy in the air made it so I could be both the first to draw and the winner of the showdown. I set down my plate with calculated carelessness, like nothing was all that important to me. "What did you want to say, anyway?" I asked, trying to fold him into someone small and insignificant. Someone whose presence I could discard as soon as our conversation ended.

He dropped his voice a few decibels, almost as a challenge. *You think you can hear over the music? You'll have to get so close to me you breathe in my peppermint gum.* "Marley is everywhere," he said. He reached across the dessert table to grab my hand. "Please, Ollie."

No one called me that anymore. I was Olivia the brave, sixteen and capable. Not Ollie the brat, eleven and scared.

"I really can't talk here," he continued. "I don't want to yell."

Our sweaty palms got stuck in the clasped position. And I didn't mind. I didn't mind. I hated myself for my severe lack of minding. Even more for letting the hand-holding be accompanied by walking. The blare of the music faded to a low thrum as we reached a hollowed alcove between twin cedars behind City Hall.

As if we traveled time in the distance between the building and the trees, we became like the little kids we once were, watching our old neighborhood friends from a place out of their reach. The tent was still in plain view, stark white against the blackened night around us. Soft string lights lined its perimeter, casting a dreamy glow on Aidy and Harrison making small talk with the Campbell twins, Bigs and Teeny.

My dear Ruby stood alone at the edge of the parking lot, legs crossed over one another as she smoked one of her pointless cigarettes. Her eyes were trained on the people walking up. Earlier in the day, I'd told her to stay outside the tent until I arrived. In all the spectacle of the actual event, I'd forgotten to find her. There she was, waiting for me. Like always.

The rest of our old friends would never bother to do that. No surprise. They always noticed my presence; never seemed to notice my absence.

It was a testament to my resilience that I didn't end up as the odd man out in the years after Marley's death. Nick explained to everyone what happened that day. How I resisted. It didn't change the fact that the whole town—and our whole group—wanted it to be me who pulled the trigger. I was an Elmer's Glue addendum to my older sister's friends. An eleven-year-old girl who could never get it right for most of them. Always making things bigger than they were. Whatever I happened to be on any given day, I was always too much of it. Too sensitive. Too tough. Too imaginative. I was the one who had to go everywhere, "because our parents said so," the ultimate indisputable argument to a group of unsupervised kids. Ranked eighth out of eight in terms of importance.

1. Marley (15 years old)
2. Aidy (14 years old)
3. Teeny (13 years old)
4. Bigs (13 years old)

5. Harrison (14 years old)
6. Ruby (12 years old)
7. Nick (11 years old)
8. Me (11 years old)

An order as fixed as Earth's rotation.

I was the youngest, the most emotional, perceived as the general worst to most everyone else in the group. But I was the one who saw what happened that day. The witness, not the villain or the victim. I was the one who got the task of representing the tragedy. Representing our whole group: the kids of Albany Lane.

I was the one who'd spent the last five years carrying Marley everywhere I went.

JULY 11

Five Years Prior

An antique clock in the shape of a birdhouse hung over the couch in Marley's living room. The small, stuffed bird that lived inside burst out every hour on the hour. I'd studied him often over the years, waiting for his grand appearance every time the big hand landed on twelve. He was an odd-looking thing. He had a mottled brown underbelly and a grayish-brown chest. A distinctive black plume jutted out from the crown of his head, with a matching black bib under his beak. His front door would swing open, and he'd slide forward on his perch to chirp out his cheery tune, a brassy smattering of notes that had gone flat over the years.

Marley's bedroom was down the hall from the clock, which meant that most of the time the bird's warbling couldn't be heard when her door was shut. In the dead stillness of the early morning of July 11, the bird sang me awake. Five a.m. on the dot.

I wiggled from my sleeping bag. Marley's room was filled with the restful breaths of the four girls and three boys who were still asleep. I tiptoed over them, careful not to wake anyone. By the time I made it into the living room, the plump, feathered thing was retreating, back to sleep for another fifty-nine minutes. I climbed up onto the couch to press my face against the glass. What happened to the stuffed bird while he sat inside that dark box? Did he listening to the tick of the hand as seconds passed? Did he watch the clock's cogs grind?

My breath fogged up my view. I pulled up my sleep shirt to wipe away the imprint of my nose. Once again I smashed my face against the clock's. The white behind the Roman numerals had yellowed over time. I looked past it, staring into the small hole in the center, my vision blurring until finally, something clicked into focus—the glass eyes of the stuffed bird, amber-rimmed with onyx pupils. I stared at him and he stared back, both of us unflinching.

The ticking clock told me it had been fifteen seconds of this standoff between the bird and me. The air felt like sandpaper on my eyes. Tears formed above my lower lashes. I would have to blink. I was only human.

The bird would win.

As I prepared to surrender, giving myself three more ticks of the clock before I would cave, the bird's eyes moved. He glanced to his left, his glass eyes growing small and worried as he examined a corner of the interior only he could see.

I blinked. I couldn't wait any longer. When I opened my eyes again, I couldn't find the bird inside his house anymore. All I saw was yellowed paper and the blurred hands of the clock, continuing to move.

2

WHENEVER AIDY TALKED ABOUT MARLEY IN PUBLIC, SHE'D say, "On July 11, I lost my best friend." That word always struck me—*lost*—like Marley was nothing more than a misplaced sock or a wallet buried in the bottom of a giant purse. It bothered me, not because it wasn't true, but because it *was*. When Marley died, she didn't leave. She was right there, but not in the way we'd been used to seeing. If only everyone else would have looked a little harder, they'd know she hadn't gone anywhere. But they left her lying dead on the floor of her parents' bedroom. They buried her and painted pictures of her and carried wallet-sized photos in their pockets to prove to people that they knew true grief. They lost sight of her and all she was. It was I who had to pick Marley up and place her on my shoulders, carrying what no one else could.

After Marley died, I was the only one who found her.

So when Nick muttered, "Did you hear what I said?" as if

he was afraid to say *Marley is everywhere* again now that it was quieter, my heart tried to reassure my pulse that it wasn't possible. Nick was like everyone else. He'd lost her too.

I sat shoulder to shoulder with him—this boy whose name I used to scribble on every spare piece of paper I could find—trying to decide which version of Olivia best suited a situation so complicated. I could put on an easy mask and make him feel strange and small for saying something as absurd as *Marley is everywhere.* Or maybe I'd get up and walk away, offended by his very presence.

In trying to decide, my free hand found a stick lying on the ground. I needed something to hold. Nick's skin touching mine burned so bright that it stunned me. For the first time in the five years since she died, what Marley wanted from me wasn't clear.

Nick coughed, clearing his throat to make himself braver, and said, "Earlier, in the tent, did you hear me?"

My ears grew hot. It wasn't right. Marley had let me go five years without him. I'd lived through 1,825 days of Nick shipped off to his alternative school and me stuck pretending for people who didn't understand. A full 43,800 hours of her guiding me through every step of my life as her proxy. I wrote her name in the dirt with my stick and jabbed the pointed end into the ground after drawing the last letter; a period for a girl who never dealt in sort-ofs or maybes.

M-A-R-L-E-Y.

"Why now?" I asked aloud. To him or to her, I didn't know, but I could guess the answer anyway. *Because it's been five years.*

As if that was really any answer at all.

Nick sat slack-jawed, chewing on words that wouldn't come. Another minute to add to the 2,628,000 that had passed between us in silence. He rapped his knuckles a single time against the wood of the tree beside him.

Once for all clear.

When we used to search our houses for interesting findings, someone usually had to stand guard. Make sure our parents weren't going to find us rummaging through their belongings. That someone was first me—the aforementioned youngest and worst—but I failed the job so often that Marley had no choice but to let me pass Nick in seniority rankings. He became our official watchman, and I became investigator number seven: best known for unearthing an old love letter written for Harrison's mom and a stack of vintage *Playboys* in the Campbells' garage. I loved my job, but Nick's—though unwanted by everyone—was most important. The sound of his single knock on the door meant we were safe to discover more secrets. *Once for all clear. Twice for get out of here.*

"I did hear you," I finally said. This was Marley's work. Nick's knock on the wood, an unconscious declaration of safety. "And I know. She never left."

"*You're* the reason I came here," Nick said to me, like there was a reason before that he'd misinterpreted. He craned his head back to see the sky. His face had ridges and grooves smooth enough for water to trickle across in steady rivers. I carved a picture of it into my palm with my fingernail, trying to remember him in his older form, in case this moment was the last we'd ever share.

The day of the accident, I made the choice to carry Marley with me always. I couldn't leave her. Nick made the choice to run away. He became a shadow on my life; our town. The usually right boy who made one very wrong choice and decided to take up residence there permanently. But here he was, drinking in the night, sitting right beside me. Telling me I was why he'd shown up.

So much for making him insignificant.

Words had been what protected me. Say I'm okay and I am. Tell the world I don't care about Nick and I don't. Always bending lower than the truths I didn't want to share. Never losing the game of limbo. But by the dried-up creek behind City Hall, between the dying cedars that leaned into one another like lovers touching foreheads, I couldn't find a single protective syllable with more power than my own mysterious feelings.

Feelings.

Of all the things to take me down.

Nick angled himself toward me. I scooted closer. He moved his hand to make room. My head inched toward his shoulder. Every centimeter was its own revelation. I didn't have to force anything. Didn't have to pretend. Didn't even have to speak. *Maybe the past really doesn't have to matter,* I thought as I laid my head on Nick's collarbone. *If this is all there is, then this is enough.*

I started to tilt my face inward. He started to tilt his down.

Wind rustled through the trees, the exact pitch of Marley's mischievous, musical laugh. It broke our shared peace like a book falling off a shelf. Nick tensed. He looked at me with eyes that said what words couldn't. *That was her.*

I scooted away. The change in distance between us was only inches, but felt suddenly insurmountable. It was all too much.

"I should go back inside," I said.

Nick stood and reached for my hand again, tilting his head toward the glow of the party. I was so used to being able to see right through people. Knowing exactly what truth would keep the real me disguised. Not with Nick. I couldn't make sense of a single thing he did.

"Walk in with me?" he asked.

I couldn't help but grab on to him. It had been so long since I'd gotten myself into real trouble.

Upon seeing Nick and me, Ruby's cigarette fell from her hand. Her fingers flopped around like live wires as she tried to find it. "Been a while," she coughed out to Nick as we came closer. Smoke released in a cloud around her face. "Need a cigarette?" Her focus flickered between the ground and the sight of Nick Cline's hand in mine.

He shook his head no.

"Fair enough," she said.

Ruby's black clothes and winged eyeliner and wine-colored ombré hair and occasional nervous cigarette habit all served to disguise how time treated her appearance like a well-preserved relic. Not much ever changed about Ruby Marquez. Soft brown skin and eyes that never judged, even when they probably should, she was the better half of me—only a year older but light-years wiser—yet still young somehow. It might've been the kindness in her heart. She picked trash up off the street, no matter how much it seemed to multiply. Looked people in the eye when they asked how her day was going. Hugged with a ferocity and intention that shot through you like a lightning bolt. Or maybe it was the unnatural gruff of her voice, a rasp she'd had all her life that was exactly as she was, too old for someone who looked so young. Or maybe it was me that kept her frozen in time. I was the childhood friend she never gave up on, even when the others did their best to stay cordially distant.

She was my only remaining ally in a post-Nick world, and here was that very Nick, holding my hand after five years of avoidance, and still she couldn't be bothered to put limitations on her love for me. She smiled at us and asked, "Headed back in?"

I gave her a nod I knew she'd read as significant.

A few purposeful foot stomps later, she found and extinguished her burning cigarette. "Cool. Let's go in together."

I became a chorus of dancing nerve endings, alive and sparking, coiling around Nick's rough hand and Ruby's warm arm and an invisible Marley slung over my shoulders.

Back under the tent, disheartened glares met me. It was all the adults that patted their own backs every memorial by being kind to me, the girl who ran screaming down Albany Lane the day Marley died. I shattered their expectations by aligning myself with the very trouble they believed they'd exorcised from my life.

They were nothing more than a shapeless entity until my eyes adjusted. I homed in on my parents' horrified expressions. *Is Olivia holding Nick Cline's hand? I told you last week that I had a bad feeling about today,* they said to each other through panicked gasps. The familiar unease of disappointing them came through like a crack in a window.

Across the tent, Aidy was still wrapped up in what was surely a riveting conversation about college life. That was all she ever talked about since coming back to Cadence after her first year. She made big gestures with her hands as Harrison watched her intently. Bigs and Teeny nodded along, their eyes following her every wrist flick. In all my years of Marley guidance, I still couldn't get those Campbell twins to listen to me like they did my big sister. Any conversation we had seemed to be stamped with the words OBLIGATORY KINDNESS DUE TO FAMILIAL RELATION TO SOMEONE WE STILL LIKE AND RESPECT.

My prolonged staring drew Aidy's attention over to me. She tugged on the sleeve of Harrison's light-blue chambray. Aidy was tall, but Harrison Shin had always been a few inches taller. They'd gone through puberty in perfect synchronicity, never straying too far from who they were to each other when Harrison moved to the neighborhood all those years ago, his mother a first-generation Korean American who'd grown up in Cadence herself and his father gone from a short battle with lung cancer. Aidy grew a chest, and Harrison grew muscles. Her voice dropped, and his did too, the two of them flawlessly key-changing from harmonized soprano and tenor to harmonized alto and bass. The neighborhood sweethearts, through and through.

Aidy tugged again on Harrison's sleeve, and he leaned over to kiss her forehead. When she swatted him away, he looked around, holding his chin high to survey for trouble. His focused stare caught the attention of the Campbell twins, who turned their puzzle-piece bodies around to see if they fit together when inverted.

If there was ever a more complementary pair than Aidy and Harrison, it was Bigs and Teeny Campbell, born two minutes and fourteen seconds apart, which seemed to be the longest stretch they ever spent away from each other. Teeny never let us forget that she was actually the larger one at birth. Born first, with dark brown skin, a full head of pitch-black hair, and a wail that made their mother cry tears of joy and their father high-five the nurses. It was such a famous story in the Campbell household, we all knew to chime in with the line, "When Teniyah Campbell spoke, the world listened," right before the part about Bigs arriving so small and silent they didn't let his parents hold him, worried something was terribly wrong. It turned out that he was fine. He knew, even at birth, that his sister was the one meant to do the talking for both of them.

All four of them caught sight of Ruby, Nick, and me in the crowd. The seven of us were the remaining kids of Albany Lane. Oldest versus youngest on either side of the tent, locked in a battle of stares.

If only they could see my upper hand. I had Marley.

I always had Marley.

"We should sit," Ruby said, daring to wave at the older kids. She led us over to a table near the DJ, where sound swallowed all possibility of conversation. A brilliant move on her part. It was a silent crusade we'd embarked upon. Discussion would only shatter the illusion that we'd meant it to be this way all along.

Nick tried to loosen his grip on my palm. I squeezed tighter.

The lights in the tent flickered.

Almost show time.

It's hard to say what purpose Marley's memorial served outside of fund-raising for Cadence's police department. Certainly not that of healing for those most affected by her death. Once a year, Officer Bricket, who had retired, had to get out the shaving razor and make himself presentable enough to walk up on stage and deal with the fact that he was out of town when his daughter was killed with his gun. Ms. DeVeau, formerly Mrs. Bricket, had to make a production out of finding a seat as far from her ex-husband as possible. If ever the two came close to one another, someone swooped in and redistributed the crowd.

The lighting changed under the tent once more, casting the audience into darkness. A spotlight shone on Mayor Bayor walking out onto the makeshift stage. After introducing himself, he held for an abnormal amount of applause. No one found his presence to be the gift he thought it was, or his name as clever, but if ever the response came close enough to satiating him, it was year five. Hands slapped together with the fury of flags caught in a windstorm. *Fix this, Mayor Bayor. Don't let our Olivia be ruined by Marley's murderer. Accidental murderer. But you know what we mean!*

He began his recycled opening statements. "Let us remember our beloved Marley Bricket. The picture of youth lost. A heavenly reminder of all that needs to be made better about the world."

Everything but a person.

I slinked my way up the edge of the tented room and over to the side of the stage. Right beside me, Marley's mom shoved her chair so hard, it flew into the parking lot. "Don't touch me!" she screamed.

"Karen, I'm not. I'm just…" Mr. Bricket said. He tried to hush himself. He thought there was still a way to placate his ex-wife. "Come on now, give me a second here." Because of Nick and me, the watchful eyes had drifted too far from the exes, who, much like unattended children, went straight to the very thing they knew they shouldn't.

"Karen, please," Mr. Bricket pleaded. He made the mistake of taking a step closer to her.

Ms. DeVeau grabbed her discarded chair. She threw it back toward Mr. Bricket. "I don't know what the protocol is here, but this man needs to be taken away!" she yelled.

Out of misguided respect, the news cameras trained themselves on the ground. No one in Cadence wanted to remember what Marley's death actually did to the living.

"Christ, Karen!" Mr. Bricket looked at two police officers—his former coworkers—walking toward him. "No, please don't come over here. I'll leave. I got it. Thank you." He buried his head into his neck and started walking out.

Mayor Bayor recovered with the exact amount of grace you'd expect from a man who'd led a one-sided mayoral campaign with the slogan: *Taxpayer. Sax Player. Vote for Bayor. Your Number One Mayor.* Three generations of Bayors had ruled our forgotten freeway town. There was no skill set required to take the title.

A lucky last name, a Cadence address, and an uncontested race did the trick. Mayor Bayor wiped forehead sweat onto the sleeve of his jacket. The streak left a California-shaped wet mark below his right elbow. He couldn't find his place in his speech, and heaved and *hmm*ed until it seemed easier to surrender. "Let's bring it back to what matters, yeah?" he said to cover. "You all know her. You've grown to love her." A dig I did not miss. "Cadence's very own Olivia Stanton!"

A hand pulled me back from walking up the stairs. Ms. DeVeau. The line of her lipstick went above her actual lips. The miscalculation of it transfixed me. "A young lady should not be up to such unbecoming things," she warned.

As I shrugged off Ms. DeVeau, I caught sight of Marley's empty, foam-board smile by the dessert table. On the other side of the tent, her new, oil-stained smile was propped up on an easel next to the DJ. I smiled back—at first out of habit.

Then out of joy.

All my life I'd been loyal to her, waiting for this moment. Carrying her when she couldn't go anywhere anymore. Honoring her by copying her words, her mannerisms, her bravery, and her poise. Mimicking her ability to spin tall tales with believability and ease. Chasing her grand schemes.

I knew in my heart she was challenging me, but I couldn't quite see how yet.

I needed to take a risk. Make my move.

"Good evening, Cadence," I started, unable to make out the faces in the crowd through the harsh glare of the spotlight.

Instead, I looked up, feeling Marley's scattered, star-teeth smile in the unseen sky above me.

She *was* everywhere.

"Marley never left us," I said into the mic, a bit too close. My last word caught reverb that rang out like a siren. "You're all liars for pretending she did."

The crowd let out a collective gasp. With one sentence, I'd erased years of work at crafting a palatable image for them. I was once again the messy little girl they all tried to forget, no longer masked by well-worded sentiments and Marley's hand-me-downs. I'd worn the truth down until it fractured completely.

I knew my cue. I always did. It was a performance Marley Bricket would want, and it was a performance I gave. Eyes welling, I ran down the center of the tent until I found the parking lot on the other side. To the crowd, I'd regressed.

To Marley, I was exactly who I was supposed to be.

She'd always been an obvious girl with a knack for the sleight of hand. Even when you watched her closely, you still missed what she was trying to do.

Like she'd done every summer when she was alive, she set out game pieces without giving all of the rules. The pageantry of her memorial, the chaos of her parents' behavior, the unexpected arrival of Nick Cline—they were all pieces of the puzzle.

It was time for her final adventure to begin.

July 11
Five Years Prior

"OLLIE, WHAT ARE YOU DOING?" MARLEY ASKED.

"Nothing," I said, hurrying down from the couch cushions. It wasn't clear who was intruding upon who. Marley always went to sleep last and woke up first. Somehow, I'd beaten her to waking.

"I hate that thing," she told me, pointing to the birdhouse clock. "My great-great-grandpa made it. My dad's mom's dad's dad, or something. All I know is that he died way before my dad was even born. I don't think we should have to keep it. But apparently, *we have to*."

"It's pretty weird," I said.

"I guess it's our state bird in there. A real California quail that my great-great-grandpa taxidermied up. Nice, huh?"

She walked to where I stood. The two of us turned to examine the clock, our heads tilting as the thinnest of the three hands ticked down each second.

"That bird's still alive, you know," Marley said. Her lips spread into a sly smile. "Come on. Let's go watch the sun rise." She'd slept in nothing but a giant white T-shirt. It hit her at the shins and hung off her right shoulder, the sleeve so wide and long on the slouching side that it reached down to her wrist. She could pull her arms inside and make a blanket out of it if she wished.

I wanted to be covered like that. Fabric that could wrap around me until I was swaddled like a baby. I didn't like being eleven. The world felt too big. The bird was dead but still alive. I'd seen it for myself. Marley knew it too. How did Marley know everything?

Neither of us had anything on our feet as we walked out her front door and down her driveway. The night before, Aidy and Teeny had braided the girls' hair. Marley's long french braid, blond and delicate, hit her exposed collarbone and snaked down the front of her shirt. It had stayed perfectly maintained, as if she hadn't slept at all. Unlike me, who tossed and turned at night. No one but Nick would ever put their sleeping bag beside mine. Not even Ruby. She was already a light sleeper, and my apparent thrashing didn't help the matter.

My two french braids had more hair outside of the plaits than in. Exactly like I felt. Straggly and messy and always finding a way to climb beyond the parameters I was given.

"I don't want to walk all the way to Cadence Park," Marley announced.

The sky, like a healing bruise, had started to lighten. "Where do you want to go?"

"I need to think." She turned onto Arbor Street. We were

headed toward the abandoned train tracks. It was the only place worth going when walking east.

"What do you need to think about?" I dared to ask. She looked sideways, taking in my every feature. I fixed my posture and lifted my chin, only seeing her through my peripherals. Glancing her way would show her I cared too much about hearing her answer.

"I have to figure something out. I'm doing the Adventure differently this year."

"Really?" I tripped over my own eagerness, stubbing my toe on a crack in the pavement.

A few years back, she'd started something she only ever called the Adventure. It was always a scavenger hunt of sorts, sending the eight of us all over Cadence in pursuit of a goal Marley never fully explained. She said we'd know when we got there. The Adventure happened every year, right around the middle of summer. Marley would show up to Cadence Park with crossword puzzles to do or riddles to solve and she'd say, "It's time."

The actual adventure itself was already different every year. Calling attention to that would only make her less likely to explain when she meant, so I bit my tongue. The only constant there'd ever been was that one thing was supposed to lead to another, and another, on and on until we reached her final destination or goal. Whatever it was. No one ever made it far enough to even know.

Instead, every year it became a game centered on who would be the last to give up altogether.

"I bet it will be great," I decided to say. "It always is." When it came down to it, we all liked having something to do. Summers in

Cadence could be listless, swelling too large with the unexplored possibilities around us.

"You're sucking up. You guys all hate it a little bit."

"Not me," I protested. "Everyone else fights too much. Especially the year you made us break up into teams."

Marley hurled a cold, choking laugh at me. "You literally pulled Aidy's hair that year."

It had been Aidy, Bigs, Nick, and Ruby on Team One and Teeny, Harrison, and me on Team Two. Marley had intentionally broken up all the strongest pairings, and she wouldn't listen to any arguments about the fact that Team One had more people. They found her first clue, a ribbon tied around her mailbox with BUGS HIDE THERE, CHILDREN PLAY THERE, WE HATE IT THERE written on it. They were supposed to leave it for our team to find, and they didn't. They figured out Marley meant the pointless, fake playground ship at Cadence Park. Aidy bragged long and loud about making it past the first round so much faster than us.

I did what I had to do to defend my team.

"Forget I said anything." Marley picked up her pace. "Trust me. The Adventure is going to have a different purpose this year."

A small pebble imprinted onto the bottom of my foot. I didn't dare dust off my arch and remove it. If I broke pace, Marley would leave me behind, and she wouldn't bother to look back.

3

IF SILENCE COULD BE SEEN, THE PARTICULAR QUIET OF THE moments following my speech took the form of an ominous figure in the corner of a dark room, lurking and unknowable. The eerie quiet chased me as I ran away from City Hall and into the surrounding area. Crooked palm trees and flickering streetlamps loomed overhead like the world beneath them was hollow, and I was all that lived inside it.

I moved so easily. Too easily, I realized. Marley wasn't with me. At least not that I could tell. She'd become such a part of me that even in her absence, I felt her like a phantom limb. I never knew where she went when she left. Or if she never left and I sometimes forgot how to hear her. Neither thought gave me much peace. What if I lost her one day too? Became like the rest of them, blissfully unaware of what was right in front of me. I second-guessed myself long enough for Nick to find me riding the current of the ditch alongside the road.

"Ollie! Wait up!" he yelled.

I slowed at the sound of his voice. He sprinted faster.

It felt so good to hear a different kind of worry attach itself to my name. And to hear it come from Nick Cline of all people.

When he caught up, he grabbed me tight. I breathed into his shirt. The fabric stopped the flow of air in my nose. That's how far inside of him I tried to burrow. Because I was not the one who would slip away. If anyone ever bothered to pay attention, I always existed as a gallery of my own heartbreak, displaying Nick Cline on the shelf right below Marley. My hands clutched his shirt so tightly that the fabric nearly ripped.

He didn't hear the story of Marley's death.

He *lived* it.

I knew this, but I'd let myself rework my truth into something that looked nicer for the general public. The reality was, Nick Cline did what Marley asked of him. Just as I did every minute of every day that followed.

We had been two magnets pulled apart by something bigger. All it took was being in the same room again to remember the power between us when united. As children, the Albany kids—aside from Ruby—hated that Nick never voted against me when it came to choosing something to do. That we seemed to understand each other without words.

Together, we'd always been unstoppable.

We started to run, fast and recklessly. Cadence belonged to only us. We grabbed on to it the same way we grabbed hands. For the first time in years, I let myself scream. I decided I could be sixteen and tear the fabric of the night with the power in my lungs. My hysteria could dance out all the way to the open desert framing our town.

High on it all, sprinting so fast the ground seemed to disintegrate, Nick yelled, "Let's go somewhere," ready to run until we didn't recognize a single thing around us. Our feet lifted from the ground, taking us up into the sky as we stepped from cloud to cloud, enveloped by the magnificence of unfiltered starlight. "There's nothing beneath us," he said.

"Nothing," I echoed.

At that, Marley's bony feet kicked into my heels. I screeched to a startling halt, gravity hurling me back to reality. As frustrating as it should've been, I felt nothing but sweet relief. She was back. She was watching. She still cared about what I did. To keep ahead of her nipping steps, my hand broke from Nick's.

Marley chased me toward the cluster of sister houses we'd always known as home. I knew better than to try to run away. I could never leave her adventures behind.

"Follow me," I called out to Nick. Right as my lungs began to burn, our pace evolved into a cautious trot. Then a secretive tiptoe. Three houses from my own, down the driveway, past the locked gate, Marley urged me over her fence and into her backyard.

The aboveground pool in the backyard didn't exist anymore, remembered instead by a sad circle of brown grass traced into the lawn. Without it, the yard somehow looked smaller. Only a measly red shed to keep it from complete despair.

"What are we doing?" Nick whispered.

Inch by inch, I pulled on Mr. Bricket's unlocked sliding door. Nick grabbed my shoulder. "Ollie, hold on."

Marley never issued a challenge without a pledge of allegiance. Even on the day she died, she'd made our group choose between swimming at her house when we weren't supposed to, or sitting inside my house watching movies, like we'd all told our parents we were going to do.

"Sorry," I said to Nick.

Marley always won.

The sliding door rumbled as I pulled it open. Not loud, but not quiet either. I approached the master bedroom, slow-motion skating down the hall to avoid creaks in the floor. The shadow of a seated Mr. Bricket stretched out onto the new hardwood to my right. If I moved as a blur, chances were good he wouldn't notice me. His shadow shape told me he held his head in his hands.

On the tips of my toes, I leapt across the doorway. My heart started beating so hard, it felt like it might break through my sternum. The hallway was dark, but I found my way to Marley's room without an issue, still pattering along on the balls of my feet.

Why now? I asked her. I wasn't ready for the Adventure to begin.

A hand brushed my hair. I gasped, half expecting to find Marley behind me. "Sorry. I can't really see," Nick breathed. I pressed my hand into his chest to collect myself. "Hey," he whispered. "I'm here."

The weight of his nearness threatened to crush me. He said, "I'll keep watch," just in time, pulling Marley's door closed to give me the space I needed.

I exhaled.

Inside Marley's world, I felt safe, as if I'd walked into a memory I could never outgrow. Save for the clothes Ms. DeVeau dropped at my doorstep almost five years prior, Marley's bedroom remained unchanged. The air held faint traces of the sugary sweet perfume she left as a fog over every room she entered. Magazine pages remained collaged over her walls, framing the vanity that carried the keys to crafting her many identities. Her collection of plush pillows, in blushing pinks and soft blues, stayed composed like an editorial spread. Her nightstand had three drawers, the bottom of which was padlocked. This was where the Adventure started.

It's time, isn't it? I asked.

A single gentle knock came from the closed door. *Once for all clear.*

The nightstand's padlock did not cooperate with my tugging. I knew it required a key, but I didn't have one to use. Even with the all clear, time was still precious. I looked around the room for something heavy. My eyes were beginning to adjust, and the night-cloaked furniture took on more color, as if it existed in the space between Kansas and Oz. A shelf above me held trophies from the many pageants Marley entered. Most were golden plastic and left behind thick dust outlines when moved. One had real weight. A "Most Photogenic" award Marley won when she was six. It jingled when I picked it up, and as I turned it over to examine why it was so much heavier than the others, coins and bills fell out of a jagged hole in the top. The figure had no head.

Two knocks on the door. *Twice for get out of here.*

I bashed the "Most Photogenic" award into the padlock, finally making a sound louder than the escalating beat of my heart. Nothing happened.

Two more quick, urgent knocks on the door.

Again, I bashed the trophy into the padlock. Nick opened the door and closed it behind him. "What are you doing?" he gasped. I hammered at the lock with the relic in my hands. The two would not do for each other what I needed. Nick tried to pick me up. "Ollie-we-have-to-go-we-will-try-again-her-dad-is-coming!"

I pounded until I'd hit my own hand more than the lock itself. Loose change flew out of the golden man like confetti. I didn't do things halfway. Giving up was not an option. Every summer I was always the last to surrender, no matter how far I'd fallen behind the others.

Mr. Bricket found us right as the lock gave in to me. He stepped into the doorway of Marley's unlit bedroom. His eyes did not fall onto Nick and me, but the room itself, as if it had newly been revealed to him as existing at all. I grabbed the notebook and folder from the drawer. There was a box still left behind. Before I could reach for it, Nick took a deep breath and grabbed it.

We bolted.

We headed toward the hilly part of Albany Lane. Both of us were fixed on a destination we didn't have to discuss. Every place held a purpose for the Albany kids. Cadence Park had always been our sacred meeting ground: a wide-open space for the eight of us to gather and consider all we'd learned that day. Nick and I found our way to it in bursts—sometimes sprinting, sometimes jogging, sometimes walking so slow that every strike against the pavement echoed. Neither of us spoke.

The park sat in front of a bowl-shaped divot of land that could've been a lake if it were anywhere other than California. Instead, the bowl held nothing but wilted grass and an exposed sewage tunnel frequented by homeless people looking for overnight cover. That night, the bowl sat unoccupied.

"What just happened?" Nick asked as he tossed himself onto his back to recover, panting from the marathon we'd done in silent unison. "We both knew we should go here."

"I know." It didn't need to be spoken, but our unpracticed connection stood to gain a little attention since being reignited. Somehow, the air smelled like the water that never filled the bowl. Salty as the ocean west of us. Expanding into my chest. Filling me up.

I was shaking.

"He let us go," Nick whispered. "I even hit my shoulder against him when we were leaving." He shot upright. "Do you think he followed us?"

"No."

Nick collapsed back down. "I can't believe this."

His eyes, always so focused, found mine. Under his unfaltering stare, I issued myself a challenge: If I could last ten seconds holding his gaze, we would never hurt each other again. Pressure built in the back of my head. He could see. All of it. His face in my heart. Marley in the curve of my slumping back. With a careless flick of the head, I looked to the swing set in the distance.

I'd lasted three seconds.

The rules of my self-appointed challenge weren't clear, I assured myself. It's not like the entire fate of something could be determined by small inconsistencies between plan and execution.

Marley, neglected too long, pressed into my spine until my shoulder blades pinched together like wings connecting. "What is she for you?" I asked Nick.

He considered this with the carefulness I forgot I remembered so well. He tilted his head back and forth, seeming to empty his ears of any thoughts that didn't attend to the question at hand. "At first it was noises, mostly. It was so loud when it happened. It used to be too much for me after that. Fireworks and stuff. But then I decided that...no, I *realized* that when I'd hear a balloon pop or something, it was her. Yelling at me to get it together. I don't know why, but it helped me to think things like that." He paused. "She yelled at me a lot." Pinches of amusement tugged his cheeks into his eyes.

Nick Cline was smiling.

And so was I.

The surprising burst of joy erased itself from his expression, replaced with his patent-pending stoicism. "I really screwed up."

"Don't say it."

"Ollie..."

"Don't."

His eyes wanted to find mine again. Maybe the challenge was a collective ten seconds of looking at him, added up over our entire lifetime. For a fraction of a quarter of a millionth of a second, I

41

stole a look. The years of silence between us wanted to be seen, acknowledged, discussed, dissected.

"Why was I the reason you came tonight?" I asked, desperate to steer the conversation.

"Because you're the only one who'd understand. Or wouldn't think I was making it up, at least. And I was right. You got it before I even explained it. No one else would ever believe that."

I gave myself another eighth of a second's worth of staring.

"Ollie, it's so much stronger now. I was eating cereal last week, and a song started playing on my shuffle. It was the one that was on when—"

He didn't have to finish that sentence. I couldn't remember what specific song was playing, not the name or who sang it or even what it sounded like, but I knew that if I ever heard it again, I'd somehow know every word. And more than that, I'd know it wasn't only a song on shuffle.

"I tried to skip it, but it kept coming on. Every few songs, it would play. Then my phone shut itself off." He paused, probably expecting me to say something about glitches or coincidences. When I didn't flinch, his eyes flashed with recognition. He remembered what it was to have someone truly understand, no matter how implausible something sounded. "Yesterday I was getting a T-shirt off the shelf inside my closet. Same place I always keep my shirts. I accidentally knocked the whole stack down. A wallet size of her school photo was at the bottom of the pile."

He was keeping his examples pretty safe. It was in the way his jaw wouldn't quite relax. How every sentence ended with an uptick, like a comma left hanging without words to follow. She was more to him, but he couldn't push it too far. He didn't want to be adrift.

I decided to throw him a life raft. If he, too, had woken up drowning in Marley that morning, he deserved a better way to float through the remainder of the night. "I take her with me everywhere," I admitted. I'd told that to everyone. Counselors, therapists, my parents, my sister. Ruby. They said they understood. They even said they believed me.

"It's normal to keep someone in your heart after you lose them. To want to honor them," they'd said.

But they didn't *know*. Not like Nick did.

"I know you do," he said. "I do too."

I squeezed my eyes shut. No crying. I couldn't give any more away. How was Marley no longer only mine?

"I knew if I could just talk to you," Nick whispered. "I was so afraid to talk to you."

I stared at the ground. *Don't, don't, don't,* I chanted, willing Nick to stop trying to discuss it. *You cannot break what is already broken. You can only make it harder to reassemble.*

"How'd you know she had that drawer?" he asked.

I looked at Marley's belongings from the drawer, scattered around me like a salt circle. "The Adventure," was all I said. I opened up the notebook I'd carried with me on our run and pushed the pages of it through my fingers like a flipbook. One contained sloppy writing that looked as if it had been scribbled with the wrong hand.

Everything is Something.

I flipped the pages once more. Some sheets were ripped out. Some had imprints of words once written on the pages above. The second-to-last sheet had a single sentence in neat block letters.

THE TOWN HOLDS THE ANSWERS.

It's time to get everyone together, I thought to myself.

Nick read over my shoulder. His breath was warm behind my ear. Steady. "We can't do this alone," he said. It was like he was inside my thoughts.

Do what? I wanted to ask, but it was futile. I knew what he meant. No Marley adventure was ever complete without all the kids of Albany Lane. It surprised me he would come to that conclusion so quickly. And that he would want to see everyone else after we'd all shut him out for five years. I had to remind myself I didn't know him anymore. That he was a wild card who seemed to be reading my mind, and that shouldn't be as comforting as it felt.

"I'll call Ruby," I told him. I should've resisted involving everyone so quickly, but it would've been too easy. I was done with easy. We'd already started. We had to see it through.

Ruby would spread the word to the rest. She would make them come.

Wordlessly, Nick collected the folder, and I the notebook and the box. We didn't look over any of it. It wasn't yet time. Instead, we tucked everything into our old safe spot inside the sewage tunnel, like the old days. Still papering the circumference of its entrance were some of our group's pictures and plans, the details of which had faded long before we returned to remember their existence. Nick touched them anyway, feeling for what he could no longer see.

We walked up the bowl and over to the swings. I made quick work of my call to Ruby. "Tell them it's about Marley and it's urgent," I said. Details would bog everything down.

"I'm on it," she told me, never requiring much context before diving headfirst into action.

Nick and I sat on the plastic seats and generated small swings. Wood chips worked their way into our shoes. Time bent back and forth between the past and the present. He'd always been gone. He never left. I'd always been gone. I never left. Young Ollie wrote our initials somewhere on the legs of the swing. My eyes sought to find the spot, to prove to myself that I always knew we'd be back here. To challenge the other challenge I'd issued myself. We wouldn't hurt each other. We were kids, but we weren't young anymore. If we wanted to build a new world for ourselves atop the wreckage of our past, we could do it.

Couldn't we?

After a long bout of quiet, much longer than most people could sustain, Nick dared to speak. "I've really missed you."

Ruby rolled up over the hill as he finished his sentence. My voice quavered as I announced, "Ruby's here," as if he couldn't already see her. As if that was all that needed to be said.

She tossed her bike onto the ground and filled the space of the third swing in one unbroken sequence. "I'm scared. But I'm excited." Her breath betrayed the ease of her action. "Everyone was talking about your exit after you left."

Running out of the memorial already felt like another life. It was the last action of the Olivia who had been created in the five years since Marley died. When Nick and I sprinted down the streets of Cadence, I'd shed that layer of me like a snake molts.

I still looked the same, but everything was different.

"I'm sure they were glad to have something new to talk about," I said back.

Ruby and Nick both laughed.

The three of us swayed back and forth. No matter how hard I tried, I couldn't unmarry my swing from Nick's. Ruby shot me a look. I squinted as if I didn't know what she meant. She clarified by glancing toward our synchronized swinging. I rolled my eyes, even though I'd noticed it too.

The Campbell twins came next. "I told everyone they had to use their bikes," Ruby said as Bigs and Teeny pedaled up. "I said it was a Marley thing." She smiled to herself. "Can't believe that worked." Even without knowing, she could sense what needed to happen.

When we were kids, Ruby loved to pedal at the back of our flock, blasting music from an iPod in a cup attached to her handlebars, always screaming the lyrics louder than the singer. Between choruses, she'd beg us to ride all the way to the southeastern edge of Cadence, where the train tracks disappeared into weeds and a handmade sign read THE POINT OF NO RETURN. Rumor had it, there was quicksand beyond the sign. We never went far enough to know for sure. Ruby always asked anyway. It was enough for her to get us onto our bikes for a long ride.

When we'd get home after a long day of pedaling around the southeastern border, Aidy would say she thought Marley made the sign herself, "to keep things interesting." I thought it didn't matter who made it, because it *was* interesting, and interesting was the best way to entertain ourselves on hot summer days when we had nothing better to do. The sign was like the longest running adventure of all.

No one but Ruby had touched their bike in five years.

"I can't believe it either," I said to her as we watched the Campbells ride over to us.

The twins, officially Xander and Teniyah Campbell, had their nicknames written on baskets in front of their handlebars, a remnant from when they received the bikes for their tenth birthdays. Immediately after Marley's accident, their parents enrolled them in a private school a few towns over. Their bikes were locked up against a fence along the side of their driveway. It was a reminder for the rest of us: Bigs and Teeny were not gone, but things were not to be as they once were. The rules had changed. No more pedaling across Cadence at all hours.

Bigs looked mighty on his small bike. He was a linebacker of a human, capable of tossing other players like discarded toys. I'd heard he was a great sportsman, but football wasn't what put him in the local newspaper so frequently. He'd taken to making miniatures out of polymer clay. So far, he'd done a replica of Cadence that sat inside City Hall, as well as a rendering of an amusement park, complete with a Ferris wheel that actually spun. Last I read, his skills had earned him a full scholarship to an art school in one of the flyover states.

Teeny maintained the height that defined her, but puberty and years of dance had carved her shape into something impressive and hard-earned. Even the way she rode her bike looked powerful, her back arched as she lifted herself from her seat, braids cascading down her back, blowing with the wind, whipping around her face but never obscuring her view. She didn't bother to pedal. She rode the momentum down the last part of the hill, lifting her hands off the bars because she could. She dismounted from her bike without breaking speed, a flawless leap that looked as impossible as it was. The bike's wheels rolled until the ledge around the wood chips stopped them.

"What's going on?" she asked.

Bigs propped her bike back up and placed his beside it.

"I'll explain once everyone's here," I told them.

The twins climbed the ladder beside the swing, sitting side by side on the edge of the rattling plastic bridge.

Aidy arrived moments later. Harrison trailed behind her. Swap out his usual athletic wear for dressy casual, toss ten inches of height and a good sixty pounds of muscle onto him and it was the same well-worn sight we all knew. Harrison Shin, for as long as he'd lived in Cadence, had always been a clip behind my sister. As the two of them pedaled closer, I realized Harrison was riding *my* bike: a lemon-yellow Schwinn with a bumblebee sticker on the left handlebar.

Our bikes used to be our flags in the sand wherever we went, declaring that area our territory for the day. We were a pile of bikes in someone's driveway, outside someone's store, in the always-empty parking lot of Cadence Park.

But for years, mine and Aidy's had sat behind dozens of boxes in our garage, buried to keep us from the Cadence we once roamed without restriction. For the same reason as the Campbells, Aidy and I were forever banned from using them, as if being able to pedal all over our town was the reason Marley stole her father's gun and died.

The strange thing was, our parents didn't get rid of our old Schwinns. It would be too much to give away something they'd spent a good deal of money on, even if they could get some money back by selling them. The bikes sat among other unusable things we didn't need but would never part with, giving my parents a twisted sense of pride in their punishment.

Aidy had broken a years-long rule to retrieve them.

Before Marley's death, it never would've occurred to our parents to take away the Schwinns. We could use them to run to the store and pick up bread and eggs for them, or to get far away from the house when they wanted space. Taking them away afterward was the only resonating punishment they'd ever given us.

Then again, everything after Marley's death had a way of resonating.

Aidy and Harrison rode over the ledge and onto the wood chips. Harrison treated my bike as a motorcycle, bending his elbows and leaning forward like he might speed off when the light turned green. Aidy stayed at attention. Parks closed at dusk. She didn't want to be breaking rules. Yet here I was—her little sister, sticking her hand in the cookie jar again.

I cleared my throat. "We found a few Marley things."

"Where? Why? How?" Harrison asked for Aidy, who'd already trained her eyes on the legs of the swing set, zoned out on the HARRISON + AIDY FOREVER she'd scribbled there so many years ago.

The first thing Marley ever taught me was that it never mattered what I said, but how I said it. In a solemn tone, I reminded the group, "It's been five years," using the same reasoning I'd sighed over only hours before.

Matters concerning Marley needed no real preface anyway. That's why they all came, on bikes no less, leaving the memorial in the chaos of my speech's aftermath. Even after five years, the promise of knowing more about Marley Bricket was always enough to do anything.

"We didn't want to keep going alone," Nick added.

"Now you two don't want to go do things on your own? That's funny," Teeny said. "Guess someone has to die for you to learn your lesson."

A tiny bubble of old Ollie popped up inside me. My fists tightened and my stance widened. I bit down on my cheek until the urge to overreact passed. In stony silence, I filtered through many reactions until I settled upon the one that never failed me. "I'm sorry," I said to her.

She didn't respond, which was as good a stalemate as any.

"There's a notebook, a folder, and a box," Nick told the group. Everyone, except for Ruby, stared at him like he was an even greater mystery than what we'd found. EXILED GROUP MEMBER REAPPEARS AFTER FIVE-YEAR ABSENCE.

Aidy folded her arms. "How did you get all of this stuff?"

The tides stood to turn with every sentence. Keeping the group united hinged upon revealing just enough to keep everyone interested without upsetting anyone's moral compass. Aidy would leave if she knew I broke into Marley's house. The rest of the older kids would do whatever Aidy did.

I pulled out one of my stronger tricks: a related statement that could be interpreted as a direct answer. "Everything's in the sewage tunnel," I said. Like magic, they all followed me without further comment toward the how of it all.

"Remember this place?" Harrison asked Aidy as we crept downhill. He seemed to be unable to keep the quiet she wished of him. "I kissed you here for the first time."

"On a dare," she countered, sounding more annoyed than sentimental. "I believe you also had to kiss Teeny. And the bottom of your own foot?"

Ruby picked up Marley's box, surely thinking of our own—filled with all the rejected trinkets we used to collect when the big kids left the room. She rubbed the lid of the new Marley box. It was plain, unpainted wood. No special puffy paint swirls and doodles on it like the one we'd made.

I took the red notebook and showed the two pages to Bigs and Teeny. Then I opened the folder. In it were six sheets of computer paper, each with a name in the header. A paper for me was on the very top of the pile.

OLLIE STANTON

Welcome to the Adventure. Eyes on your own paper, please.

I started this in my notebook, but it's much easier to type. Words find me faster this way. Plus, I can erase the sentences I don't want. Isn't that powerful? To erase things and have them disappear for good.

Congratulations on getting here. I trust you will do what I wish, and I trust you will find this at the right time. You have a knack for getting the goods. Consider this your belated props. Well, maybe. If you're here, you probably haven't gotten to everything else yet.

Come on, Ollie. Make the right choices. Now's not the time to mess things up.

Remember, to pay attention to me is to pay attention to details. Everything is Something.

So go on and make something memorable.

What are you waiting for?

Love always,

Marley

JULY 11

Five Years Prior

WHEN WE ARRIVED AT ARBOR STREET'S DEAD END, DESERT and weeds waiting beyond the road, Marley climbed onto the aluminum barrier intended to stop cars from driving into the desert. It was a precarious balance, I learned. And it hurt. Much more than the pebble in my foot had. The top of the barrier had a fine edge. Staying put required looping my legs into the space between the two rails, then leaning backward to counteract the forward pull. The threat of falling was constant. The only way to hold still was to let the railing dig into the back of my thighs.

Farther to the left of where we sat, the abandoned train tracks were a little nicer. The tracks here had been swallowed up by brambles and covered in sand, only peeking out in sad fragments. Farther to the right of us was the POINT OF NO RETURN sign. We were in the undesirable middle ground.

"Cadence is different, isn't it?" Marley asked. She looked comfortable atop the barrier. Balanced and carefree.

I thought again of the bird. "Yeah," I said.

Marley laughed like I was so obvious. Like I'd ever do anything but agree with her. "Maybe *we're* different. Not this place." She cupped the railing with her palms. "I wouldn't know. I've never been anywhere else."

"Neither have I." I took a deep breath. I wasn't a follower. I had my own thoughts, and I'd prove it. "I think it's both. This place is special, and so are we. Me and you."

"Oh, Ollie." She patted my head. I don't know how. My hands were glued to the rail. If I let go, I'd fall. "You'll learn."

"I'll learn what?"

She shook off the thought. "It's so ugly here," she said, even though the sky was turning pinkish-orange, and I was positive neither of us had ever witnessed anything more magnificent than the lazy rise of that morning's sun.

I tried again to be brave. Challenge her. "I think it's beautiful."

"No, you don't," she informed me. "You're what? Nine? You don't know any better. Wait 'til you're fifteen like I am. You'll get it."

She knew full well that I was eleven—she'd given me a very nice handmade birthday card earlier in the year—so I said nothing about her error. Because she was the oldest, she always hurled my youth against me when she didn't have a better point to make. "You don't know any better either. You just said so."

"I was exaggerating. My mom's driven me to other states for

pageants. Nevada and Arizona, mostly. Utah once. You've barely left Cadence."

Of all the things she'd said to me, this hurt the most. How could I leave Cadence? I only had a bicycle. The next town was more than ten miles away. Leaving Cadence wasn't up to me.

I wouldn't want to, anyhow. Things were different here. I had no proof other than what my heart knew to be true. I'd really meant it when I said that Cadence was special, and so were we. Marley also saw the life inside that long-dead bird. That couldn't be how it was in every town.

"Plus," Marley continued, paying me no mind, "I can see what isn't even here. If I close my eyes, I can see the whole world at once."

"I don't have to close my eyes to do that," I told her. If I wanted, I could make the mountains shrink into nothing. I could pull the tide of the Pacific Ocean in until it washed up to where we sat, hundreds of miles from shore. I could make its frothy waves clean our dirty feet. I could rescue that California quail from his perch and set him free, watching him fly until he disappeared into the clouds. My imagination always lifted me up above reality and into a better, brighter world.

"I know," Marley said, and nothing more.

The sun woke up right in front of our eyes. I closed mine to feel the warmth of the morning glow press against my lids.

That's when Marley pushed me.

If my hands weren't death-gripping the rail and my feet weren't hooked below me, I would have fallen onto my head. Instead, I hung upside down like a bat.

Marley's laugh was casual. "I thought you didn't have to close your eyes," she said, teasing.

I started to cry. I didn't mean to be so scared, but the fall had jolted my heart. I couldn't find my breath.

Marley hopped down. She put her hands beneath my armpits and lowered me to the ground, then picked me up until I stood face-to-face with her. When she saw my tears, she softened. "Oh, Ollie. I knew you wouldn't hit the ground. You were holding the rail so tight, your knuckles were purple." She hugged me until I was almost hidden inside her arms. "I'm sorry."

"It's okay," I lied.

4

"WHAT DOES YOURS SAY?" AND "I'M NOT SUPPOSED TO SHOW anyone," and "This is so much to take," and "Let me read it," and "What's going on?" and "I don't want to share mine yet," and "Let's show each other. It's not like Marley is here to know," and "What was that you said?"

Bigs cleared his throat to stop a fight from breaking out. The entire group fell quiet at the promise of words from his oft-sealed lips. "We should do whatever the letters say. It's from *Marley*." He said her name the way the rest of Cadence feared, like tears threatened to burst out. Or worse, a real memory might slip through his clenched teeth. I hadn't heard it said like that since her funeral, the last day I remember that kind of sentimentality being not only acceptable, but welcomed.

Our seven sets of eyes found one another, like dots connecting, tracing the outline of Marley's silhouette between us.

Teeny sighed at her brother. "Can everyone tell me if theirs also says this is the Adventure, though? I need to know I'm not the only one."

Everyone nodded.

"My letter also says for me to tell you all that the tunnel goes farther than we know," Harrison said.

Our attention moved to the tunnel. Going inside meant no going back. As if there was a choice. Every millisecond in Marley's absence had been leading up to this. Year five. Cadence Park. The Albany kids huddled together in the bottom of the bowl. I never pictured it as such, but living it, I knew it couldn't happen any other way. It was year five, after all. Everything had to be bigger.

In a group of our size, discussion did not last long before someone sprung to action. Two choices remained: follow or defy. Precious Ruby flew into the depths of the opaque hole. No doubt farther than we'd ever gone. One of the only warnings we'd ever received in the days before Marley died came from Officer Bricket about that very tunnel.

"It's filthy and filled with rodents and shit. Actual shit," he'd said. "If you go too far, you're stuck in a maze. Don't screw around in there, you hear me?"

Marley snickered at him.

"Marls, look me in the eye and say you aren't going to go in there."

"I won't, Dad."

"Look at me and promise!"

She ran across the room and pressed her nose to his, grabbing his cheeks with her flour-covered hands. We were in the middle of baking her melatonin cookies. "I promise!"

Of course, we'd already been in the tunnel long before that moment—years before—finding most of what he said to be true. It was dank with a smell that lived up to its fame. To prove my loyalty, I got tasked with the investigation. On my hands and knees, I crawled through the hole. Several feet in, it dropped off into a walkway. I did not step down into it, only confirmed its existence. The edge of the entrance served us fine, although I'd always figured Marley hid her best scavenger hunt clues deep inside there, knowing we wouldn't enter again.

Officer Bricket's warning came after a dead body was found somewhere deep in the workings of the tunnel system. A homeless man had stumbled upon him and ran out of the hole screaming. The dead man's eyes were in his outstretched hands. They said he looked like he was reaching for something above him. Nothing of a nature that gruesomely strange had happened before or since, and they ruled it as an accidental death by drug consumption.

There were no memorials for that stiff-armed corpse with his hands to the gods. No paintings. Not even a wooden cross hammered into the dry dirt of the bowl.

The image of his death flickered into my head, and I had to crawl into the hole after Ruby. To have her back, quite literally. Right on my heels, Nick followed. The flashlight from his phone sputtered out faint assistance. I yelled Ruby's name. She replied with a gasp. Soft, but noticeable. Her own phone's light gave faint promise of the upcoming ledge and walkway. I switched from bear-crawl to scoot, letting my feet find the drop-off first. It came and still I thumped down. Nick remembered me enough to know not to ask if I was okay. Instead, he came up behind me and brushed his hand against my back to clean off the dirt. We came to where Ruby stood. The cell phone's brightness carved new shadows into her full cheeks. Her eyes filled with tears as she read the words spray-painted low on the wall.

You didn't love me like I asked of you.

Still I love you back.

Beneath it, in a little hole chinked into the concrete to avoid the trickle of water running through the walkway, was the head of the trophy I'd used in Marley's bedroom and a wallet-sized copy of her freshman year school photo.

Nick gasped at the sight of the picture. His body trembled beside mine.

"It's really happening," Ruby whispered.

From farther up the walkway came an unexpected sound. It echoed down to where we stood. Startled, my elbow jammed into Nick, causing his phone to fly out of his grasp and land facedown. Ruby pulled her hands to her chest as a protective instinct. With both of their phone's lights swallowed, the blackness gasped out more mysterious noises.

"We can come back tomorrow." Nick found his phone as he spoke. Only a pat or two before it returned to the safety of his grasp. We ran down the walkway, which seemed infinite on the return.

When we collided into the rest of the group inside the tunnels, I let out a small scream. "The noises. Was that you guys?" I asked once I realized. Fear made me sound petulant, and the indignant tears I hadn't dealt with in forever resurfaced with a vengeance.

Harrison scoffed. "What do you mean?"

Nick pushed through them and kept moving toward the exit. "Let's go back outside anyway."

"C'mon," Ruby said with a head nod. "We'll explain out there."

"This is so ridiculous," Harrison said under his breath. "I can't believe we're doing this."

"Stop muttering," Aidy warned him. I awarded ten mental points to my sister for finding her backbone and shoving it in Harrison's face as often as she could, though it struck me that the two made a bitter pair. Where a deep and full history elevated some relationships, it seemed to be souring theirs.

Back out quicker than we climbed in, I learned Teeny had not joined us. She sat in the lowest part of the bowl with a paper in her hands. "Hey!" I screamed. "You're not supposed to be reading that!" I ran and snatched the paper—Aidy's paper—from her hands.

"Don't act like you wouldn't do the same thing if you got the chance," she said.

"You're right," I admitted, tamping down my unwarranted frustration. Teeny's respect was always best earned through honesty. I hoped she could see how hard I worked to be better. I returned the paper to Aidy.

"How much did you read?" Aidy asked Teeny.

"The first few lines."

I would never leave my paper behind. I'd folded it down to a tiny square and tucked it into my bra, where I knew it would not be compromised. In remembering my letter's actual contents, it really was not so private as to be worthy of hiding. If Teeny had read mine, there would be nothing to be that angry about.

Everything is Something, Marley whispered in my mind, reciting the last line from my letter. So much had happened in the last few hours. I felt the delirium of staying up all night and it was barely ten o'clock. "Let's go through all of this tomorrow," I said.

"Is this really happening?" Teeny asked no one in particular. "This can't be happening."

Nearly everyone but me had asked that question. We had letters. A notebook. A box. Messages spray-painted on concrete walls.

What more proof did they need?

Yes, it was happening.

They'd lost more than Marley in the years since she died. They'd lost their sense of adventure too. Of course they had.

She was our adventure.

"All this time," Harrison whispered. "We never looked."

Aidy crossed her arms. "We cannot be upset with ourselves for not looking for letters we had no idea Marley wrote. It's not like she ever mentioned when her little scavenger hunts were going to start. We didn't know she'd had one already planned before the accident."

"We could've tried," Harrison replied. "The Adventure always started sometime in July. We knew that much, at least. It makes sense there would be stuff left. It's not like she let any of us in on how she planned each one."

"What were we going to do? Leave her funeral and go hang out in the sewers?" Aidy stalked off, only a few feet. She wasn't done. Whenever she got emotional, she became unbearably logical. "We were all very young. We had no idea what we were doing most of the time. Continuing to behave the same way we did before we lost Marley wouldn't have helped any of us," she said. Two tears rolled down her cheeks. "I won't put up with any pitying behavior from any of you."

"You're right," Harrison countered, his voice soft. "But we're older now. This is different."

"It's scary, is what it is," Teeny said. "This kind of stuff gives me goose bumps. Letters from someone who died. It makes it seem..."

"I know," Harrison agreed, cutting her off. "I used to think about the Adventure all the time. If she'd planned another one before she..."

No one would finish a single thought.

"I always kind of wished there was more from her we never found, but I don't know if I mean that now that we're here." He turned to Aidy. "Didn't I say that to you before? That I wanted to find stuff from her?"

Aidy shrugged. "Maybe. I don't know."

"Let's look at the rest of it tomorrow," I suggested again.

"We should definitely look at the rest of it tomorrow," Aidy echoed. "This is a lot to handle in one night. On the anniversary, no less."

Half of the group looked at me. Half looked at Aidy. I swallowed back words. It was *my* idea to wait until tomorrow.

"Who should keep the box while we wait?" Nick's hand brushed against the small of my back.

"Ruby?" Bigs suggested.

The group nodded. Aidy was the best choice, but since I was her sister, and most of them didn't trust me farther than they could throw me, Ruby made the most sense. She wouldn't look inside until we all agreed someone should. The one thing we'd learned from the great Team One and Team Two debacle was that we had to share the things meant to be shared and keep what we got from them to ourselves.

We walked up the bowl and over to the playground, past the idling swings and swaying bridge. One by one, everyone mounted their bikes and waited, until only Harrison, Nick, and I were without.

"You'll have to walk," Aidy told Harrison. He shot a look to me.

What could I do? The bike was mine.

It was smaller than I remembered, even with the seat hiked up as high as possible to accommodate Harrison's six-foot frame. Climbing onto it, I felt like Little Ollie yet again—young and small and unsure of my purpose in our group.

That wasn't who I was. But I'd shed the skin of the me I'd been for five years. It was time to become the newest version of myself. The one Marley had prepared me to be. I didn't know if I was ready yet, but I had to try.

I walked my bike to the spot that once belonged to Marley herself. She always pedaled at the tip of our *V*, her soft blond hair spiraling through the wind, thrashing across her rosy cheeks. "Close your eyes!" she'd scream as we rode across an intersection.

Now, it was me.

To my surprise, everyone else fell into their old positions, leaving me up front. Teeny was on my left. Aidy was on my right. Bigs rode behind his sister, and Ruby rode at the back, the box in her basket. The *V* was misshapen without Harrison and Nick.

"I'll just run," Harrison said.

"Sounds good," Aidy told him.

Nick didn't even bother to come close to the rest of us, instead heading off with a small bob of the head.

The formation wasn't exactly right, but it would have to do. My legs burned the instant I began pedaling. I pushed on, turning onto Albany, pedaling up the hill and over. As delicate wind pressed into my face, a tear rolled down my cheek. The kids of Albany Lane, united again.

"Close your eyes!" I screamed, my voice sounding like Marley's.

And they did.

JULY 11

Five Years Prior

EVERYONE WAS STILL ASLEEP BY THE TIME MARLEY AND I made it back to her house. Even her mom. Her dad had gone out of town for a week, something we weren't allowed to ask any questions about. When Officer Bricket was home, his fights with Mrs. Bricket underscored every sleepover, an erratic heartbeat beneath our less-than-innocent games of Truth or Dare and Never Have I Ever.

There was a hose in Marley's backyard, meant for rinsing feet after pool time. Her dad was so strict about it I once took off for home in the middle of his reprimands, barefoot and belittled. Marley picked my foot up as I rested my hand on the side of her house. The hose blasted icy cold water onto my sole. "Don't scream," Marley warned. I bit my lip to keep from yelping out. "It's clean now," she announced. I stepped my left foot onto the towel beside the hose while Marley washed my right.

When we repeated the process on her, she smiled. "I love cold water," she told me. "Wakes you up like nothing else."

We went into her house through the back sliding door that was always unlocked. "Let's pretend to sleep for at least another hour," she whispered as we crept down the hallway, past her parents' bedroom, into her own.

I wondered why it was necessary but decided not to ask. I was always wondering with her and rarely asking. I hoped one day that would change. Or maybe the questions would start to answer themselves.

The air inside her bedroom had grown thick from the warmth of bodies. The night before, we'd draped colorful sheets from bookshelf to bookshelf, tenting her bedroom. We'd hung string lights in random patterns across the cotton ceiling and rolled out our sleeping bags underneath. There wasn't enough room on the floor for all of us, so Marley slept in her bed. Only Aidy was allowed to share it with her.

It was getting harder to have sleepovers. Marley's dad thought it was inappropriate for the boys to stay over. With him out of town, we knew it was one of our last chances to have one before the rest of our parents started to feel the same way as Officer Bricket.

We got away with a lot by having such a wide age gap between the eight of us. Most of our parents figured the younger kids kept the older kids from having too much fun, like we were built-in narcs and they were somehow authority figures. In reality, it was just easier on our parents for us to move as such a large unit.

Strength in numbers among us meant less for them to keep track of during summertime.

My spot on the floor was right beside Nick, as always. I took a wide step over Bigs and another over Teeny, scooted around Ruby, and settled back in. I was careful not to wake Nick, who had his arm extended over my open spot as if he were saving it for me. I picked his arm up at the elbow and moved it enough to shimmy into my sleeping bag.

I lay on my back to examine the man-made constellations overhead. They didn't shine as bright in the early morning light, but still my finger traced across the glowing bulbs, drawing my own versions of the Big Dipper and the Little Dipper and Orion's Belt. The only ones I knew.

Marley cleared her throat. My cue to close my eyes and pretend to sleep.

I must have been very convincing, because after a while, Marley opened one of her nightstand drawers and took out her journal. I watched her through slitted eyes as she wrote and wrote, her hand scribbling faster than my thoughts could even form.

5

Sleep found and held me into early afternoon, when I awoke to Aidy perched on the edge of my bed, using the absolute bare minimum space required to hold her up without falling. "Mom and Dad want to talk to us," she said.

It was inevitable. A weak-brewed coffee of a speech poured hot down our throats, as it usually was on the day following trouble. The ritual of receiving our punishment actually excited me. It had been so long, I was interested to see how different it would be.

I'd forgotten to charge my cell phone overnight. The dead device would likely be the cost of my bail, so I dug through the pile of belongings closest to my bed and grabbed it as my offering. Piles of clothes, papers, empty bowls, cups, and other random things populated my bedroom floor. My mom always got on my case about cleaning. I liked the mess. Occasionally,

I'd shift it around into more visually appealing piles for her, but ridding myself of it entirely meant doing hard work for a temporary outcome. The mess would eventually return. Best to leave it be.

Aidy tried her best to sidestep everything, tripping over herself to follow me out of my room and down the hallway into Dad's office. Always his office. To communicate that this was *official business.*

Dad sat in his old leather chair, like old times, leaning into the rickety back that was sure to someday break under such undue stress. He had his hands folded across his lap and an unreadable expression on his face. Mom stood beside him with the pads of her fingers pressed into the desk. They exchanged a look as we walked in, Mom twisting her wedding ring around her finger while Dad raised his eyebrows.

"Hi, girls," he started. "I'd say morning, but you slept right through that."

I faked a laugh to ease the tension. "I was pretty tired."

"We'll make this short," Dad assured.

"I'm not going to fall asleep during this, I promise."

He didn't seem to get the joke. He had a look of concentration I recognized in myself sometimes, like when I hadn't studied for a test but needed to come up with an answer to something I swear I'd never been taught.

"Your dad and I spent a lot of time talking about the best course of action for today," Mom interjected. "Olivia, your behavior at the memorial was inexcusable." As she went over the details, I handed over my cell phone in lieu of a response. She took it but did not accept it as full payment. "Ms. DeVeau fell apart after you went running out. I know you're young, but you need to try and understand what that woman's been through."

I understood pretty perfectly.

"As soon as we're done here, you'll get dressed and walk over to her house and apologize," she said.

Now I was listening. "I don't even know where she lives," I lied. Right after the divorce, Ms. DeVeau bought the house next to the railroad tracks on Arbor Street. She had the exterior painted a shade of soft orange she wanted to read as authentic California. She also took up gardening. Her excessive yard work didn't impress anyone in our drought-ridden town, but she had a lifetime my-child-died-and-is-now-Cadence's-legacy pass and got to do whatever she so pleased.

"You won't be alone. Aidy will be going with you," Mom added.

"What?" Aidy and I both asked in unison. Aidy held a near-exempt status herself. The punishments she received never extended beyond stern words and restricted computer use, and now that she was a collegiate nineteen-year-old, I assumed her days of being reprimanded were nothing but a memory.

"For one, you left the memorial with the keys to our car in your purse. Not only that, but on our unexpected little walk home, Dad and I saw you and Harrison pedaling down Albany on bikes we told you were never to be used again."

"You can't be serious. I was fourteen when you said that!" Aidy protested.

"Aidy, you are in no place to argue with us," Mom said. The edge in her voice meant there was a story, some trouble I hadn't yet heard about. "The both of you made us look like bad parents in front of the entire town."

"Mom, I didn't do anything! I went and found Olivia, and I'm somehow in trouble for that?" Aidy could not hide her disdain for me. We'd been told for years that when we got older, we'd not only love each other, but *like* each other. Judging by the angry glare she hurled at me, we were still waiting to find that bridge, much less cross it.

Part of me hoped she'd keep digging her own little hole with Mom and Dad. It used to be me that made it worse. I could never stop myself from yelling about how unfair they were being. I was always the first to cry, which they assumed made me the guiltiest. Aidy once broke four bowls at once—I had no idea how—and *I* had to mow people's lawns for two weeks to pay for the damage, all because when asked if I did it, I protested so much that snot bubbles formed in my nose from crying.

Carrying Marley made me calmer. There were more important things to fight about. More effective ways to handle myself. At the same time, Aidy was right. She hadn't done anything wrong. Not on purpose, at least.

"She was helping me with something," I said in her defense.

Mom let out a sigh so long and steady, it almost sounded melodic. She rolled her head toward my dad, her neck muscles straining.

Dad took this as his cue to reenter the conversation. "Girls, when you're under our roof, you play by our rules. No cell phones for a week. Aidy, your iPad is mine. Olivia, you're not to use the house laptop. Neither of you are to leave here while we're at work, and you need to check in with us from the house phone every two hours."

"Come on!" Aidy shrieked.

"Every hour," Dad countered, even though he knew it wouldn't stick.

"Is that all?" I asked.

Dad looked to Mom, nodding to ease a hesitant sentence out of her lips. "We made a few calls while you were asleep," she said to me. "You'll be returning to Camp Califree at the end of the month."

She wanted this to resonate. Be a big moment where I broke down weeping, grateful. What could be better than gigantic slides that tossed me into a wide-open lake? Relay races and tugs-of-war and Pizza Fridays? Suntans and curfews and loosely structured days spent hugging other kids who'd experienced real trauma and grief?

Summer in Cadence was better. My messy bedroom and my messy friends. Marley.

"Whatever," I whispered, clenching my teeth to keep from crying. It would do me no good to protest, even though my every breath seemed to be laced with searing rebuttals. I knew I should show them joy, but I was too tired to perform that much.

I should've seen this coming. I'd been out in public with Nick Cline. I'd run out of the memorial crying. I hadn't meant to make my own perfect storm, and yet there I sat in the eye of it, watching the chaos swirl around me with stunning efficiency. I stalked out of the office and back to the comfort of my bedroom, shutting my door and locking it behind me. I had to come up with a way to get out of camp.

The Adventure had only just begun.

I couldn't miss a single day.

JULY 11

Five Years Prior

MRS. BRICKET OPENED MARLEY'S DOOR AT EXACTLY EIGHT IN the morning. The hinges squeaked to announce her presence right as the quail started his song, cheerful and off-key as ever.

"Marley," she called out in a hushed yell. "I need to go to work. The Stantons said you're all spending the afternoon at their house. Please eat breakfast there. I don't have enough food for all of you."

Marley didn't answer her mother. She pretended to sleep, which was ridiculous, because she'd been painting her nails mere moments before. The bottle was open on her nightstand and the room was sharp with the unmistakable metallic scent that only came from fresh polish in a closed space.

"Marley, I know you hear me. Can you please acknowledge your mother?"

Marley started fake snoring.

All of us were awake. Our collectively held breaths pressed down on the silence, everyone wondering how far Marley would push her disrespect.

"I've got it, Mrs. Bricket," Aidy said. "I'll tell her."

"Thank you, Aidy, but I'd prefer for my daughter to tell me herself." She snapped her fingers. "Come on, Marley. Don't be a brat. I'm not in the mood."

I turned my back from the door, rolling toward Marley's bed. When I opened my eyes, Marley did too. She was on her side, facing me. She winked at me before she stretched her limbs and yawned, as if she'd just come to. "Morning, everyone," she said in a husky whisper. She sat up. "Oh. Hi, Mommy. Good morning. You look lovely."

Mrs. Bricket combed down her pencil skirt. It was mint green, starting above her navel and landing right below the knees. She'd tucked a flowy white blouse into it, the kind that had a bow built into the neckline. Her hair was almost the same shade as Marley's, like bleached wheat rinsed in champagne, and she had it pulled into a low ponytail. I wasn't sure what her job was. Something that made her dress up a few mornings a week and drive forty miles each way. That's all I'd learned.

"Did you hear me?" Mrs. Bricket asked.

Marley gave her a coy grin. "Oh, no. I was sound asleep. What is it?"

"You need to take your friends to the Stantons'. I've already texted all of their parents letting them know that's where they'll be. Please eat breakfast there."

"Perfect. Sounds amazing. Will do."

"And clean up your room before you go," Mrs. Bricket added.

"Mm-hmm."

"All right. See you later." Mrs. Bricket started closing the door. "Please be good, Marley."

Marley blew her mother a kiss. "Of course."

"Love you," her mom said in a clipped rush, shutting the door as Marley answered with a "Love you too."

Mrs. Bricket's heels clacked along on the hardwood of the hallway. Once the sound of her steps disappeared, Marley picked up her cherry-red polish and finished painting her left hand.

"Do you guys wanna swim here today?" she asked, a mischievous smirk plastered across her face.

6

MY CURTAINS FAILED TO MAKE MY ROOM DARK ENOUGH. Light still snuck in through slits I couldn't seem to cover, even by pinning together the thick, black fabric designed to block everything out. I rushed into my cocoon all the same, hoping it would be good enough. That was all anyone ever settled for anyway.

By the time I'd caught my breath and mellowed out, hours had passed. The sun still waved at me through the curtain slits, but softer. An entire day of the Adventure was almost done slipping away from me, all because of Camp Califree.

I pressed my door open an inch at a time, needing to be in control of when my family realized I'd come back around. I tiptoed down the stairs, unsure of what awaited me. Mom sat on the couch watching reality TV. Aidy lounged beside her in the recliner. Without her phone to stare at, she gazed blankly at the television.

To my mom, I said, "I'm sorry. I didn't think before I acted. I know better. You're only doing what's best for me. I'm excited to go back to camp."

"Olivia," she cooed. "My baby girl. It's gonna be fun, isn't it?"

"Absolutely." I hugged her. "I'm sorry," I repeated. When dealing with my mom, repetition did wonders for my authenticity.

"It'll be good for the soul," Mom said. "We all need breaks sometimes."

I was sixteen. I didn't have a job. It was summer. What I needed a break from wasn't something I wanted to hear her explain. "We do."

"We should go," Aidy interrupted. "I don't want to do this tomorrow."

I sensed challenge in her voice. "Where?"

"To Ms. DeVeau's."

I'd forgotten. At the sound of my unchecked gasp, Mom closed her eyes to pray for my obedience.

"I'll run and change, and then I'm ready," I told Aidy. If I wanted to win the war of Camp Califree, I had to lose some battles.

In my bedroom, stacks of folded clothing decorated the floor in front of my dresser. In the wreckage I found a slouchy gray shirt and black leggings to replace my sleepwear. I hurried to pull my hair into a ponytail, threw on sandals, then headed for our front door.

On the walk to Ms. DeVeau's, Aidy kept her eyes trained on the ground. She had on black polka-dotted shorts and a black V-neck tucked into the high waistband. Shiny black flats on her feet to tie it all together. Classic as ever. She handled each crack in Albany Lane with graceful high-kneed steps, artful in her avoidance of the many uncertainties in her presence. Like sisters do, we moved in time with one another, even our breathing the same, a soft chest-lifting hum, rising with the incline.

"You're really excited for camp?" she asked.

"Of course."

"I thought you hated it the first time."

"I was young then. I didn't understand the point."

"But you do now?"

"Of course," I lied again.

"Mom and Dad never sent *me* to camp," she muttered.

Her words were a match tossed right to the embers inside my belly. "Oh. Did you see someone die too, and I missed it, Aidy?"

"I did, actually, Olivia. I was there too."

"Yeah, but you didn't actually see it happen." She had no idea. No one had any idea.

"I didn't realize the camp application required actually witnessing the exact instance someone was lost."

Lost. Of course. "You're more than welcome to go in my place," I told her. "Be sure to pack your cutest swimsuits. Don't eat the meat. Request cabin four. They have the warmest showers. Oh, and rumor has it that it's rigged and the blue team wins the color war every year."

"Why aren't you ever grateful for the chances you're given?"

"Chances for what? Please explain. I'd love to hear this."

"Olivia, stop."

"You started it," I said with a scowl.

We turned at the second intersection and followed the flatter street until it tapered off to make space for the railroad track that no longer operated. The end of daylight was fading the sky into the magic orange Ms. DeVeau wished her house mimicked.

Aidy stopped our momentum to press her hand into my elbow crease. "Wait. What are we going to say to her?"

I recalled the trace of lip liner on Ms. DeVeau's skin at the memorial. Her taut face scolding me. "I figured we'd listen and go from there," I started. "Say whatever she wants us to say, so we can get out as soon as possible."

"Okay," Aidy said as she bobbed her head. "That could work. Yeah."

"It always works."

We proceeded up the two concrete steps. Aidy knocked. I looked around. Nothing of note in the small front yard, save for the beautiful garden that shouldn't exist. Footsteps pattered close then stopped. Ten seconds passed between the halted movement and the door opening. Ms. DeVeau revealed herself to us, wrapped up like a present in a satin robe that didn't seem like it would do much good after a shower. Her face was bare and scrubbed pink. "Come in, girls," she said.

Her house smelled like expensive floral candles. They burned on otherwise-empty tables scattered throughout. The layout went straight back, and she led us through the front room, dining room, and kitchen. Each area felt staged, all done up in rustic whites, ready for a catalog shoot. Not a single personal touch was in sight, save for a black and white 8x10 of Marley as a toddler, birthday cake frosting streaking her plump cheeks. We reached an enclosed porch on the back of her house where Ms. DeVeau had iced tea waiting for us, along with sliced cucumbers and peppers.

"Sit down," she said.

Aidy and I joined up shoulder to shoulder on one of the love seats.

"Your mother called this morning to say you'd be stopping by. I almost put this all away, and well, here you are." Ms. DeVeau evaluated Aidy and me with no discretion, starting at our feet and dragging her eyes up. "As you both get older, you'd really never know the two of you were related." She looked from Aidy to me until we met in a deadlock stare. "Except maybe in the nose?"

If it was chess she wanted to play, I was no pawn. "Maybe."

Aidy grabbed a cucumber and began nibbling its edges. With a sly shimmy she masked as a full-body cough, she moved into me. *Don't you dare abandon the plan,* her arm said to my side.

Ms. DeVeau joined Aidy and me on the love seat. A matching one waited across from us, empty, like a mirror into a world where we didn't have to pretend this way for each other.

Ms. DeVeau's hand found the top of mine. "Little Olivia," she started. Her breath was raw as her skin and smelled of coffee. "If there is anything I want to say, it's that I believe in you."

Aidy's fear dampened my urge to laugh at the way Ms. DeVeau tried to pick me up by the nape of my neck. "Thank you," I said instead. "That means a lot coming from you."

"Being around the Cline boy again won't do you any good.

No one blames him for what happened. Marley should never have had such easy access to her father's gun. That was the real problem," Ms. DeVeau said with a rehearsed flick of her hand, like she'd spoken that exact statement too many times to muster up any feeling behind it. "But Nick's had such trouble acclimating since then. I don't want that for you." She stroked my hair. "You were always Marley's little admirer." As Aidy reached for more cucumber, Ms. DeVeau said, "And you, Aidy. You're her sister. You should be watching out the way Marley would."

If there was ever a time to see the resemblance between us Stanton girls, it was at that exact moment, as our brows scrunched to meet the bridges of our apparently similar noses. Aidy could do no better or worse than Marley, for she was not Marley. She was Aidy. *My* sister. And she did not belong in judgmental sentences falling from any lips other than my own.

"She does," I warned.

"Well, she needs to do a better job. You turned my daughter's memorial into your own little show."

The local news segment showed Cadence's art teacher talking about her new oil portrait of Marley, a few crowd shots from earlier in the night, and a short clip of Mayor Bayor's introduction. Those who didn't attend would never know how many truly interesting things occurred. And those who did attend kept the interesting parts hidden away, like they always did. It was no wonder we spent our childhood raiding our houses. Adults loved secrets. Kids loved learning them.

Aidy leaned forward to see Ms. DeVeau across the couch.

"You're the one who threw your chair," she muttered. "Don't you think that was kind of distracting too?"

I wanted to throw my arms around my sister. Squeeze her so tight, her newfound truth-telling got stuck in the top half of her body, forever spilling out of her mouth. But Ms. DeVeau clenched the flesh of my back to absorb the shock of the blow. I wiggled out of her hold and stood.

"Yes. We're all very emotional," I assured. "What happened can't be changed. Marley is who's important, anyway. If anyone deserves the apology, it's her." I stepped down into the backyard. "I'm sorry, Marley," I said to nothing and no one.

The trees swayed, a random breeze shaking down delicate leaves like Marley's shoulders used to shake when she found something hilarious.

The real Marley was laughing.

Satisfied, I walked back up and said, "If you'll excuse Aidy and me, we have a few other things to take care of before our curfew. We Stanton girls get very busy in July."

Aidy rose, eyes on the ground. "Thanks," she muttered to Ms. DeVeau.

"Yes, thank you," I added.

Once inside the house, we ran. Once out the other side, we laughed. Sprinting and giggling, we kept our quick pace until we knew we were out of sight.

JULY 11

Five Years Prior

OUR SLEEPING BAGS HAD BEEN ROLLED UP AND STACKED IN A triangular formation next to the Brickets' front door. Aidy stood in front of them as if she got to decide who was worthy of getting theirs returned.

"We have to go to my house," she said. "It's not a discussion. All of our parents think that's where we're gonna be." She folded her arms. "If we don't do this, they're not gonna let us have sleepovers and stuff anymore."

Teeny laughed at her. "We've been on borrowed time for a while now. How you and Harrison have tricked them into thinking you're just *best friends* is beyond me."

Aidy blushed. She hated when anyone pointed out this out. We lied to our parents all the time, but Aidy had it in her head that she only lied when necessary. Otherwise, she handcuffed herself to the *rules* and acted like she didn't have a key.

"We told them that's where we were going today. So that's where we're going. End of story," she scoffed.

It was rare for anyone to disagree with Marley Bricket. It was usually me to do it. Of course, my disagreements got written off by the rest of the group without so much as a vote. If anything, I served to strengthen whatever point Marley happened to be making. But Aidy was number two, the de facto leader whenever Marley wasn't around. Her defiance made the morning memorable.

"I'm sorry, when has that *ever* mattered?" Marley countered. "Didn't your parents lie to everyone else anyway? They're not even gonna be there!"

"Only for a few hours! They're out visiting family friends. They'll be back by one. Two at the latest."

Marley laughed. "Aidy, it's barely nine in the morning." She readjusted her sleep shirt to make it drape from her shoulder again. "We never get to look around my house. If my mom's gone, my dad is here. This is the first time in forever they're both out at the same time and we're all around. I'm not passing this up. Plus, it's gonna be hot out. I want to swim."

"We got a new air conditioner, and my dad made homemade Popsicles last night," Aidy countered.

A snorty, judgy giggle slipped out of me without warning.

Marley took it as bait. "Even your little sister knows how ridiculous that sounds." She walked over and draped an arm across me. Claiming me. "Tell you what? Me and Ollie are staying. Right, Ollie?"

"Of course," I said.

"Anyone else that wants to join us is more than welcome," Marley added. "If you're desperate for homemade Popsicles and AC, by all means, join Aidy. Sounds like a *lovely* afternoon."

Teeny swerved around Aidy to grab her sleeping bag. She slung it over her shoulder, grabbed Bigs's, and opened the door. "I'm taking my stuff home. Then I'm meeting Aidy at her house. Like I've told you a hundred times, my mom will know I went swimming if my hair is wet," she said as she stared at Marley. "We're not getting in trouble today. We're supposed to get a puppy by the end of the week. Nobody's messing that up for me." She was so small, both bags covered her entire body. "Love you all or whatever. Goodbye."

Bigs bowed his head and walked to the door. "See you guys later." He stepped back to give Marley a hug. "Hope you find something," he told her.

"Oh, I will," she promised, looking Aidy dead in the eye.

The Campbell twins exited, leaving only Aidy, Harrison, Ruby, Nick, and me.

"Let's go then, Aidy," Harrison said. "I'll make us breakfast." He grabbed his bag and left without a goodbye, heading three doors down to my house.

Aidy didn't follow. She cocked her head at me. "You're really staying?" When I didn't move, she clicked her tongue behind her teeth. "I'm going home and calling Mom and Dad, then. I'm not gonna get in trouble for you." She swirled around and hurried out, leaving her sleeping bag behind.

"Such drama," Marley said with a shake of her head. Her eyes lingered on the shut door. "Glad we're done with them for now. Don't need that dark energy clouding up my day. My little friends, let's get down to the real business. We have much to do."

"Actually," Ruby croaked out. A fine line of sweat beaded up on her forehead, right where her braids began. Her hair, onyx black and too thick to all be held at once, had recently been cut above her shoulders. The two braids Teeny put in the night before wound back into two little buns, one on either side of her head, with short pieces clinging to the back of her neck. "I'm gonna go over to Ollie's."

I gasped. Ruby had a crush on Marley that everyone, including Marley, knew about. Ruby told me that sometimes it was like her feelings for Marley lassoed around her throat and she forgot how to breathe. I could see it then, how much effort she put into each inhale, her hands holding her ribs and pressing tight, trying to push the breath up and out.

"I'll explain more later," she whispered to me. "Love you." She hurried out quickly, leaving her sleeping bag behind. I decided I'd bring it over to her later to get the scoop.

Only Marley, Nick, and I remained.

And Nick didn't leave.

7

AIDY AND I HEADED THE WRONG WAY. WE ENDED UP FAR OUT on the railroad tracks, nearing the famous POINT OF NO RETURN sign. The sun lowered with each step. Aidy stopped to stare. I matched her actions as a little sister should, the two of us holding our hands above our eyes to appreciate the beauty of Cadence on the cusp, flirting with night. We stood at the southeastern border, our backs to the open desert behind us, our eyes looking due west at our hometown.

Aidy laughed at herself. "Can you believe I said that to Marley's mom?"

"I really can't."

"She was making me so mad! Her fight with Mr. Bricket was outrageous. Way more people were talking about that. What you did made people kind of—I don't know. Sad, I guess."

My breath dragged. "Yeah."

Aidy dropped her visor hands to look at me. "Are you okay, though?"

"Obviously."

She tossed a curious glance over her shoulder. "So, then..." she started.

"Nick," I responded. His name had been on her lips since she'd woken me up that afternoon, and she'd yet to work up the courage to say it aloud. I had to do it for her, because I always had to be the one to handle the hard things. I was glad for the opportunity. I liked getting the chance to say his name without having to follow it with a reflection on what he'd done or how he'd failed to overcome it.

"Nick," Aidy repeated, and his name once again became more story than title, the details of which unfolded in flashes of memories. Our neighbor Nick, the boy with a face so precious grown women couldn't help but pinch it. Little Nicky Cline, the boy in my day care. The boy in my homeroom. The boy knocking on the door to ask if Ollie could come outside to play. The boy standing next to me in every photo from the first eleven years of my life. The boy who disappeared without an apology.

Nick Cline, the boy who killed Marley.

By accident, of course.

But terrible. So terrible.

"He showed up to the memorial. And I said hi. And, yeah," I started.

"So you said hi and that was all that needed to be said to hold his hand and run off to Cadence Park together?"

"No."

"But you did it anyway?"

"Obviously."

"Olivia, I really don't understand."

"That makes two of us."

"After all this time, he gets away with it because he's cute?"

"What? Ew. No. Why would you say something like that?"

"There is no person on this planet who has hurt you more than him."

"That's not true."

"Name one."

"It isn't about naming people. It's about a misunderstanding."

"Misunderstanding? What could be misunderstood about Nick pressing a gun into Marley's gut, shooting her in front of you, and running away?"

I couldn't get away from Aidy fast enough. Her contempt for what she didn't understand. Her lack of empathy. She did not see Marley die. She did not know the way Marley coerced Nick and me into obeying her. She did not know what I knew.

"Olivia, wait," Aidy called out, chasing after me. "Is there something I don't know?"

Everything, I thought.

When I didn't answer, Aidy fumbled for words. "About that day. Was it...did...did Marley...know..." I didn't dare fill in that blank. Instead, I raised my eyebrows at her the way Dad had at me earlier in the day. She gritted her teeth and pressed on. "Did Marley know the gun was loaded?"

"Don't be gross, Aidy."

"Olivia, there's letters. A box that maybe has her stuff. Tell me that doesn't look like suicide."

"Okay, I will. It doesn't look like suicide. Thank you. Goodbye."

"Come on. At least tell me how you even knew to find this stuff."

It was going to be hard work to keep her off the scent of what had really happened, so I decided to share a different truth. "I remembered something Marley said about the Adventure."

"That's not even possible. She never told any of us about it. You'd be the last person she'd ever give information to." Aidy always chose the worst times to belittle me, knowing the exact buttons to push to make me hot with rage.

"Oh yeah? Then how come I'm the one who knows the most?"

"Fine. *If* that's true, what did she say, exactly?"

She was always insulting my capacity for secret-keeping. "She said that it was going to be really different that year," I told her. "It wasn't going to have the same goal or something. No. Same purpose. She used that word. *Purpose.*"

"The only thing different about that year is Marley died, Olivia." Aidy stared at me. "Come on. You can't tell me you don't see it."

Nothing's gonna happen, I heard as a memory, Marley whispering to Nick before he pulled the trigger. *Everything is Something,* my letter had said. If everything was something, then Marley must've known what nothing meant, because even nothing was something, and nothing happened to Marley, exactly like she said it would.

"No," I whispered. Then my whisper became a statement. "No." Then a command. "No." Then a scream. "No! You don't get to do this, Aidy!" I stalked off, tears streaming down my face. "You have no idea!"

"Then tell me!"

"Leave me alone! I want to be alone!" I kept walking, not bothering to look back.

Marley, I need a sign. Let me know she's wrong.

The breeze stilled. My shoulders lightened.

Marley was lost.

And so was I.

part two

TITANIUM LIES

8

Aidy left me at the edge of the tracks, pressed between two rusted prongs of the train's horizontal ladder. It seemed like I too would rot away, destined to become another artifact of a town that never let things go. Every street in Cadence had its own life, filled with children that became blood by address association. Every house its own story, passed from generation to generation. No matter how time weathered our town, Cadence crossed its arms and remained unchanged by the growth of the world around us. All residents accepted this destiny.

Except Marley.

We made her the very symbol of the place she tried to escape. In all the years she'd been on my shoulders, in my mind, my heart, in everything I ever did or said, she never once told me she wanted to leave the world altogether.

Why? I kept asking, over and over.

She wouldn't answer. My imagination had always lifted me up, and now it dropped me down lower than I'd ever been. If given enough time, I might've let my questions cocoon me until I hatched into a person who knew the answers. Marley couldn't hide from me forever. I'd made myself her home.

She had to come back home.

Aidy, however, would not allow me to disappear into my own confusion. Though she left me, in a fit of tears no less, she did not abandon me. She sent Ruby in her place, and soon Ruby was beside me on the ground. She grabbed my hand and squeezed.

"What do we need to do now?" she asked. My Ruby, always ready, the girl who could pick up a movie halfway and stick with it through the credits.

"Understand," I told her.

"Hmm." She looked at me and then the sky, trying to see what it was that I saw.

"Aidy thinks Marley knew the gun was loaded."

"How could Aidy know that? She wasn't there," Ruby said, running a hand along the side of my face to wipe off my tears.

"I know." I leaned my head onto her shoulder.

She reached into the pocket of her jeans and pulled out her letter, her eyes searching for mine in the dark like fingers hoping to link into a promise. "You know what? I know it says *eyes on your own paper*, but what the hell, Marley's dead and we're all screwed because of it." She turned on her phone's flashlight. We sat up and huddled close, letting the light show us her letter.

RUBY MARQUEZ

Welcome to the Adventure. Eyes on your own paper, please.

When was the last time you thought of that day you and Ollie were sucking on the Gatorade bottles and you did it for too long? You had that red mustache on your upper lip that turned into a bruise. It didn't fade for a week and a half.

The whole time it was there, you'd catch sight of yourself in a mirror or something and you'd laugh. If that were me, I swear I would have had to move to a different country. Or buy that concealer that's made to cover up tattoos. I love that you didn't seem to care. I'm sorry that mean kid at the park made fun of you for it.

Really proves that our Cadence is not the same Cadence everyone else has, I guess. It's so weird to think that. All of these other people our age, one or two streets over, getting a whole different life. That could've been any of us. We could be strangers. Or enemies. All because we lived in a different house. Or a different body. This place feels like it's ours, but it belongs to a lot of other people too. And they don't treat it the same way we do.

I like to believe we'd all find our way to each other no matter what. Don't you think? Promise me that's true. That we'll all stay together. People trust you like they trust therapists. If you were the type to gossip, I'd never write this stuff down. Of course, if you were the talking type, you wouldn't know what you know in the first place. What a weird catch. You have to stay bottled up to keep the trust. But I need you to use that trust to make sure we don't lose each other. We can't lose each other.

Anyway, know that I love you.

You are a part of me forever.

Love always,

Marley

JULY 11

Five Years Prior

"Can you believe my mom didn't want to feed everyone?" Marley said as she rummaged through her kitchen cabinets in pursuit of something breakfast-like for the three of us. "That's so rude."

"There are a lot of us. My parents always get mad about it too," I told her.

"That's the thing. All of our families do it. It's only fair. And it was our turn." She found a box of strawberry Pop-Tarts hidden behind bags of rice in her pantry closet. "Aha! I knew my dad had these in here." She tossed a packet to Nick and me.

Nick had been quieter than usual, ever since the day before. He and I had stuffed ourselves inside the Campbells' towel closet during a game of hide-and-seek. To fit, he'd scooted his back against the wall. I came in face-first, my back to the door. Our heads were ducked low to keep from hitting the shelf above us, and we ended up cheek to cheek. He barely breathed. I tried to laugh, but I couldn't.

It wasn't funny.

"Here," Nick said, pointing the opened Pop-Tart pouch toward me. He wrapped the foil back to better show the contents. "Pick which one looks better."

"They look the same."

"I want you to have the one you like more," he said.

"What if you hate the other one?"

"Didn't you just say they're the same?"

"Yeah, but what if you can taste the fact that I didn't choose that one?"

He smiled. His grin was toothier than he wanted it to be. He fought it often, covering his mouth with his hand or turning his cheek. But not then. He shone his joy on me like a blazing star breaking through pitch-black infinity. "Hurry up and pick. I want to know what your hate tastes like."

It sounded inappropriate somehow, even though he'd meant it innocently, and there was no double meaning our eleven-year-old minds could scrounge up. Still, the both of us broke our gaze to look at anything but each other. I reached my hand into the Pop-Tart pouch and pulled out the first one my fingers found. Nick took the other.

After his first bite, Marley wrapped her braid around her pinkie. "Go on, Nicky. Tell us what Ollie's hate tastes like. Is it..." She paused to raise her eyebrows. "Sweet?" Only Marley could make an awkward situation unbearable and enjoyable all at once.

Nick didn't give an answer.

Marley sauntered out of the kitchen with a laugh, leaving us to chew our Pop-Tarts in silence. I finished my half. Nick finished his. He used his hands to dust up the crumbs we'd shed, then crumpled up the pouch and threw it away.

"I still liked it," he told me when he came back to his seat.

It took me a full thirty-six ticks of the birdhouse clock to decide what I thought that meant. What Ruby told me about feelings became more than an idea. They didn't lasso my throat, though. Instead, my heart outgrew my chest, but it couldn't break through, so it pounded against my rib cage, furious and unruly, demanding some kind of action I was nowhere near ready to take.

"Quick," he said. "Be a chair!"

We played this game every so often. Usually when we didn't know what else to do. I stepped down from my actual chair and then bent at my knees and hips, extending my arms forward to be a human chair. After a few seconds, I came back with, "Quick! Be a lamp!"

Nick stepped away from his seat and stood stock straight with his arms pinned to his sides. "Quick! Be a paper towel!" he told me.

The goal was always to start easy and keep going until the objects got more and more obscure. He'd taken a major leap between lamp and paper towel, but I gave it my best effort. There wasn't really a way to lose, anyway. I lay down on the kitchen floor face-first, spreading myself out as much as possible.

"I see it, I see it," he assured.

"Quick! Be a pen cap!" I called out.

Marley returned, right as Nick began folding himself in half, his fingers reaching for his toes. "You guys are so weird," she said. She'd taken down her braid and put on her bikini, cherry red like her nails. Fire against her icy skin. "Go get dressed. We've got stuff to do."

I stood. Dusted off the Pop-Tart crumbs on my chest.

"I can't believe you were face-first on this gross floor," Marley said as Nick and I headed toward her bedroom.

"She doesn't know what it takes to be a paper towel," Nick whispered, saving me from all-consuming embarrassment.

All of the Albany kids left spare swimsuits in a drawer in Marley's room. She was the only one of us with a pool. It made sense to keep some stuff at her house. But when I pulled open the drawer, I cursed myself for my tie-dyed peace-sign tankini, sun faded and baggy from overuse. Where was my cherry-red two-piece with a padded top and drawstring bottom?

Only in my mind.

Nick took out his board shorts. "Today's gonna be good," he said as he left to change in the bathroom.

I undressed in front of Marley's mirror, slipping into my old suit. Maybe it didn't fit. Maybe it was old. But it was mine. I could make it wonderful.

No. Today's going to be amazing, I thought to myself, a ghost of a smile traced onto my puckered lips.

I loved getting into trouble with Marley and Nick.

9

I stared at Ruby's paper like the words were going to rearrange into something easier to decipher. "Mine's pretty strange," she said. "I never knew she thought like that. I can't think of a time she was ever embarrassed. The Marley I remember was like—"

"Unstoppable."

"Yeah." Ruby examined her paper. "You know what else is weird? She says I'm in on everyone's business. I mean, I *am* good at keeping secrets, but I don't know that many. I know things like Aidy and Harrison lost their virginity to each other on the pool table in your attic."

"I told you that."

"That's what I mean."

"I think she's trying to say she knows you'll listen."

"That's my clue, then, isn't it?"

"I'd say so."

Ruby smiled to herself. "Her clues never made a lot of sense. She plucked this stuff straight from her head like we were all wired into her brain. No wonder we never finished a single Adventure." She wrapped her arms around her knees. "Remember the year that everyone got mailed a different pair of something? I got a pepper shaker from the Campbells' table. Did I ever tell you that? When I figured out which one of our houses it came from, I stole their salt shaker and brought the pair to Marley. She was like, *Okay? So what?* and didn't tell me anything else. I'm pretty sure she counted it as me giving up."

I hadn't heard the story before. Not even Ruby shared her memories of Marley with me anymore.

I got mailed a sock that year, and I spent most of the following days sneaking into my friends' bedrooms to rummage through their underwear drawers. I never found the matching one, but folded into a rolled pair of Bigs's socks, I discovered a picture of some boy from the sleepaway camp he and Teeny went to at the start of every summer. There was a heart drawn around the boy's face. A photo of Teeny with her arm around that same boy was prominently framed in Teeny's room. She talked about him (and to him) almost every day after she got back, until the school year came, and their long-distance camp romance had to go where all summertime activities went: into hibernation. Bigs never said a word about him. When the next year's sleepaway camp came around, neither did Teeny.

Ruby read her letter one more time, then folded it up and tucked it into the pocket of her ripped jeans.

"Aidy thinks because there are letters, it means Marley planned to die." I tried my hardest to make each syllable sound ridiculous and implausible, but my throat was too dry. I sounded naive. Sputtering, I fought to find the courage to explain what Marley had told me about the Adventure having a different purpose.

"*Purpose?* She used that word?" Ruby asked.

"Yeah. But when she said it, I took it as meaning she'd have a different goal or something. I can't really explain right now." I paused. "I see how that sort of proves Aidy's point. But it's not possible." Another wave of upset began to wash over me. Tears rolled down my cheeks as my breath came out in hiccups.

Ruby found herself stopped up. "Olivia, the message on the wall in the sewer. *You didn't love me like I asked of you. Still I love you back.*"

I fixated on the dark outline of raised land to my right, imagining the sky as the ground and the ground as the sky. I wanted the world to flip me over and empty out my hurt like loose change falling from pockets. In trying to form a response to Ruby, I couldn't inhale without choking. No single thought of mine made sense.

"Aidy might be right," Ruby said. She pulled me in close. "Hey. Listen." She whispered our oldest, most private saying: "No stops."

There used to be days we Albany kids did things boys versus girls. Who knows why. Everyone hated it. The older girls complained Ruby and I messed things up because we were too little and didn't understand how to work hard. The older boys were mad they had two fewer bodies on their team. One day, moments before beginning a relay race down Albany, as Marley and Aidy and Teeny yelled at us to pull our weight, I suggested that Ruby and I have our own team instead. The older girls agreed with such little hesitation that Marley got a crick in her neck from nodding so aggressively.

"No stops," I said to Ruby as she crouched low. She would have to run the relay twice to keep things fair.

"No stops," she repeated back. A razor's edge of determination glinted in her eyes, ready to slice everyone's expectations.

What I said, I meant literally. If we were going to beat everyone else, she could not stop for anything. After we won, it became more. Our secret code for staying in the race in whatever way applied. *Keep running. Even when everything hurts. You'll find a finish line. It may not be the one you set out for, but wherever you end up, it's still ahead of where you were.*

"Aidy told me about Camp Califree. Don't worry. We've got time," Ruby assured, wrapping her arm around me. She could feel me pulling away, so she switched focus. "It was nice, wasn't it? Everyone on the bikes again, riding down Albany."

Suddenly I was furious with myself for being so relaxed. Maybe Marley stopped showing up because I bored her, taking too long to get everything together. Maybe I'd gotten the Adventure so far off track already that I'd lost her, just like the rest of them. I searched the desert for some piece of her to assure me.

I found nothing.

"We have to keep going," I said to Ruby. I had to make everything right. If Marley wanted to die, I needed to know for sure.

If she didn't, I needed to show everyone what she meant by the Adventure having a different purpose. And I had to do it all before Camp Califree.

"Would I ever do anything less?" Ruby dipped her head. "Would I? We're gonna finish this one. We've got that whole box of stuff to look over. And I want to get back to the tunnel during the day. If there's more for you to find, you're gonna find it. If I'm the one who's supposed to know secrets, then I'm gonna know them." In her lowest, steadiest voice, she asked, "What do you say?"

I didn't answer.

"Olivia Stanton, what do you say?"

"No stops."

"What was that?"

"No stops."

She stood tall and cupped her hand behind her ear. "I can't hear you!"

"NO STOPS!"

"There she is. Now let's get out of here. We're nearly past"—she put on her spookiest voice—"the Point of No Return."

That was true. And Ruby pointing it out meant Marley wasn't as far away from me as she felt.

We started walking toward Albany Lane.

"Did Aidy tell you we're grounded?" I said after a while.

"When I tried texting you, and you didn't respond, that wasn't really anything new. But when you didn't answer my calls, I figured something was up. Is that why Aidy had to call me from your house phone?" Ruby asked, but I didn't have to answer. She already knew. She laughed so hard, it startled me. I couldn't help but laugh with her. She found her next question—"Are you supposed to be home right now?"—so hilarious she had to hunch over and clutch her ribs. "Sometimes I can't believe how much I love you," she said.

"I can't believe it either," I said back.

JULY 11

Five Years Prior

"You guys, come here!" Marley yelled.

Nick and I ended our game of Marco Polo without question. We jumped over the pool's edge and raced each other to the towels draped over the railing on the other side. It took me five easy strides to beat him.

"Good job," he said when he reached me. His eyes fell to his feet. At first I thought he was embarrassed, but it was far from the first time he'd lost a race to me. We'd been outside for a few hours and color had already bloomed on his cheeks and his shoulders.

Suddenly, my cheeks warmed too. "Thanks," I said back. I usually preferred to air-dry, but I snapped up a towel, wrapping it around my newfound self-consciousness.

The back screen door squeaked as it slid open. Too excited to bother washing them, our unrinsed feet tracked grass through the hallway and into the master bedroom, where Marley stood on the bed, hiding something with her right hand and holding a strange object in her left.

"I hit the jackpot," she said.

I pretended to marvel at whatever she held in her left hand. It looked a little like a miniature rocket. "Everyone else will wish they came to swim with us," I told her, hoping I sounded confident enough to disguise my cluelessness.

Marley turned the rocket on, which prompted Nick to shove my shoulder. As soon as I shoved back, the only response I could muster, Marley tossed the rocket onto a nightstand.

"Come on, Ollie. It's a vibrator!" she scolded.

I didn't know what that meant, not exactly, but I laughed like I did. "So cool," I said.

"Please, it's not even the best part," Marley scoffed. She held her free hand up in the air. "Nicky, look."

My spit turned thick as peanut butter. "I'm going back to the pool," I said as I swallowed back. I hated when she treated me like Little Ollie.

"Please stay," Nick pleaded. Panic set fire in the blacks of his eyes. He'd already seen what I had yet to notice.

Marley's hand was no longer held high. It was wrapped around her back to join the other. She looked at once vulnerable and fearless, standing tall on her parents' bed in her bright red bikini. I leaned all my weight to one side so I could see what she was holding.

"It's not loaded. I checked," she whispered, showing us the gun.

10

IN SLEEP, I FELL. DOWN AND DOWN FROM HEIGHTS unquantifiable. Once awake, I remained suspended, like I'd tripped but the ground never caught me. When I entered the kitchen, Dad and Aidy put an abrupt stop to their hushed conversation.

"Morning," I said to them both.

"I made pancakes," Dad said. "They're on the counter." As I prepared a plate for myself, he stood to hold a private conference with me, mere feet from Aidy, who did her part and pretended not to be interested. "Were we not clear about the rules of your punishment?"

I might have cowered in the face of his intimidation, but I could always see what was meant to be hidden, like the way his hand did not firmly hold the refrigerator door. How his eyes searched the space around my body, incapable of keeping me in clear view. "You were," I said with a smile.

He wanted to ask where I'd been the night before, but I'd given him kindness when he expected a challenge. He didn't know what move to use next, so he said, "Don't let it happen again," and patted my back. On his walk back to the table, he reconsidered, adding, "Looks like Camp Califree's got some new staff. The woman I spoke with on the phone said they've made quite a few changes since you were last there. They've completely redone the ropes course, apparently."

It was a smart play, but I was in no mood for a real match, so I nodded and said, "Cool," in the type of voice adults use to mock teenage apathy.

I sat next to Aidy and poured syrup over my chocolate chip pancakes. Dad sipped at his coffee. After a weighted beat, I said, "You look nice today."

"We're meeting three investors for lunch this afternoon. Have to give them the goods." Knowing that statement was as dignified an exit as any, he let it simmer, then kissed our foreheads and said his goodbyes. "Enjoy your day indoors. Maybe you can get to cleaning up the mess you made in my garage. We should've given those bikes to Goodwill a long time ago."

Ha.

Once Dad left, Aidy started tapping her fingers on the table to fill the silence. She liked to test my mood by testing my patience. She used small motions, thinking herself unobvious.

"I'm all good," I said to her.

"Dad told me he's having Mr. Jimenez watch the house."

"To make sure we don't leave?"

"Yeah," she said as she phased out her finger tapping. She

sighed into her last bite of pancake, covering the bottom of her face with a hand and grabbing for her napkin after each bite, chewing like her presence offended the world.

"Perfect," I muttered. Another obstacle to face.

An expectant quiet simmered. With Aidy and me, fights somehow made us closer. The extra layer of friction between us played out like a game we both won. The person who first made it better got the pride of being the bigger person. The other person got the satisfaction of surrender.

Through shielded mouth, Aidy surprised me by saying, "We'll use the back door." She was trying to be the one to make it better between us.

"You still want to do the Adventure?" I asked, needing the satisfaction of her surrender.

With a careful dab at her lips, she cleaned off her last bite of food and stood to put her plate in the dishwasher. "We have to make sure we don't go onto Albany. At least not until the first intersection. Mr. Jimenez won't notice. It's not like he ever leaves his house."

"So we're going the Marley way." I was careful not to sound too interested. I thought Aidy would be done with all of it. I certainly didn't think she'd want me to come with her. Then again, I'd proven to know more than her. She needed me.

If they wanted to finish, they all needed me.

"Mm-hmm," she answered in a measured tone.

Bursting, I shoveled down the last of my pancakes and dialed Ruby on the house phone. She'd meet us at Cadence Park in a half hour.

Aidy and I went into our rooms to change. We both emerged in jean shorts caked with mud that could never be washed out. Shirts that smelled like they'd been folded away for years.

I felt renewed. I could get the Adventure back. Prove to Aidy it was all for something different.

Going the Marley way meant crawling through the hole we dug under our wooden fence; sprinting full speed through the yard of the haunted house next to ours; hopping over Miss Sherry's chain-link fence; marching through the cluster of trees in her yard; shimmying under the hole we made on the other side, the one we couldn't get quite deep enough, and that always made our clothes filthy; pressing against the wooden planks of the next fence to keep from getting scratched by the shrubbery forming a perimeter around Marley's yard; jumping over Marley's gate; taking the walkway between her house and the one on the corner, and following until it spit us out on Arbor Street. A complicated path that had become an exact science once upon a time, well-worn from constant use.

As we emerged onto Arbor Street, we headed toward Harrison's. His house was across the intersection, on the other side of Albany. Out of Old Mr. Jimenez's sight.

Nick lived diagonal from Harrison. Through many different distractions—skipping and jumping and humming and being a generally annoying little sister—I'd taken care to keep Aidy from remembering this fact. It was easy to do. We'd all gotten very used to ignoring the entire idea of Nick Cline. He went to his different school. He lived on a different schedule. Even though he was only a block away, he was more of a ghost to me than Marley would ever be.

"Do you want Mr. Jimenez to catch us?" Aidy whisper-yelled as we sprinted across Arbor.

"Oh, please! He's so old; he can't hear anything anymore!" I screamed back.

We skipped up onto the sidewalk. My eyes were on my feet, watching as I toppled off the tips of my toes. Aidy's steps fell out of sync with mine. She'd noticed something across the street.

Nick.

He kneeled in his driveway, pumping air into the tires of his old bike.

Our sister rhythm slowed. I quit humming. Aidy took a sharp left into Harrison's driveway. I turned right.

"Ollie," Nick said as I walked up, genuine surprise in his voice.

My hands dug into the pockets of my jean shorts. There was stray change in the left side, along with a pen that had dried out. The right had bits of shredded paper. "Fancy meeting you here."

"I didn't hear from you yesterday," he said. "I was gonna ride over to your house."

Uneven heat spread through me, overcooking my center. I suppressed a smile. I wanted to look at him, but out in the open like that, I couldn't bring myself to add any time toward taking in his face. "Good thing you didn't. We're under house arrest."

Nick laughed. "Seems to be going well."

"Old Mr. Jimenez is supervising. Can't get anything by him."

"Definitely not." Nick looked left, then right, filling time with movements, contemplating what to say. Finally, he asked, "What's the house arrest for?" He squinted, fighting daylight to see me better.

You and Marley, I thought to myself. The only two people ever getting me into trouble. "A few things," I said instead. "Shouldn't be a problem. Not until Saturday, at least."

"Why?"

"No work for my parents then."

He held his hand up to shield the sun. "That gives me five days."

"Us," I corrected, playing the game better than him. "That gives *us* five days." I used the brightness of the sun as an excuse to close my eyes and settle.

Nick laughed again. Our interaction seemed to keep him in a constant state of confused amusement. I wished it did the same for me. "Quick!" he yelled, startling me. "Be a girl under house arrest!"

I folded my arms. "That's not the game, and you know it." When he didn't budge, I relented. I sat crisscross on the pavement and examined my fingernails. "Quick! Be a boy fixing his bike!"

He scooted away from his real bike, instead miming a wrench, turning it over and over in the air. "This spoke." He wiped sweat from his brow. "Always giving me trouble."

I couldn't give in. It was too easy. I had to fight him at every turn. "Oh, there's dialogue now?" I asked, standing again. The sun's warmth glowed red through my closed eyelids. If I watched him, I would cave.

"The rules are always changing, Ollie. Quick! Be a person who tells me what she's doing with the rest of the day."

My heels snapped into the earth, denting the ground with the force of the motion. I opened my eyes, seeing Nick see me. I wouldn't lie to him. "Meeting Ruby at the park. She's got the box."

Nick stood. "Can I come?"

The older I got, the more the desire to make a mess became an active choice. And it was a choice I could taste in my spit. Salty and metallic. "Sure," I said. Bringing Nick along was not playing fair. If Aidy and I remained locked in battle mode, neither of us benefited. Fights were only satisfying in the aftermath.

But I couldn't deny that Nick started this with me. No matter how everyone else tried to revise history, he was an Albany kid like the rest of us. If we were going on an Adventure in the name of Marley Bricket, Nick deserved to be a part of it.

"Let's go." I pointed to Harrison's house.

Nick tossed his bike into his open garage, and we walked across the street. It felt so surreal to be together, knocking on Harrison's front door—once for all clear—like it was only another Adventure day. Like, if we pretended hard enough, we could actually erase the vacant years between us.

Harrison's mom answered the door. "Hello, Ms. Shin," Nick said, as formal and polite as always.

The softness in his voice melted into her like butter. She hugged him tight. "It's so good to see you," she whispered into his hair. She let go, taking him in, then hugged him again. "Harry! Aidy! Nick and Olivia are here!" She turned to me. "Staying in or going out?"

"Out," I said. "Cadence Park."

She hugged me as tight as she'd hugged Nick. She loved to bake, I remembered, smelling the flour on her. My eyes suddenly watered as she continued to squeeze me as if I were her own child. As if she loved me as I was, not for what I pretended to be.

I'd made myself forget her baking. Her white chocolate chip macadamia nut cookies. The three-tiered strawberry cake she made for my tenth birthday. She'd covered the cake in lavender frosting and made a fondant lion for the top, my name in lavender letters running across the crown of the lion's glorious mane. My parents hadn't asked her to make it; she brought it over to my party unprompted and without fanfare, setting it down in secret and refusing to take credit for its majesty. I knew it was from her because days before, she'd asked me my favorite animal. She wouldn't accept *I love all animals* as an answer.

"There isn't one you like more than the others? Like me, I love otters." She had a beautiful laugh, musical and easy. "Their little whiskers make me happy."

I'd always fancied myself a lion. Drove Aidy up a wall when I'd walk around our house on all fours, roaring at her. Refusing to speak. She'd assume I was pretending to be a house cat and would tell me to go live under a porch with the other strays. I could never get her to see the world as grandly as I did.

"A lion," I'd told Ms. Shin that day.

Right then, she'd mussed up my hair until my bangs pointed toward the ceiling. "Ah, yes. There it is. Your mane," she'd said, grinning. She winked at me as she pressed my hair flat. "Go play now."

I'd roared at her as I left.

When she released our hug, I resisted the urge to tousle her hair like old times. Her voice dropped to a whisper. "I don't care what the other people here say. This is what you all should be doing. Harry's been inside all day since he got back from college. He should be getting sunshine. That's what everyone forgets. You kids were out getting sun and fresh air every single day."

She was making a reference to the Marley day. We were not the only kids in Cadence to be unsupervised during summertime, but we were the most famous. The rest of the town held airs of superiority over our families. Opinions on the rightness of our parents' actions were shared freely and often. They were forever branded the *Albany parents*, code for negligent.

"It's so good to see you," I told her, using the voice that made me sound like an adult. The one I used at all the memorials. She didn't attend them, so she didn't know.

Harrison and Aidy came from the hallway. Harrison kissed Ms. Shin's cheek. "Bye, Mom. Love you."

"Be good," she said to us as we left, patting my head two times more than she pat the others. On a whim, I flashed her my claws.

With a wide grin, she clawed back.

Tension wrapped taut around Nick, Aidy, Harrison, and me. One millisecond of attention toward it, and we would all snap in half. We invented the longest, most out-of-the-way route to the park, letting the need to avoid Mr. Jimenez take all of our energy, even though deep down we all knew we were putting an obscene amount of work into hiding from a man who had become so withdrawn since the Marley day that he sometimes got the mail in his underwear, seeming to forget he could be seen.

It was such sweet, tangible relief to finally arrive at Cadence Park. I basked in its plastic glory: The sun scorching the red slide, making it unusable. Two young kids running across the blue bridge. Ruby sitting on a swing, holding Marley's box.

I felt another twinge of victory. Aidy was outnumbered. I had more allies. I tried not to let it make me too bold, but I couldn't help but jog over to Ruby.

"Where are your bikes?" Ruby asked as we hugged.

"We couldn't take them through the Marley way."

"Ah. Bigs and Teeny aren't coming," she told me. I should've been upset, but without them, the balance stayed tipped in my favor. "Not yet," she clarified. "They have these things called jobs."

"Never heard of it."

"I think it's sort of like when I babysit my brothers. Except you get paid."

Aidy walked up, Harrison and Nick right behind. "I was hoping they'd be off today. I wanted to ask if their aunt is hiring."

Harrison touched her shoulder. "At her hotel?"

"No, I wanted to ask if she's hiring somewhere else." She brushed him off, her voice oozing with sarcasm. "Yes. At her hotel."

"Why do you need a job, anyway?" I asked.

"Mom and Dad want me to find something paid to do for the, uh, rest of summer."

I perked up at this information. So far, I knew that Aidy had some sort of conflict with our parents. Now, a requirement to find another job before she went back to school. I bookmarked the knowledge, promising to return to it when I had more time.

"Why didn't you ask them about it when we were at the memorial?" Harrison asked. "We were talking about their work before Olivia…gave her speech." Without meaning to, he cut the conversation off at the jugular. He must've forgotten I was there until it was too late, and he had to course correct.

I wondered what he would've said if I wasn't around.

Before Olivia…caused a scene? Before Olivia…ruined everything?

Swollen with all the words I kept inside, a sound kind of like *eh* snuck out of my mouth.

Ruby laughed. Her quick clip of amusement read like an admission of the awkwardness that consumed all of us.

"Hey," Harrison said. His tone was strange and soft.

I turned around to find Aidy crying. She caught my gaze then walked off in the direction of the bowl. Harrison started to follow. "Don't," she warned him, the blow as heavy and blunt as a hammer.

I knew my cue.

I always did.

I followed her. She stopped when she reached the sewage tunnel. It looked grosser in the daytime. Especially the dampness in the middle—a dark pool of mysterious liquid with no pleasant explanation for its presence.

"You've got to stop doing this," she told me as she sat on the edge of the tunnel entrance, careful to avoid the suspicious wetness.

"What do you mean?" I asked, playing innocent.

123

"Hurting people then acting like nothing's wrong."

Here, conversation built momentum easily.

I said, "I never told you I'd stop talking to Nick," which made Aidy toss her hands up and sigh out, "Forgive me for hoping Ruby knocked some sense into you."

She knew it was a ludicrous statement, so I called her out on it with a "Why does it bother you so much anyway? It's not your life." It's one of the worst points to argue, because it discredits people for caring, but I was working on impulse, and didn't have time to craft a response with more care.

Aidy knew it wasn't my best work, so she got smarter with a "You act like you're the only one who notices things."

I gave that my most incredulous "What does that mean?" response.

Our walk to the park had been the cautious uphill climb of a roller coaster. Now we were flying down, breathless and unsettled.

"It's not good for you to be around him."

"How could you possibly know that? I don't even know that. I haven't been around him in years."

Aidy buried her hands in her hair. "We're running in circles with this. Go ahead and remind me why you haven't seen him. What was it again?" She went right where I knew she'd go with it. As if she didn't drive the point home hard enough the night before. "Oh yeah, that's right. He shot Marley then ran away. You were never the same after that." She stopped. Restarted. "You're not the same."

"Of course, I'm not the same!" I shouted. "Are any of us?"

"I'm tired of this! I don't know how to talk to you without making you mad!"

"I'm not mad! I'm defending myself!"

"That's what you always say," she informed me.

"I didn't realize you were the expert on all things to do with my life. You know, I like my therapist, but it sounds like you've got me all figured out. Maybe I should start going to you instead. Save Mom and Dad a few bucks. Maybe you can be my camp counselor too. Something tells me you'd love that."

"Olivia, I'm just being your big sister. Will you ever let me be that?"

I was a lion, I reminded myself. I had a mane, hidden away. I had razor-sharp teeth that could clamp down on Aidy's flesh and leave a mark that would never fade away. I buried my nails into my palms, trying to latch onto a different kind of hurt. "You're obviously an expert on relationships. Anyone with two eyes can see the love between you and Harrison," I said. Despite my best efforts not to bite, I was weak. If I didn't get a pass with Nick, she didn't get one with Harrison.

Aidy whispered something indecipherable. From her face, I could see it was a concession.

I collapsed onto the grass in front of the tunnel, overwhelmed. It would always hit me all at once, and never when I expected. The world shrank until everything around me became small, and I remained the same size. I didn't fit.

The dark calmed me best, but I was out in the open, under the sun's constant observation. I focused only on my breath and my body, watching my rib cage expand. I released the air that filled my lungs in the slowest, steadiest stream manageable. Over and over I did nothing but breathe. My breath became paintings, poetry. People. Sound. Whatever it needed to be to return the world around me to its proper proportions. It would be too much to tell Aidy I was okay. To embrace my own falsity.

Once the world had halfway restored itself, I tried to apologize, but couldn't find words beyond the generic "I'm sorry" I shelled out to everyone. She deserved more from me.

"I'm sorry too," she said back. "We're not so good at this." After a beat, she said, "I don't know if I love Harrison enough," once again letting me win.

She was always being my big sister. It amazed me she couldn't see that.

"I know," I told her, my voice dry and unpracticed. I said it not to be mean, but to let her know she carried the loss of her relationship as I carried Marley. Invisible to everyone who didn't know how to look. Painfully obvious to those of us that did.

"He's every part of my life. He's Cadence. He's college. At this point, we're basically one person."

She was nearly a foot taller than me. Her hair was more like Dad's, but with Mom's coloring—soft curls in an incredible shade of red that made strangers stop her on the street. My hair was more like Mom's, but with Dad's coloring—that weird texture between wavy and straight, all a shade of walnut brown. We didn't need to look alike to resemble one another. I knew what it was to be unable to escape someone.

There was a safe way to play out our conversation. I could've fed her the lines I'd conditioned myself to say. Something like, "You need to do what's right for you," or, "All that matters is that you're happy," but I wanted to tell her something authentic, which I hoped she'd know was the rarest gift I had to give. I dug around inside my thoughts until I found a truth I believed. "When you're locked in a room with no exit, rearrange the furniture."

She looked at me with a curious squint. "You're too old to be sixteen," she told me.

"I was born too old," I said back.

JULY 11

Five Years Prior

MARLEY JUMPED OFF THE BED AND SAUNTERED TOWARD Nick, wrapping his stubby fingers around the black metal. "Officer Cline, I'm so sorry that I've been causing trouble," she purred.

"How did you get this?" Nick asked.

"Guess my dad forgot it."

Marley maneuvered Nick's fingers until he was holding the object properly. It was foreign in his unskilled hands. Crude. He fidgeted as Marley positioned the tip to point at her.

"Don't let it touch me!" she yelled. She reached for one of her parents' decorative pillows and held it over her chest. "Okay, try again."

"This is a bad idea," I mumbled. Marley's dad was the most intimidating person I'd ever met. I figured he would have no problem arresting me just for looking at his misplaced weapon.

"Yeah. I don't wanna do this," Nick said.

"Oh, you're fine," Marley told him, guiding the gun back to

her pillow-covered gut. "You know how Ollie is." She flashed her most mischievous, cutting smile. "Pull the trigger. Nothing's gonna happen."

I pouted to myself, contemplating my next move. Marley was playing a game of chicken with Nick and me. Testing us because we were the youngest. We couldn't cave.

My frustration bubbled up into my cheeks. And then, of course, my eyes. Reluctant tears only made me angrier. Indignant, I tried to let my stare burn holes through the pillow Marley held.

Its casing was golden, much like her parents' bedding, with flowers embroidered in the same delicate shade. Each detail was so subtle that you had to be up close to notice, particularly the flaxen petals of the roses, which seemed to be spun from strands of Marley's hair. She held the pillow over her body so casually, her eyebrows raised into impish arches, no mind to the contempt I lasered at her. Only serenity. She knew she'd won.

She always won.

Then, like the unexpected clap of a firework on the fifth of July, or the startling pop of a blown-out tire, a heavy, booming sound shocked me like I'd touched an electric current.

Marley collapsed with a resounding thud, landing in the fetal position atop a decorative rug. Viscous red liquid poured out from a hole in the pillow, saturating every texture around her rag-doll body.

11

FULL ON THE PROMISE WE'D BE BETTER TO EACH OTHER, Aidy and I walked back up the bowl. Ruby still sat on the swing. She twisted side to side to let herself spin. Harrison stood nearby, staring at his phone. Nick squatted on the edge of the playground, arms wrapped around his knees as he looked outwards.

It struck me then, the magnitude of what I'd already accomplished. I was no longer the tagalong sister fighting for some semblance of dominance. I had united these people. They were all waiting for me to come back before we continued with the Adventure.

Whether they liked it or not, I had become their leader.

1. Me (16 years old)
2. Aidy (19 years old)
3. Ruby (17 years old)

4. Teeny (18 years old)
5. Bigs (18 years old)
6. Harrison (19 years old)
7. Nick (16 years old)

Without the tension between us Stanton sisters, a new problem popped up. No one knew what to do about Nick. For five years Cadence had labeled him a pariah. As the only other person in the room the day Marley died, I guided that narrative more than I ever realized. I allowed Nick to have that title, just as I allowed it to be crossed out. The problem for everyone, including myself, was that I didn't know with what to replace it.

Who was Nick Cline to me now?

Who was he to everyone?

It hurt me to watch him, but leaders had to do things they didn't like. I was going to give my role everything I had. With each step made toward the playground, I stayed locked on his face, ticking down agonizing seconds.

Two nights before, we'd run down dark streets together, holding hands and screaming. That memory did not touch me. It stretched so far out of the realm of things I expected that it took on the hazy, warm film of a fantasy. It was the sight of him huddled up that wrecked me. Being an older version of the Nick Cline he'd always been. The same Nick Cline who would've known how much it hurt me not to speak for five years.

I'd let the years between us float into the abstract, dazzled by the promise of adventure and the thrill of his surprise presence. That high had worn off. All that remained was the Olivia I'd become.

This newest Olivia Stanton, five years older and stronger and better, did not let people hurt her. She did not wait for apologies. She marched up to Nick and said, "Hey, stand up," in a voice so harsh and firm it sounded almost cartoonish. "Apologize to everyone."

In his head, Nick asked *for what?* then thought better of it, because after standing, he took a defensive step back, then two deliberate steps forward.

Once again, we circled around Ruby on the swing. This time, all attention fell to Nick. Uncomfortable as can be, he let his guard down for me to see he was sorry, so sorry, but he didn't want to say it like this. *Why hadn't I let him say it the other night? Why did I need to make this so hard?* His stare burned into the side of my face, desperate for my acknowledgment.

I leaned against the swing set to keep myself steady. "You don't get to choose the easiest way for this to go," I told him, like, *I get it. I hear you.*

"I…" He faltered.

"You left all of us behind. We would've been there for you," I said.

Not that everyone was there for me either, but presenting a united front strengthened the illusion. Heat from his steady gaze crawled down my neck until red patches started to form along my collarbone.

"It didn't seem like you wanted me around anymore," he said.

To expel the fire burning my skin, I yelled, "You didn't ask me!"

The younger neighborhood kids at the park stopped to stare.

"I..." he started again. He looked to Aidy. "I tried."

"What do you mean?"

"I tried to talk to you, Ollie."

"This is enough," Aidy snapped. "Can you say the actual words, like she's asking you to do? Do you have to make everything a whole thing?"

Nick nodded. "I'm sorry I haven't talked to you guys." His low, steady tone accentuated how ridiculous my previous yelling sounded. "I really am. I've missed you every single day. It just seemed too complicated... It doesn't matter now. Know that I'm probably sorrier than it seems. I'm not great with this whole speech stuff. I can't sleep most nights because of Marley and what happened to her." He stopped. "What I did to her."

I had to look up.

He bit his lip, hard, leaving the indent of his teeth on the pucker of skin above his chin. "If there are pieces of her she left behind, we need to find them. It might make life easier for us. Or maybe it makes it harder. It's Marley. It probably makes it harder. I guess we don't know yet. We've never finished one of her Adventures before. But I need something to change, because this way isn't working so great. I'm the one person who didn't know better. Everyone would've done things differently that day. I can't tell you how many times I've run the moment through my head, making different choices. No matter how many times I do it, the end result is still the same. She dies." His teeth pressed back into the imprints, freshening the marks. "If you need me to say sorry once an hour every hour until time runs out, I'll do it, if it means I get to be around. Whatever I have to do, I'll do. Even if that still makes me the only person in the world who doesn't know better. At least I'm good at being that."

I recognized what he was doing. So much so that I could barely breathe. He was me, spitting out the words the world required. Admitting complete defeat so the tables turned back onto the rest of us. It was the very art form I'd spent five years mastering. He proved how fine-tuned his skills were by being the one to push us forward. By carrying that burden too. "If that's enough for all of you—I'm sure it's not—but if it's a start, then we should do what we came here to do. She always used to tell us that if we ever finished the Adventure, the prize we'd get would be amazing. I've been thinking about that nonstop. We need to go back into the tunnels. And find whatever's in that box," he said. "We deserve something good."

His magic worked, of course. Charming in his perseverance, he finalized the removal of his outcast status. FORMER DISAPPOINTMENT EMBRACED BY OLD FRIENDS AFTER WELL-WORDED APOLOGY.

But he knew about Marley. He knew about pliable truths. He knew the Adventure was meant to be good, not cause more hurt.

Nick knew everything I knew.

When it came to feelings, that was a feeling I did not like.

Harrison was the first to soften. "I'm so sorry, man." He patted Nick on the back. "Thanks for saying that. It was really big of you." He bowed his head like the action could actually wipe the slate clean. "What do you think we should do first?" Not only did Harrison forgive Nick, he lent him my title, pushing Nick into a leadership role he had not earned. The destiny of a When rubbed right in my face.

Every piece of my being knew the whole thing angered me beyond reason, but I could do nothing to act on it. If at that exact second someone suggested I drop the entire Marley subject and go live under a pile of blankets forever, I'd have signed a lifelong contract in my blood. I could focus on nothing but the idea that Nick shared everything I considered unshareable. He knew she never left, but did he carry her too? How many Marleys existed now that she was gone?

By unanimous vote, the group decided to explore the tunnel first. Somehow, my left hand raised in agreement. It's possible I even spoke. The world moved at a pace I couldn't follow. Too fast and too slow and too up and too down. Nick suggested the box be opened when Bigs and Teeny were back from work. I agreed to that too.

We'll wait because we're one team, everyone else thought. Their synchronicity instilled faith that we were on the right track. That all internal trouble had been navigated. Suddenly I wasn't even required to unite this group. They had Nick Cline, boy wonder.

He walked ahead. I ran around him. I went into the tunnel first. He pressed his hand into my back. Every move was attack or counter. Our battle was constant. I fought without thinking. Without hearing the guides I'd used to keep my life in check.

I made sure not to fall off the tunnel ledge again. Before Nick could even spot the drop-off, my legs stretched out and caught the ground. I hoped my grace did not go unnoticed. And wished for a memory that would never exist. "Remember that time Nick Cline fell?" I imagined asking Ruby. I'd have to use his full name because he'd be so far out of our lexicon that she'd need the reminder.

He didn't fall, of course. He landed with the same lightness as me.

Similar, I told myself. *We are not the same.* He might've known about Marley, but he didn't carry her, I decided. He wasn't strong enough.

Daylight helped make the first part of the tunnels less ominous. It was still too dim to be comfortable, but not as unsettling as our last visit. "So, you found the letters and stuff in the sewer?" Harrison asked once we returned to the scene of the spray-painted message.

If only he noticed how little muscle contractions in my stomach betrayed me. It was hard to catch me in my own untruths. I was usually my only alibi. But of course Nick knew, because he seemed to exist solely to disrupt my entire self-image. So, to Harrison, I said, "Yep," as a throwaway word, using it as a test for Nick. *Agree with me and I'll speak to you again. Give me back my power.*

"All right here, all this time," Nick told everyone. He sounded so wrapped up in the memory that even I believed him.

I had to continue the lie, to prove I was better at it. "Kind of incredible no one touched it."

"Yeah, really. How was it not rained out?" Harrison asked, still oblivious. "We hardly ever get rain, but still. Five years is a long time."

Lies worked best when hazy. Undetailed. I'd call inconsistencies to the forefront, all because of Nick. He started to speak, prepared to cover for me, but I barreled over him with my liveliest, surest tone. "It was tucked into a dry little corner right before the drop-off. There's this crevice you can't really see. I was crawling in here for old times' sake, I guess, and I touched it by accident. Not sure why I even thought to look further. Guess I had Marley on the mind because of the memorial, and I thought *what would she do?*"

Nick did not get to rescue me. He did not get a debt in his favor.

"Smart," Harrison said. He turned his flashlight onto the wall. "You didn't love me like I asked of you," he read. "Still I love you back."

"Whoa," Aidy said, nearly breathless.

"Do you think that's a clue?" Harrison asked.

"Well, yeah. And a pretty obvious one," she answered, smug as ever.

I could feel her trying to shift the conversation toward whether or not Marley meant to die, so I took a risk. I reached into Harrison's back pocket and yanked out his Marley letter. "Sorry, what was it your letter said again?"

"Hey! Give that back!" He snatched the paper from me. But my strategy worked. He started reading. "My clue says: *The tunnel goes farther than we know. Walk until the dead man's eyes see*

137

you leave." He returned his letter to his back pocket, tucking it in with his wallet.

"Oh my God," Ruby whispered to herself. "That guy they found dead down here. Remember that? He was holding his eyes in his hands."

There was a collective shudder.

"The eyes were looking up," I said.

The group was trained on me, waiting for more. I raised my eyebrows to coax the answer out of someone's mouth.

Aidy read me. "You think we need to find an exit that goes back up," she said.

"Ooooooh." Ruby nodded her head. "Of course. His hands were reaching up. That's good, Olivia."

My answer was a nod to farther down the tunnels. Leaders didn't always explain. They taught. Didn't see Nick doing much of that.

Harrison took my cue and started walking. When we reached a crossroads, he stopped to examine the three tunnels that lay ahead. "Which way?" he asked.

He'd backpedaled, leaving me at the front of our pack. Various cell phones cast weak streaks of light in all directions. Not much could be made out from where we stood, loosely huddled like Scooby-Doo characters.

"I know this is like Horror Movie No-No 101, but I think we have to split up," Aidy said. Everyone waited for her elaboration. "We'll do it once, and find whatever we're looking for, instead of coming back over and over. I don't know about the rest of you, but I'm not doing this again."

It was three tunnels for five people. Everyone in this group had a set companion, and though mine sometimes fluctuated, it would end up Nick and me, I knew. The story wrote itself. Ruby would think we needed a moment alone, so she'd volunteer to go on her own. Harrison and Aidy would be paired up without acknowledgment. If Bigs and Teeny were here, they'd go together. It was the way things went.

To be more unique, I had to not only surprise Nick, but myself. No one could know what I would do next. Nick might've been a When, but I was a What If.

What if little Ollie Stanton turned out to be the one meant for greatness after all?

"I'll go with Harrison," I said in answer to the expectation. It was the most surprising option available. The only way to keep the Nick battle in my favor.

Harrison recoiled like I'd punched him in the gut. "Uh," he said, looking to Aidy.

"I'll go with Nick," she countered. She thought this was the start of another fight between her and me.

I hadn't meant to upset her. Still, I found myself throwing kindling to the flame. "That's fine," I said.

To have something to contribute, Ruby said, "I don't mind being by myself."

So it became Harrison and me down the left tunnel, Ruby up the center, Aidy and Nick to the right. Harrison and I spent the first few minutes listening to the pipes above us creak and rattle as we walked. It sounded like a constant stream of semitrucks driving over our heads. The farther we got, the more distant the noise became, and with it came the expectation of conversation to replace it.

It turned out I had no clue what to say to Harrison Shin. Everything I knew of him came from Aidy's stories, mixed with a touch of the constant colorless interactions we had. *Hey, Olivia. Hi, Harrison. How's school? Good. How about for you? Good.*

I always imagined his dreams to be as simple as our conversations. He wanted to marry Aidy. Get a good job. Buy a house in Cadence. My image of him floated as a mirage in front of us. As I contemplated it, Little Ollie emerged next to him, peace sign tankini stained with blood, struggling under the weight of an imaginary Marley wrapped around her neck. She cried out for help. Over and over.

"I'm sorry," I said to Harrison, compelled by the memory of my younger self. Harrison had been hard for me to know. He belonged to Aidy almost entirely, and I'd accepted that for as long as I'd known him.

"For what?" He cast light onto the concrete walls in pursuit of another message, pretending to find our mission more interesting than an apology from me.

"I haven't always been fair to you," I started.

"Oh," he said, stunned.

"I know, I'm being weird. But let me talk for a second." I took a deep breath. It smelled terrible where we were. "I don't like it when people accept only one idea of who I am. I do that to you. I'm sorry," I said again. My magic words fell from my lips before

I could consider the consequences of renovating my impression of him.

He stopped and shone his cell phone on me. Stark in the light, I fought the urge to cower. "Thank you for saying that. I have no idea why you did, but it means a lot to me." He was being so earnest, it made me squirm. The two of us never communicated this way. My opinion of him was a veil I wasn't supposed to lift. I'd pledged allegiance to my sister on the first day of my life. If her boyfriend bothered her, he had to bother me too. That was the unspoken contract of our sisterhood.

But I didn't want to know only cardboard versions of the Albany kids. I didn't want to do to them what had been done to me for so many years.

Before I could find a response that both honored Aidy and expressed my appreciation of our ability to look past what we knew of each other, Harrison turned his phone's light toward himself. "Shit, shit, shit," he muttered.

"What's wrong?"

"Shit," he said again. "My letter." He began patting the wet, filthy ground, gagging as his frenzied hands grazed over discarded condom wrappers and various piles of unidentifiable muck.

I stood frozen, observing in horror and fascination. Once it occurred to me that holding myself like a statue would not be the choice of someone who didn't know where the letter had gone, I crouched down to duck waddle around in pursuit of the paper.

"It's just," he started, his voice rising.

"What?"

He didn't answer. Not on the second time either. By the third time I repeated the question, he managed a squeak that trickled with the possibility of tears. "Marley." He was nearing the height of hysteria now. "I need that letter. I can't lose it." His face folded into a pile of grief. "It's the only piece of her that's mine."

"It's all right," I cooed, my heart hammering so hard, its foundation started to crack, breaking into my newfound Harrison soft spot. "We'll find it. It's probably back by the first entrance. We'll keep moving now, then go back and look a little later. Okay?"

"But what if there are more clues in there that I missed?" He made circles around himself like a cat chasing his tail. "What if it had the answer to why she wanted to die?"

I stopped moving.

"Every little piece matters," he continued. "I didn't spend enough time reading it. She said we didn't love her like she asked. I should have memorized what my letter said. How could I lose it?"

Aidy had gotten to him. She'd spread her theory like a contagious disease, and Harrison was infected. As I staggered back, my foot pressed into a piece of paper.

Harrison's letter.

Marley, Marley, Marley. What are you doing? I wondered as I picked it up. One corner was wet from my shoe, but it was otherwise unscathed.

"You found it," Harrison whispered in awe. He wrapped his arms around me. "Thank you."

I had no idea the last time we'd so much as brushed shoulders, let alone hugged. It was strange to let his gratitude envelop me. It made me feel unsteady. I didn't want to give in and hold him too tight, but I didn't want to push back either. There was no reason to perform with my head pressed into his chest.

I pulled back and tried to return his letter. My sweaty palm had softened the paper, dulling the dry edges and bleeding the ink where my shoe had dampened the corner.

Harrison pushed the letter away. "Will you hold on to it for me until we get outside? I don't want it to fall out again."

I tucked it deep into the front pocket of my shorts.

We kept walking. With each new step, the smell worsened and the tunnel darkened. Even with Harrison's cell phone light as a guide, there was nothing to see. We walked side by side for fear of separating. We didn't speak. We couldn't. Opening our mouths and taking in the air seemed hazardous. I clutched onto his shirt. The muscles in his arms pressed up through the fabric. The sturdiness of him was a comfort.

I couldn't see that there was something sticking up a few paces ahead.

When I reached whatever it was, I tripped. Stumbling toward the ground, my hand wrapped around his shirt, Harrison went down with me. Our faces splashed into liquid. We bolted upright, spitting and spitting to eliminate the tangy taste of whatever lay on the ground. Thicker liquid trickled down my nose and flirted with my lips. Blood, I recognized. I did my best to snuff it out, pinching my nostrils with one hand, wiping my face with the other, still spitting. My bottom was wet with whatever I sat in, seeping through the denim of my shorts.

Harrison's spitting took up more weight. He'd begun throwing up, and through unexpected fortune, managed to do it without splashing me. I settled into my misery until it became unbearable, knowing I could turn it into motivation. If finding his letter was a gift from Marley, this was a punishment.

"Come on. Get up." I patted to my left until I found Harrison and yanked him up alongside me. "We can't stay here." He was so much taller than me that my arm started burning, but I didn't dare release, needing the touch to assure me he wouldn't leave.

"Do you still have my letter?"

I patted my pocket. "It's here."

The hole we walked through blackened, anthropomorphizing into a vicious beast, eager to swallow us whole. Somewhere along the walk, a genuine connection formed in the poignant hush between us. We were disappearing into this hungry void, covered in vomit and blood and tears and who knows what else. The darkness became so complete that I no longer remembered how to be anything other than afraid. In the absence of other feelings, that fear became soothing.

A wall shattered our tragic mutual resignation. An actual wall. My free hand could not fathom its wholeness after infinitely reaching for nothing. The cold concrete startled me so much that I screamed out, my shrill voice bouncing around me, offending my own ears. We'd walked into the space between another crossroads. Once backed away a bit, subtle differences in our surroundings manifested. Two circular shapes blotted out of the void: one on the left, one on the right.

Come on, Ollie. Make the right choices, my letter had said.

On impulse, I sprinted down the right side, possessed by the promise of freedom and the belief that this was a way out of the mess we'd made.

I expected Harrison to be behind me. Instead, cries of "Ollie! Ollie!" echoed off the walls.

The wrong name for the wrong girl. I wasn't her anymore.

Turning back, even a little, would've disoriented me, so I remained steadfast, my insides thick and syrupy, swirling like a washing machine. *No stops,* I repeated to myself. Harrison should've known how this went. Follow or defy. And he didn't follow.

With arms stretched out in anticipation, I hit another wall. This one was fixed with metal bars that seemed to be for climbing. Each bar led to another, to another, and so on, until my head bumped into a ceiling. I pushed up, meeting resistance. Pushing again, sunlight shoved its way in like an unwelcome guest, nearly knocking me back down.

My eyes could not adjust to the change. Squeezing my lids tight enough to make my cheeks almost touch my eyebrows, I shoved the cover to the side and flopped stomach-first onto the sand in front of me. For a while I lay like that, easing up my squint in concentrated bursts, trying to train myself to see daylight again. The surface of the sand was hot, but the farther I burrowed into it, the cooler it became.

I tried to open my eyes all the way. I was not ready for the pierce of the sun, but I forced myself to keep looking, fighting so hard against my body's reflexes that my eyes furiously watered.

I was in the desert, which I should've known from the sand and shrubs, but had not registered.

Inch by inch, I crawled forward, my whole body splayed out like a corpse. The sky was pure and blue, not a single cloud in sight. To know Marley was to know this kind of day as the exact color of her eyes. In blinking desperation, I pieced together the world around me. A desert, I told myself again, then scolded my ignorance. There was always more to see. I spotted a sign staked into the ground in the near distance. Like a newborn foal, I clambered toward it until my eyes could make out the words: THE POINT OF NO RETURN.

I'd passed the point of no return.

The quicksand was not sand at all, but a sewer lid. In sweet relief, I collapsed back down and pulled Harrison's letter out of my pocket, careful not to stain it with the blood still dripping from my nose.

HARRISON SHIN

Welcome to the Adventure. Eyes on your own paper, please.

I'll never forget the day you moved onto Albany. We were all so excited to have another kid on the street. Especially Bigs. After Nick told us a new boy was moving in across from him, Bigs was the one who said we should ride our bikes over and check you out. Did you know that? Then Aidy took you on your own tour of the town without the rest of us. And that was that.

It's so weird to think about. How did it take you only

a day to know you liked her? It's taken me a whole lifetime to decide on one single thing I like that much.

Don't ask what it is.

I admire so much in you. You're always around, living your life, keeping everything together. I know you're like in love with Aidy. Your dad passed away. You keep Cap'n Crunch in a plastic bag in your pocket at all times. You're pretty good at tennis. You're ridiculously strong. And of course, there was that one time you saw a snake in your backyard and you freaked out. That's my number one favorite memory of you. I'm pretty sure it was a garden snake, but you were hunched over in a corner like it was about to reach out and grab you. Tiny little Ollie had to be the one to catch it. So good.

It's been years, and that's pretty much all I've got. I should be able to embarrass you with your deepest secret or something. I'll look at you when I'm trying to start some trouble and I'll be like, "Hmm. I've got nothing worth saying."

How do you do that? People find LOTS of things to say about me, even when I try to copy exactly what you do. Be in the room. Laugh at the jokes. Enjoy the company. Keep up a good appearance and stay out of drama. No one lets me get away with that.

Although I have to say, it's kind of fun to be more than that. Sometimes.

Sometimes it's the best thing in the whole world.

Sometimes it's not.

Tell the group the tunnel goes farther than we know. Walk until the dead man's eyes see you leave.

Love always,

Marley

JULY 11

Five Years Prior

MY HEAD SCREAMED. MY HEART SCREAMED. I SCREAMED. MY voice became louder than noise itself. Still barefoot, I sprinted out the door and down the street, my towel flying off and landing in the center of Albany Lane. The only word I could come up with was "Help!" I yelled it a thousand times in a thousand ways, my desperation begging for understanding, hoping for someone to fix the mess we'd made.

Aidy appeared at the edge of our driveway with Harrison and the Campbell twins. They took off toward the Bricket house before I could reach them. Spectators flitted blinds and pulled back curtains as I ran my voice ragged and hoarse, screaming to drown out the ringing in my ears. Black pavement scorched my feet, forcing my aimless yelling indoors.

One creak of our aging floorboards, sounding too much like a softened gunshot in my frenzied state of mind, broke my stream of wails. It was Ruby, with her big umber eyes widened in curious fear. She came from my bedroom holding our secret box: a collection of trinkets we'd taken while raiding our houses for hidden treasures. One of our stolen cigarettes, formerly property of my mom, filled a space between her unwashed fingers. She liked the habit more than I did. When Marley tried to teach us, I didn't smoke it right, and I had no interest in learning the proper technique. It was gross and it burned my lungs. How anyone found enjoyment in it seemed mystifying to me.

Ruby said she only did it when she was stressed—which I think was something she'd heard my mom say while trying to quit—but I didn't have time to wonder what had Ruby worried enough to sneak off into my room and smoke. I was crying too hard.

"What's wrong?" she cooed, the habit furthering the husky undertone of her voice.

I knew she wouldn't smoke if my parents had gotten home, so I did what I'd wished to do so many times before—snatched her lit cigarette and put it out. It burned a shadowy mark into the carpet at the edge of my bedroom doorway. I grabbed her hand and dragged her along. She matched my wordless panic without question.

Outside, a good portion of our block had emerged from their windowsill perches. Contempt seeped from every seam of their breezy layers and crooked robes. They were grandparents and recluses. We were the rascals of Albany Lane. Marley was fifteen, Aidy was fourteen, Bigs and Teeny were thirteen, Ruby was twelve, and Nick and I were eleven. Our unattractive ages rendered us too old to be babysat, but too young to be so self-sufficient. Still, an unspoken trust permeated throughout all of Cadence. All residents granted the town's children permission to roam without any real supervision, just as they had, and the generation before, and the one before that, and so on and so forth.

"What was that sound?" Old Mr. Jimenez, in his worn khaki shorts, half-buttoned Hawaiian shirt, and beige ball cap, asked me with a heavy undertone of disdain. "Are you setting off fireworks? Where are your parents? It isn't—"

"Leave us alone!" Ruby shouted in protection.

We continued toward Marley's, running down the street and around to the back of her house. The screen door was open. Bloodstained footprints, tracked in reverse, led us to the master bedroom.

Looking at the size of the prints in comparison to mine, sometimes stepping in one to measure the heel of it to my toe, I knew they were Nick's, but there was no time to wonder where he'd gone.

Marley's dead body lay in front of us.

12

EVERYTHING AROUND ME LOOKED LIKE TEXTBOOK CADENCE, the same exterior I'd seen nearly every single day of my life, washed out by the sun, strangled by dry heat. The ancient train tracks had disappeared completely. Rocky sand and starved shrubbery left little indication of where they'd once been. I walked up and down, feeling for what was left of them.

After such a long bout with Harrison in the dark, my thoughts turned inside out in the startling brightness. To me, the letters read as sentimental. They highlighted what was best about each of us. They gave us each a task.

That didn't seem despairing. Did it?

Chasing the Adventure five years later wasn't supposed to mean rewriting history. But words could do that. Take on new life in different minds. Turn themselves into monsters when they might have been conceived as angels.

We were a team, but I was the leader. I needed to gather up every piece of Marley spread out across every inch of this place before anyone else got to it. It was possible to both share the information and control what people thought of it. I watched Marley do it all the time. But if the Albany kids started finding things without me, they might continue to mishandle Marley's memory. They wouldn't even discuss her at all until I brought us together again, and this is how they chose to revisit what she'd been to us? I had to show them they were wrong.

The tunnel had led me back up, like Harrison's letter said. The next clue was here. At the point of no return.

Perfect.

Every year, Marley scolded us when we inevitably gave up on finishing her scavenger hunt. "Ugh. It's so obvious," she'd say when the last of us surrendered. The last being me. Always. I'd have to give my verbal resignation because adventures ended with summer. I'd walk to her house at six thirty in the morning on the first day of the new school year and tell her I hadn't found anything else. What she didn't know is that I always kept searching even after that point, trying to squeeze meaning out of misplaced rocks in our driveway or even holes in my shirt. Papers discarded in the trash. Everything.

I started digging into the ground beneath the POINT OF NO RETURN sign. Sweat mixed with the blood falling from my face. Red drops dripped onto my clenched fists. After a while, something grazed the tips of my fingers. Soft and solid. Distinctly different. My digging took on new fervor. Right beneath the surface was a third of a journal: the front side leather bound, the back side sheets of paper dangling off binding. I pressed its sand-stained cover to my chest.

Marley's journal.

In my mind, her words propped up and became a movie playing on fast-forward. The Albany kids were nowhere to be found on the first pages. Marley painted vignettes of the life she lived without us. Late nights with her dad in their shed, working on a project she never referred to with any specificity. Memories of drives to pageants all across the coast, her mom forcing her to eat only cottage cheese the entire weekend. Impressions of a fight between her parents as she overheard it from her bedroom. That particular entry devolved into direct quotes, each getting scratchier and more urgent, Marley fighting to keep pace with the crescendoing argument.

MOM: *You didn't love me like I asked of you.*

DAD: *I could say the same.*

MOM: *You know it's not the same.*

DAD: *Karen.*

MOM: *Don't try to compare. The sickest part is that still, I love you back, even though I know it's not a good idea.*

Why can't my mom see that the way she feels about my dad is the exact way I feel about her? You didn't love me like I asked of you. Still I love you back. But it doesn't seem to be enough. Nothing is ever enough.

Harrison was wrong. Those words in the tunnel weren't about us. They were about Marley's parents. My eyelids grew heavy with angry tears. I pushed the pages into the band of my shorts and stood, Marley's journal like a weapon I brandished for show. Aidy had tainted my thoughts. I couldn't help but filter every word of the journal through what Aidy had said. She made Marley seem sad to me. And hurt. Lost. Confused. Ignored.

I hated Aidy for that. So much. More than I could handle.

In my anger I stalked off, headed toward Arbor Street. Under my breath, I rehearsed different phrases. *What happened with you and Marley? What did you do to her? Why couldn't you love her like she asked?* The incessant practicing made my tongue melt the words into unrecognizable blobs. I started running to chase off self-doubt. My speed built to a pace that required all of my focus. I ran until my words no longer had sound at all.

The blood that dripped onto my knuckles was still wet, leaving red stamps on the cream-colored lacquer of her front door. "Ms. DeVeau!" I called out. I pressed my ear to the wood to hear something. Anything. I imagined Ms. DeVeau manifesting in her living room, teleported from wherever she was by the sheer urgency with which I continued knocking.

"Karen!" I tried, testing out her first name. Willing myself to be the kind of person she had to answer. "Karen, it's Olivia Stanton. I need to talk to you!"

"Olivia!" a voice called out from behind me.

Terror froze me in place. The sharpness in tone, coated in confidence, sprinkled with the faintest traces of affection. It was Teeny.

"Olivia, I know you can hear me!" she yelled. "Get over here! You've got people blowing up my phone asking me to look for you."

I turned around.

"Didn't I tell you she'd be over this way?" Teeny asked Bigs as she waved me down. She was in the passenger seat of their shared car, an impeccably maintained silver Honda Civic they'd been gifted with two years ago, right around their sixteenth birthday. I knew about it from Aidy. In fact, I got almost all of my Campbell twins information from her.

"Yes, I see you," Teeny said. "You see me. Please come over here." Teeny gasped as I got closer. "What did you do to your face?" I opened the back door. "Hold on a second." She tossed a magazine into the back seat. "Rip this up and sit on it. You're filthy."

Bigs and Teeny wore khaki pants and matching blue polos with their aunt's hotel name monogrammed onto the front right corner. On a different day, it would've made me laugh to see the two of them dressed alike, something their parents used to force upon them as young children.

I couldn't muster up amusement anymore. After I covered my seating area, I rested my elbow atop the ledge of the passenger window and used it as a kickstand for my face, watching my chance for answers turn into a heat-choked blur of scenery. "Thanks for finding me," I forced myself to say. Putting aside what I'd wanted to do, it meant a lot that they would go out and look for me.

"We'd just left the hotel when Ruby called me five times in a row," Teeny said. "I looked at Bigs and said, *Can't she send me a text?* But she kept calling, and I got scared that—" She stopped. "Well, I answered then. It's a good thing we were only working the morning shift."

"Are you all right?" Bigs asked.

Explaining myself felt like a courtesy I owed his kindness. "I fell in the tunnels."

"Ruby said she came up over by the school," Teeny told me. "She tried to call you, but your parents have your phone? You were down there without a single way to talk to anyone? You're lucky I guessed you were over by Marley's mom's house! I don't know how I knew that. I said to Bigs, *I bet she found her way out to the train tracks.* You were always trying to go to the train tracks." She wore a satisfied smile, showcasing it in the rearview mirror for me to see. "Little Ollie, still thinking you're so tough."

She was misremembering history. It was Ruby who loved the tracks.

I didn't love anything.

Teeny started to travel down the road of reminiscing until something drastic snatched up the sentence she meant to say and replaced it with one more urgent. "Where's Harrison?"

Where is Harrison? I wondered with the same newfound panic. "I don't know."

"Ruby said he'd be with you."

"The tunnels split again. Aidy wanted us to cover as much ground as we could, so I—I left him."

Teeny shook her head. "You left him? Down there all alone?"

"Did you try calling him?" I asked.

Teeny shot me a look.

Bigs redirected our conversation. "She called him twice. It didn't ring. Where do you think he'd end up?"

A helplessness started to consume me. "I really don't know. You said Ruby came out by the haunted house? What about Aidy and Nick?"

"She tried calling Aidy when we were looking for you," Bigs said. "No answer."

"Aidy doesn't have her phone either," I admitted.

Teeny looked at me as if I'd failed an un-failable test. The shame I felt rivaled anything I'd ever experienced with my parents. This was true disappointment. Letting down the people who included me in their life by choice, not genetic obligation.

"Do either of you have Nick's number?" I asked.

"Do you?" Teeny let that rhetorical question sit. "First, you were lost, now everybody's lost except for you. The Adventure's about as successful as it usually is, huh?"

The Adventure had deteriorated with such rapidity that in trying to figure out when the downfall began, all my memories seemed clouded with doom. I reminded myself I was the only one with Marley's journal. I was the only one with fingers to point at people who may have hurt her. I could still get ahead of this, and the outcome would still be worth the price being paid. It had to be.

Bigs pulled into Cadence Park's parking lot. In the distance, Ruby stood at the concession stand over by the park district. The girl who was usually behind the counter was out front, helping Ruby clean herself up. The physical tenderness between the two of them told me more than Ruby had in quite some time. I took in the situation with a different kind of curiosity. Last we spoke of concession-stand girl, Ruby decided it wasn't worth it to try and pursue her.

Her Marley letter was right. Ruby could keep secrets locked inside of her.

I never thought she kept them from me.

A sudden, flaming embarrassment over how I'd made her worry burned through me. I conjured up an image of her talking to concession-stand girl in between phone calls to Teeny. In my imagined scenario, Ruby was complaining about my shortcomings, thinking to herself, *Finally, a person I can confide in about Olivia.*

When she saw me get out of the car, she ran over. "Why were you so worried?" I found myself asking once she reached me. If no one else had returned, why was it me she sent Teeny and Bigs to find on the streets?

"I had this terrible feeling you'd gotten hurt," she told me as she rested her head on my neck. She pulled back to look at my face. "Looks like I was right."

There would be nights I felt scared—of the dark, of the future, of the past, of nothing in particular—and my usually useless cell phone would ring, Ruby's gravelly voice on the other end, telling me she'd been thinking of me.

"What happened?" she asked. "Where's Harrison?"

"I left him," I told her. It was a retaliation best suited to the situation building in my head. Scare her off. Let there be no more secrets for her to tell someone else. Let there be no more things for anyone to misinterpret.

"I thought that might happen. My path split a few times. I made guesses. I didn't find anything." She touched Marley's journal poking out of my shorts. "You did, though. I knew you would."

My disposition became a collapsible chair, folding inside itself. "It's not really much," I lied, having no way to back it up. I'd been so surprised by Teeny and Bigs—so caught up in trying to confront Ms. DeVeau—that I'd forgotten to hide the journal. Everyone would expect to have a chance to read it. Ruby would know that I'd lied to her. The failures to come made me so weak my knees buckled.

Ruby placed her hands on my shoulders to steady me. "Come on. Emery has a first aid kit at her stand. We need to clean you up." She said her name as if we spoke it often. As if life post-Marley had always been Ruby, Ollie, and Emery, yet another group of *-ee* girls, arms interwoven, skipping through Cadence Park.

I took a step back, leaving Ruby's arms reaching for nothing. "What about Aidy and Nick?" I asked. "What about Harrison? It's them we should we worried about."

Ruby pulled her hands in and buried them under her backpack straps. "Aidy called me from Nick's phone before you got here. She thinks they found what Marley was talking about in Harrison's letter. They're bringing it back with them."

No. No. No.

"Aidy has your number memorized?" I asked.

"Of course," she said with a breeziness that tried to blow the follow-up questions away. *Of course she does, Olivia. You never know when she'll have to call me, wherever she is, with whatever phone is closest. You Stanton girls never seem to have your cell phones on you.*

160

"Harrison's down there all alone. We both fell. He might be more hurt than I am," I said, trying again to scare her off. Couldn't she see by now that everyone and everything that got close to me eventually broke? It was only a matter of time before her number was up.

"Then I'll go in again and look for him. You shouldn't. Your face is already bruising. And your legs are bleeding too."

I looked down. There were little pebbles embedded into my kneecaps. Blood traced their edges. My clothing, already ragged, now looked post-apocalyptic. "Oh," was all I managed to say.

"Come on," Ruby said. "It's okay."

She placed her hand on my back and guided me to Emery, who did her part and waved, one-third of the famous trio that never was. "Hey," she said, careful to sound both comfortable and concerned, like, *You don't look great right now, but I can help. I'm not worried. Well, I am, but only in the way that makes me worried about your injuries, not in the way that says anything bad has actually happened or will happen. Okay? Friend to friend!*

She had the smile of someone who'd once been embarrassed by her braces. Her teeth looked to be perfect, and when she found something funny enough to lose self-consciousness, like Ruby's joke about my injury being what it takes to be the friend of a bicyclist, she showed them. But for me, as she wiped my knee with an antiseptic, she pursed her top lip over the enamel as she grinned for my approval. "Does this hurt?"

"I'm fine," I said through gritted teeth.

Ruby explained to Teeny and Bigs how we decided to wait for them before looking inside the box.

Shifting my eyes. Fidgeting with my seat. Rolling my wrists for no good reason. I tried everything short of actually talking. I wanted to communicate to Ruby that Emery shouldn't be overhearing this. Our Albany kid activities had always been covert. We operated under a strict code of honor that never needed to be mentioned, for it was always understood. We were a self-contained unit. In school, my friends in my grade were casual. There were no sleepovers. No talks of our childhood. They knew my relation to Marley—I was her post-death representative, after all—but they never talked about her to me. I only saw Ruby at lunch and in between classes. That's what I got for being the youngest of all of us. Forever a grade, or two, or three, or four, behind everyone.

Well, everyone but Nick, but he was at his other school.

As I thought it, he and Aidy came up from over the hilly part of Albany. My alliances shifted so much, so thoughtlessly, that until I saw him, I didn't realize he was the only one who could ever fully understand. He wouldn't misinterpret the Adventure. He wouldn't find someone else to tell his secrets to. He didn't have siblings or other friends. He had me. And we had Marley. A Marley no one else could find.

It wasn't that I didn't like that feeling, I realized. I was afraid of it. And I hated to be scared.

Aidy started running when she saw me. "What happened?" She looked every bit the part of a frantic parent as she dropped beside Emery to examine my knees. She took her inventory then leaned into my face, touching my apparently bruising skin with a firm tenderness, applying more pressure than she should, but not so much that I would cry out in pain.

"I'm okay," I said, a parody of myself.

"What are we going to tell Mom and Dad?" she asked.

"The phone call," we said together, both of us remembering the element of our punishment we'd let slip away. Aidy turned to Teeny. "What time is it?"

"Why?" Teeny observed the two of us, her very body a shield, leaning back and away, desperate not to catch whatever problems we had.

Bigs showed Aidy his phone screen. "We have to go," Aidy announced upon seeing it. "We'll be back soon."

Her behavior was classic. We both knew our punishments to be somewhat decorative. We were, after all, standing next to Cadence Park when we were supposed to be inside our house. Yet she treated their rules for us as if we were legally bound to them.

"The Campbells have a car," I reminded her as she tugged me along.

She had an internal debate with herself over what was easier, even though it was obvious the drive was the better choice. They could let us out at Arbor Street and we'd sneak back into our house the very way we came out.

"Hey, Bigs, could you drive us?" I decided for both of us. "And maybe, if you didn't mind, wait a second while we get cleaned up and call our parents?"

"Can we all go home first? We're still in our work uniforms," Teeny said. "An eight-to-one shift and straight to search for you."

"We'll drop you off. You can call us when you're ready to get picked up again," Bigs told me.

Lucky for me, Aidy didn't notice Harrison had not yet resurfaced. As we walked to the Civic, I nodded at Ruby like *Go find him,* which she understood. How convenient that she could read my body language then. Entire plans could be hatched through simple gestures and ignored through grand ones. We went in opposite directions, Ruby back down the bowl, us siblings into the car. Nick and Emery stayed stationary between us.

Bigs and Teeny dropped us off at Arbor Street. Aidy and I snuck back in the Marley way. As we shimmied and crawled, the pain of my fall started to settle. My head throbbed. My knees buzzed. Fighting against it as best I could, I took my shoes off before entering through our back door and tiptoed over to the house phone, containing my mess as much as possible.

Mom answered on the first ring. "Hey, Mom. I'm checking in like you asked," I said, my voice as wobbly as a three-legged chair.

"Oh," she said, not noticing. "Thank you, honey. I'll let your father know. I've got to go already, but call again in two more hours."

"Of course," Aidy said over my shoulder.

"All right, love you girls. Talk soon."

"Love you too." I rolled my eyes as I hung up. "Of course," I said, mocking not Aidy, but our mom, trying to regain my strength through the power of my sarcasm. "Of course she forgot."

"Oh well. We did it. Makes us look better that we remembered. We only have two more hours before we have to do it again, so go shower. You're going to flip out over what we found."

In a matter of hours, our roles had reversed. She was excited, ready to keep going. I was exhausted, overwhelmed by the gravity of what I was piecing together.

Once in the bathroom, my own face surprised me. The bruises already starting to form under my eyes looked like two faint Cheshire cat grins, smiling at my every miscalculation. The bridge of my nose was a little flatter and wider than usual. Seeing it made the pain multiply, no longer a vague headache, but a concentrated nose ache.

"Aidy!" I called out. A swelling, starting in the base of my stomach, pushed upward. My voice cracked as I shouted my sister's name again.

She burst into the room, yelling, "What?"

"Is it broken?" I asked her, hearing myself from outside my own mind, finding my hysteria to be an exact match for Harrison's earlier fit.

She tried putting her hands on the sides of my arms. Her wheels spun with ways to placate me. "I don't think so," she told me. "It's not bleeding anymore, and it's not crooked or anything, so why don't you shower and taken an ibuprofen, and we'll put ice on it once you're done. Okay? It really doesn't look as bad as it probably feels. I promise." She started to walk out, trying to trick me with her lack of urgency. She closed the bathroom door, then opened it again seconds later. "Are you having any trouble breathing?"

I inhaled. The air inside my nose moved like it was sneaking in the Marley way, compressing itself between narrow corridors. It was uncomfortable, but it moved. "Not really."

"Okay." She closed the door. She opened it again. "Keep breathing, then." She closed the door a third, final time.

I took two ibuprofens and watched myself swallow them, taking in my fractured image until it became something worth appreciating. I turned away from the mirror to remove my filthy clothes, convincing myself that every unexpected hiccup had to be a necessary piece of the bigger picture.

Good thing Marley thrived on theatrics.

I stepped into the bathtub and squatted in front of the spout. The water ran over my hands until they were clean. I pulled out the knob. Dirt and filth began waterfalling off my back, slinking into the drain. As my skin revealed itself again, I decided the water was washing away not only the dirt, but the pain itself.

By the time I climbed out, Aidy had already removed my dirty clothes from the floor. In the distance clapped the unmistakable thunder of a new garbage bag being opened. Wrapped in a towel, I walked out to find Aidy, already changed, shoving my bloody shirt and shorts into the black plastic.

"Your face looks better," she told me, even though she hadn't once looked up from her work. "The Campbells will be back in ten minutes. Get changed. We'll ice on the car ride." When she finally noticed I hadn't moved from watching her, she said, "I'm gonna hide this in the shrubs. We'll throw it out for real when we're allowed to go out the front door."

I made quick work of changing.

By its third use, the Marley way had started to give in to our new size, even as I carried a bag of frozen peas with me to ice my nose. Aidy and I came out onto Arbor Street, where the Campbells' Honda waited like our getaway car.

Back at Cadence Park, Emery and Nick still held conference near the concession stand.

"Where's Ruby?" I wondered aloud. At the same time, Aidy asked, "Where's Harrison?" Her eyes bored into me as she unbuckled her seat belt. Bigs didn't even have time to park before she'd opened her door and started running.

"Well, that's not good," Bigs said, because Bigs always said the truth in its simplest form.

"Better start admitting what you know," Teeny told me, because Teeny always knew how to say what her brother couldn't.

We got out of the car and met everyone at the concession stand. When the Campbells and I approached, Emery was almost done explaining to Aidy what happened to Harrison and Ruby. "I've been sending her texts, but they're not going through, which makes me think she's still down there."

I kept my distance, knowing Aidy's fury would be directed at me. "Well?" she said, cocking her head in my direction.

My throat swelled. There was nothing to say that would explain my actions. I brought my bag of peas back up to my face. Poor Harrison. I shouldn't have left him. Why had I left him? Why couldn't I make good choices when they mattered most?

"Don't hide," Aidy scolded. "Why'd you leave him?"

"I don't know." I couldn't look her in the eye.

"This is bad, Olivia. Do you realize that? It's so bad."

"So we're clear, I'm not ever going down there," Teeny

informed us. She said it to lessen the tension. I loved her all the more for it. If I was an investigator, and Nick a watchman, maybe Teeny was actually a defuser, in charge of deciding which bombs exploded and which got to be disabled.

"No one's going down there," Emery challenged.

Everyone looked at her like, *Who are you to decide?* Even though I was making a glorious mess, that solidarity surged through me. Against outsiders, we Albany kids still had one another's back.

"I'm calling public services for help," Emery said. "Ruby and your friend are down there, and they might be as hurt as Olivia is. We can't leave them and expect it all to work out. We need a maintenance man or something to go down there."

Teeny grabbed the phone out of Emery's hand. "Look, I don't know you that well. I've seen you around at school, and Ruby seems to like you a lot, which means you're good people. But you have to understand, this is between us." She used her index finger to draw lines of energy between the Albany kids. "We know it's bad. But we've got a reputation in this town, and I'm not about to prove everyone right. You might not understand this, but I'm telling you that if something was really wrong with either of them, I think we'd be able to feel it." She handed the cell phone back as a truce of sorts. "We know it isn't wise doing to do this without help. I promise you that. But know that even Ruby would agree with me. Involving other people will only make all of this worse."

Emery pursed her lips, still skeptical.

"How about this?" Bigs asked. "If you don't hear from Ruby in the next half hour, come find us, and we'll go from there. Yeah?"

Emery agreed to that. We left her behind as we marched along, single file down into the bowl, carrying items both physical and mental, ready to be unpacked.

Once out of Emery's earshot, Aidy unleashed. "I can't believe you! Not a single mention of my missing boyfriend. Is he hurt too?"

"He might be," I muttered.

"Dammit, Olivia." Aidy cursed again. Then she yelled out "Let me think for a second!" even though no one else was talking. "Ugh, let's show them. That's what we're supposed to do anyway. Share what we find," she said to someone. "Maybe it'll help."

I followed the path of her eyes over to Nick. He removed his backpack from his shoulders and unzipped the top. Ragged, rolled-up blueprint paper sprung up, decompressed. He pulled it taut to reveal a map.

It was Cadence, California, with Xs over places we'd already been, and Xs over places we'd yet to explore.

JULY 11

Five Years Prior

MARLEY BRICKET ALWAYS HAD A WAY OF BEING COY. SHE presented a calculated yet attainable distance from the rest of us, which we all aided. She'd been to high school: a much-coveted, little understood land of promise and mystery. Still, she chose our neighborhood group for the summer. We did whatever was needed to keep it that way. We laid ourselves out like red carpet for her to walk all over.

Want to eat the last cupcake even though Harrison didn't have one and you've had two already? Go ahead. Need to put your dirty clothes in my laundry pile so your mom doesn't yell at you for spilling rum on your shirt? Sign me up.

The trade-off was daily excitement. A new game to play. Better, more scandalous things to talk about: kissing, and drinking, and what our parents did when we weren't home. Learning what no one else would teach us. Seeing what no one else could dare to imagine.

There was never a dull moment with Marley Bricket around.

That space we'd provided her with, out of respect and fear and admiration, expanded into an empty ocean of blue marble swirls in her eyes. A startling vacancy covered up all of her trademark mischief. She—of scandalous red bikinis and house raids and endless adventure—was dead. We all knew it, yet Aidy sat with one hand pressed over Marley's bullet wound, her phone up to her ear, and told a 911 dispatcher things like, "She isn't responding yet," and, "Just a little blood."

The same Aidy—who called my parents to tell them how I was breaking the rules and going to Marley's to swim—was bending truth.

That's how bad it was.

Ruby rushed to Marley's other side and held her hand. I wanted to copy. Earn my spot in the group through dedication, not blood relation to our second-in-command. I agreed to be called Ollie instead of Olivia, so I could have an -ee name like the other girls. I gave up both soccer and softball, so I didn't miss out on any house raids, or trips to the park, or spontaneous relay races down Albany. I stopped watching TV. I didn't have favorite musicians or movies. I'd given everything to our group, and still my instincts were wrong. I forgot to call 911. I didn't think to hold Marley's dead hand. I wanted to hide her under the bed until I found a way to reverse time.

With Nick missing, I stood in as villain: a human sponge that soaked up all blame in the room, bloating beneath my hideous peace sign tankini from absorbing every inch of desperation and confusion. Harrison grabbed on to a bed post and stared at blood pooling around his feet. Bigs and Teeny hugged. Better together than apart, they always fit into every ridge of each other until it looked as if they formed one person.

They all looked at me that day as if every bad thought they'd ever had about me had been proven right. I was bad news. I could kill someone.

Of course, I didn't do it. No one knew that yet. Aidy continued her 911 call and futile resuscitation attempts. The iPod played mindless music. I howled big ugly cries over and over until finally an adult appeared: Old Mr. Jimenez.

"Dios mío," he whispered to himself. He sounded as young as one of us, his words reduced to desperate whimpers. He ran over to help, muttering prayers and pressing harder on the bullet wound, trying to stop the blood.

Nobody knew what to do.

I needed to throw up. Another terrible reaction to the terrible, terrible mess I'd made. It didn't seem right to use the bathroom connected to the room where Marley lay dead, and I didn't have time to make it to the other one, so for some unexplainable reason I ran out to the pool and pushed up on the ledge. Overshooting my jump, I ended up face-first in chlorine and my own vomit: regurgitated red freeze pop mixed with Coke.

Once the day finished emptying itself from my insides, I scooted along the ledge to dunk my head in an untainted area. Opening my eyes underwater, I saw the blue of Marley's skin and eyes in the abyss around me. Flashes of her golden hair in the streaks of sunlight streaming in like thin daggers. The soaked crimson floral of the pillow in my vomit floating overhead. Primary colors summed up Marley's demise, linking her to everything I'd ever see again.

She was everywhere.

I let my head sink lower, considering what it would be like to stay under and erase all of it. Her blue wouldn't let me. It screamed for justice, floating me back up to the surface for air. I emerged with a huge gasp, slumping down alongside the pool to drain my nostrils of chlorine and mucus. In a violent fit of cough-crying, Marley's final words wove into the incessant noise inside my head.

Pull the trigger. Nothing's gonna happen.

I saw Nothing happen to her. When the light went out in her eyes, Nothing crept in.

That day, Nothing took hold of Marley and kept her.

13

"How'd you find this?" and "I almost want to cry," and "Please don't," and "It's so detailed," and "Up in the tree," and "Which tree?" and "Does it matter?" and "No," and "It was Nick's idea to go up there."

And then so soft, almost missed, "I remember her drawing that." Everyone turned to Bigs. He took the map from Nick's hands. It was large and had been rolled into a spiral for so long that it kept curling back up like a reluctant child. "She kept it in the shed." He folded the sentence into himself as if reabsorbing every word. "It was some project she was working on. She never told me why she was doing it. Just that she was."

Each person cast their eyes downward, containing their jealousy, remembering Marley's very stern command that we were no longer allowed in her shed.

"She made me promise not to tell anyone," Bigs continued.

We all knew a Marley promise was not to be broken. Our envy sat like a cloud over the sun. "But my letter said to share something no one else but me knows. So there you go." He turned like he was going to walk away, then pivoted again. "Before we do anything else with this map, why don't we go back to where Olivia got out? We need to look for Harrison and Ruby. Or I can go down into the tunnels and try to find them. We can't keep going while they're missing," he said.

"No!" Teeny yelled. "No one's going back there. We'll go out to the desert and look for them."

Like always, it was follow or defy.

We all followed.

After a brief and silent car ride in the Campbells' Civic, Bigs parked at the end of Ms. DeVeau's street. Her orange house mocked me with its solitude. If only the twins hadn't found me, I could've gotten her to talk. I know I could have.

I pushed the thought away and led the group out into the open land, where the sun kept a steady eye on us, its golden face tracking our every step.

"*The Point of No Return*," Teeny remarked when we reached the sign. "Never thought I'd see the day we ended up here. If there really is quicksand, I'm out."

Everyone chuckled, even Aidy, who'd always had trouble committing to an angry posture for an extended period of time. I led them all to the sewer entrance. The cover was still ajar, but it looked to be in the exact position I'd left it. Even my belly-flop sand imprint appeared fresh and untouched.

175

"Harrison!" Aidy started yelling, leaning so far over the hole, everyone seemed to fear she'd fall in. We each took a reaching step toward her. "Harrison!"

Then, incredibly, we heard the faintest whisper of a "Yeah?"

Aidy did topple over, but Bigs was so close behind, he caught her by the shirt. She responded by pretending it didn't happen, and yelled, "Are you hurt? Is Ruby with you?"

It was impossible to understand what Harrison said back, so I told everyone, "I'll go down and get him. I owe him that."

No one protested. Not even Teeny, for all her claims that we were to stay aboveground. Aidy reapplied her forgotten scowl as I took off my backpack and set down my frozen peas. She kept her snarled face fixed on me until I disappeared out of view.

Back down the ladder and into the tunnel, I yelled Harrison's name, following the sound of his voice like it was a game of Marco Polo. "You got me," he said when I somehow ended up with a fistful of his hair in my hand.

I startled, leaping back, trying to see his form amid the blackness, but finding nothing. The proof of him seemed more impossible than my Marley. "What are you doing?" I asked.

"I'm sitting."

"So I've learned."

"I can't leave."

"Because you're hurt?"

"No."

"Well, I'm here to help."

He laughed at that one.

"I shouldn't have left you," I said.

"Can you go now?"

I tried to use the power of my imagination to implant Harrison-like features onto the amorphous shadow using his voice. Sloping nose. Slender cheeks. Cutting jaw. Full eyebrows that grew in perfect arches. Brown eyes.

"What are you doing?" he asked.

"Imagining you," I said.

"That's very weird."

"So is sitting alone in a sewer."

"Touché."

We went quiet.

Not until Harrison said, "Yeah, I know, I'm crying," did I realize he was. The throaty, snotty sound of his tears pushed to the forefront of sounds around me.

"Oh, wow. You are," I said.

"Don't even start."

"I'm not. I swear."

For another yawning stretch of time, our cloaked world became consumed by his ragged breaths. Each of his inhales sounded gasping and hopeful, determined to be the one fresh and full enough to renew him. Eventually, he found the breath that was, and said, through a jerky sniffle, "For as long as I've known you, you've done things that should make me mad. But I never am." He wiped his nose on what I could only guess was his arm. "I haven't seen you much since I went to college. Not that we were close before that. I'm not trying to rewrite history. But I realized something down here. You've been a part of my life for as long as I've lived in Cadence, and that's the only life that's ever mattered to me. You're not only my girlfriend's sister. You're my family."

I listened on, stunned.

"I should be pissed at you," he continued, "but more than anything, I didn't want to be the one who lost you. And my damn letter. Turns out I didn't really lose either one, but I wasn't the one to find them either."

I wanted so much to sit and cry with him. To thank him for his honesty. To live in this world where sight didn't matter and secrets were commonplace.

"Listen, everyone's aboveground waiting for you, so let's get going. We're doing this thing," I said, stifling myself, trying not to lose the bigger picture.

"I'm not going anywhere."

I started pulling on what felt like his collar. As hard as I tugged, I couldn't get him to move.

"Ruby tried this too. I sent her away."

"I'm more stubborn."

"I know." He sighed as I continued tugging anyway. "I don't think you understand how embarrassing this is. I told everyone to go into these tunnels, and it turned into a huge mess. I'm not going up there and seeing all of them."

"Harrison, you have no idea how much I get it. I'm the one who started this all, and look at me, I'm still going." I lowered myself down in front of the black mass that I'd come to under-stand was his body and probed around for his armpits.

"What in the hell?"

The darkness amplified all sounds. Two wet pops of air released out of the corners of his mouth. I could hear him smiling. It was a reluctant smile, but a smile nonetheless. He didn't seem to be ticklish, or I was doing a terrible job at trying, but the motion had the appropriate effect either way. He started jerking left to right until he shot upward. "Fine! Fine! Enough of that! Let's go!" he said, faint amusement in his words.

He placed a hand on my shoulder, letting me lead him out. As I began my climb up the ladder, Aidy and Bigs and Teeny and Nick nearly blocked out the light with their heads staring down at me.

No. There was one more person.

"You're back," I said to Ruby as she offered a hand to pull me out. The sight of her was such a relief that I couldn't hold on to my earlier frustration. I understood exactly how Harrison felt. I didn't want to be the one who lost her, but it hurt not to be the one who found her.

"Harrison kicked me out of there a while ago, so I was out in the desert, digging around to find more stuff for you," she told me. "You know, just trying to know all the secrets I'm supposed to know."

The tears I had suppressed earlier sprang up to my eyes.

I accidentally stepped back onto Harrison's hand. "You're already failing to make life aboveground seem better!" he yelled as he winced, which made me even more emotional. His fake irritation was another relief.

"He looks worse than you," Teeny told me once Harrison fully resurfaced.

It was true, but only because I'd showered and changed. Harrison had to crouch to readjust to the sunlight. "How do humans do this?" he cursed as he rubbed his eyes. "It's so bright!"

Ruby hugged me. After Harrison had properly recovered, she hugged him too. "I didn't know what to think after I left you."

"Yep," was all he said back, directed at Ruby but meant for me, a tiny incision of a word, small and painful as a paper cut.

"If you're really okay, then let's get on with it," I said, absorbing the pain. This was how we behaved on land. Our camaraderie was another secret we'd keep underneath.

Suddenly, Aidy leapt forward to kiss Harrison. It was hard to say who was more surprised: her, him, or the rest of us. Ruby coughed, making sure all eyes were averted, letting them have their strange moment in peace.

"The second Bigs spotted me, he told me Emery was really scared," Ruby said. "I wasn't getting any reception farther out." She turned to catch my dodgy gaze. "I know, I know. I promise I'll tell you all about her soon."

Truces were being dealt out left and right. Maybe everything really was okay again, I convinced myself.

It was a beautiful ten seconds of ignorance.

Aidy stepped away from Harrison. "I've already discussed this with most of you one-on-one, but it's time we talked about it as a group." She looked me square in the face. "I think Marley knew the gun was loaded."

My stomach roiled. It was happening, and I couldn't stop it. I had nothing but a third of a journal that seemed to further her theory. Anything I told them would turn this into more of a disaster, so I bit back tears instead, doing my best to keep my expression steady.

"I do too," Harrison added, backing her up. "That message spray-painted on the wall really made me believe. With the school picture and the trophy head. It was like she was saying we didn't see her right, or something."

"I agree," Teeny said.

Ruby pulled her head back until her vertebrae stacked up into a neat column. "I'd never considered it until Olivia said it the other night. Now I can't let it go."

"Aidy said it, actually. I repeated it," I muttered, not wanting my name to be tied to any of this.

The ground gave out beneath me. I plunged down, lower than the sewers, past the center of the earth, out the other side. I floated through imaginary stars, waiting for gravity. Where was my anchor?

Where was my Marley?

"Her letters might be her way of saying goodbye," Ruby said. "One last adventure. The map you guys found is probably all the places she left the clues, in case we couldn't find everything without it. If she knew she wouldn't be with us, she probably wanted to make sure we actually figured it all out this time. Don't you think?" Ruby walked over to Nick, who'd been holding the blueprint paper since we got to the desert. "Look. We've already found stuff here, here, and here." She left her finger on the POINT OF NO RETURN spot on the map and gestured to Marley's journal poking out of the bag I'd brought with me. I couldn't believe I'd let it out of my sight. "We should start looking at the places on the map we haven't been to yet. See what else we can find."

She could've kept going, but no one was listening to her anymore.

As children, our scavenger hunts and adventures, both official and spontaneous, were always fun. Harmless. We were young and unaware of how the little things we found were part of a bigger life. We'd gather around the love letter for Harrison's mom and giggle for hours. Someone had a crush on Ms. Shin! We'd dance in Ms. DeVeau's shoes. We'd ruffle through Mr. Campbell's paperwork and hold fake court cases. We'd smoke a few of my mom's old cigarettes and flush the remaining ones down the toilet. We'd chase Marley's clues into our houses and other buildings in Cadence.

We blew through our town like tornadoes, trying to find something interesting to sweep up.

With this, we weren't peeking into the world of our paper-doll parents. We were cracking open a life we never dressed up with cutouts. A life that existed inside every wide shot of our childhood. Every close-up. Never in the background. Never out of focus. Tattooed onto our every early memory was Marley Bricket.

Despite my wishes, we were no longer having one last adventure. We were examining why she left us.

The idea stirred around, dissolving into the individual memories of our collective whole, tainting their color and weight.

Marley meant to do this? And she made Nick do it for her? And she tried to tell us like this, but we didn't notice? We didn't know? How did we not know?

Nick crumpled down. He stared into the earth with a glazed expression, bewildered and wounded, the very idea so inconceivable he could nothing but let it envelop him. Everyone else cast sideways glances, knowing he had the right to be the most upset and wanting to watch the way he took it in, but knowing it was inappropriate.

To pull the focus off Nick, Bigs said, "If this is true, then I'm so mad at myself." Tears trickled down his cheeks. "I helped her draw some of that map." He tried to stop himself from continuing, but a quiet fury blazed off him, pushing against the steel trap of his mouth, forcing him to follow through. "If it was all to tell me she wanted to die, and she never gave me a chance to stop her, then I'm so mad I could scream. Why do *I* have to say the things no one knows, if she never did? I don't want any of this. It hurts too much." He pulled his typed letter out of his pocket and tossed it to the ground.

Teeny saved her brother with a hug. They clicked into position, two people forever capable of completing one another.

"You can't stop halfway," I begged him. "No one can." On sheer instinct, no Marley guiding me, I prepared myself to attempt a rescue mission. I didn't know how to steer us through something so insurmountable, couldn't see any way back to solid ground as I listlessly floated, but trying was the only option. If this was truly what was meant to happen, I had to find a finish line. "We're in the middle of where we were and where we're going. Each way seems too far. Going back means forgetting everything we've already done. We have to go forward."

Ruby grabbed my hand. "No stops," she whispered in solidarity.

Teeny pulled herself away from her brother. "You know what, Olivia? You're right. We go out every year and throw a party for her. And it might need to be a whole other thing. We might be needing to say something different. Something that some other kid in Cadence might need to hear. I can't sit on a maybe for the rest of my life. Not when it comes to saving someone else's life."

Nick and I locked in on each other. He knew, as I did, that the true decision fell in his hands. He stood to change the most from seeing this through. "I'm with you, whatever we do," he told me.

New tears formed, the kind that never fell, just hovered around my eyelids. They were made of fear. And sorrow. Regret. Relief. Reluctance and apprehension and eagerness. It was a volatile combination of contrasts. I wanted to keep going as much as I knew it would be even more painful than I ever anticipated. A pain I couldn't pretend I washed off in the shower.

I almost said, "I'm sorry," right then and there, as a precursor for what was to come, but Judge Aidy interrupted to bring her gavel down on the matter. "No sense in guessing about it anymore," she said. "Let's open the box and see what we actually have."

A solemn Ruby slid her backpack from her shoulders to remove the box. The lifting of the lid was a sacred job I assumed had no clear successor until everyone looked to me. Chose me. In spite of everything, they still treated me as the leader.

I took a deep breath and pulled the wooden lid up, slowly and delicately. I was never the type to rip off a bandage. Inside, there was bagged confetti and rolled-up streamers. Several boxed string lights. And tiny flashlights.

"I don't get it," Teeny whispered, speaking the thought on most everyone's mind. "But it's also giving me chills. Didn't I just say something about throwing her a party? I mean, I know I meant it differently, but still, this is too much."

"This is all for me," Aidy said. Her face had a greenish tint.

"How do you know that?"

"My letter asked me to throw a party. A sleepover."

Sleepovers didn't mean what they did when we were younger. Even though we still had the same age difference between us, both Aidy and Harrison were going to be twenty in less than a year. Teeny and Bigs were headed to college. Ruby was about to be a senior. Nick and I were going to be juniors. It was a whole different game.

"Why does she want you to throw a sleepover?" Harrison asked Aidy.

"I don't have to explain," Aidy scolded, her harshness a surprise to even herself. She doubled down on it. "My letter was for me. Eyes on your own paper, remember?" Reigniting her annoyance with him seemed to help her cope. She stopped holding her stomach. "Can I see the map?" she asked Nick. "Yeah, okay," she said as she reviewed it, taking inventory of more than one thing.

My inability to read her had me self-conscious. She seemed ahead of a curve I hadn't even seen. "What is it?" I asked.

She kept looking at the map. "The haunted house next door to us. That's where I'll do it. It's marked on here."

"Why would we want to have a party right now?" Harrison asked. "And at the haunted house?"

"It's what's next," Aidy snapped.

The last time we'd been inside the haunted house was at least six years before. After many late nights pondering and mythologizing the consequence of entering the hallowed home, we'd finally worked up the courage to go inside. We'd all stood in the first room—a narrow entryway with two door frames on each side and a staircase up the center—and counted to ten. To see if we'd last.

"Come on," Marley said by the time we'd reached the number four. "Ollie, go up the stairs."

"No." I steeled myself against Nick's side. He clutched my elbow, silently agreeing I didn't have to do it.

Marley clomped off ahead. "Ugh. Fine. Follow me."

We did. The house had been vacant as long as I'd been alive, and though a For Sale sign remained a permanent fixture in the yard, the real estate agent didn't put much effort into upkeep. The whole place was creaky and barren and reeking of isolation.

We'd spent years putting backstory into the house's vacancy, imagining a place filled with ghosts of past residents, trapped by the tragedy of their death and the irresistible pull of Cadence, California. The stories kept us up in the early hours, each of us trying to one-up the other with imagined gore and despair.

But the so-called haunted house did not welcome us with a possessive hug. It did not whisper with voices long gone, desperate

186

to be heard. And it certainly did not provoke the goose bumps such a storied place required. It just sat, a collection of windows and walls and floors and ceilings. Even my memories of that day had nothing substantial behind them. We wandered around empty rooms, desperate to find a story that didn't want to exist.

Still, any time we pedaled by in the days that followed, someone inevitably said something like, "Whoa, I swear I saw someone in the window," even though saying it became like chewing on stale bread.

We'd spent so much time forcing magic on that house, and we were going back to see if it had finally worked. I prayed it had.

"How are we gonna do this?" Teeny asked Aidy. "You're grounded." She seemed pleased to have something trivial to worry about. A question less weighted to ask.

"And why?" Harrison pleaded.

"I know," Aidy said to Teeny. "We can make it work, though. And Harrison, stop asking that. We didn't ask you why your letter said to go through the tunnels, we just did it. So shut up already."

Bigs and Teeny exchanged a quick glance. Ruby pressed herself into my side.

"Uh," I started, trying to rescue Aidy. "We should probably, well, uh, I guess we have everything we need now. Maybe we should go home for a while? Is that a bad idea? We can look at the other spots on the map too." I wanted a chance to collect myself. I needed time to make a plan.

"A break would be good," Aidy said. She started gathering everything up.

Bigs and Teeny said goodbye to us. Bigs didn't bother to grab his discarded letter. He left it lying in the sand in a crumpled heap as he walked to his car. I picked it up and shoved it into my bra. If he didn't want it anymore, I definitely did. I needed everything I could take.

"We'll call Ruby from our house phone and have her spread the plans to everyone later," I announced, bolstering myself up with the supply of false confidence I always kept stocked. No one could know how far this had slipped away from me.

"That's it?" Harrison asked. "We're gonna agree we think Marley died by suicide then head home for a bit to chill?"

Aidy started clapping. "Bravo! You got it all in one try!"

"Can I talk to you?" he asked her, low and serious.

"Isn't that what we're doing right now?"

"Alone," he whispered, succeeding at pulling off a calm but sincere command.

Aidy could only push so far. "Fine. We'll walk back together." She picked up the box and tucked it under her arm. "Don't get caught, Olivia. Not now."

"I won't," I warned back.

Nick stepped up. "Wanna walk with me?"

Bigs and Teeny were already pulling out of the parking lot. Ruby chased them down to ask for a ride to Emery.

The choice was all but made for me. Not that I minded. I needed a good distraction. Besides, the battle between Nick and me had only been allies fighting for dominance. When he allowed everyone to continue on with this, he'd surrendered to me. In fact, he'd been trying to surrender to me every time we spoke. But a challenge was always more irresistible, and our years apart required constant affirmation that he wouldn't leave again. I asked him, "Are you sure you want to walk with me?" needing another little boost.

He laughed the same laugh he always did. A quiet chuckle at every obstacle I gave him to climb over. "I'm sure," he said. "How's your nose?"

Thanks to medicine, and Marley, I'd almost forgotten about it. I covered it with the bag of no longer-frozen peas I'd picked back up. "It doesn't hurt as much anymore."

"I'm sorry that happened."

"I've had worse," I said, as if he didn't already know. He was there the day I broke my wrist jumping over a fence in his backyard. And the time I gashed my thigh climbing over another fence around the corner from where we stood. Me and fences.

Nick and I started the walk back to Albany. His pace was slow and calculated. I had to drag my feet to keep from breaking ahead.

"I'm going to say it before you stop me. And because you need to know," he said.

To protest seemed futile.

"I didn't abandon you. I came to your house. A few times. Aidy told me you didn't want to see me again."

Aidy, Aidy, Aidy. Conversations about Nick post-Marley never went well. But in the early days, I'd cried to her, wondering where he was, wondering why he didn't try to talk to me. She said nothing of Nick coming over.

"I didn't believe her," he continued. "I came back when I knew you were home from camp. I could never seem to catch you. It was always Aidy telling me the same thing. And you didn't try to find me or anything. After a while, I decided she must've been right."

Aidy listened. She supported.

She built me a titanium backbone made of lies.

"It wasn't like anyone was really trying to talk to me after it happened anyway." His feet kicked harder into the ground. "Especially not the kids at my new school. My story was too hardcore even for the alternative school." He tried out a laugh that sounded more like a cough. "Not that I didn't earn my way into that place with the other stuff I did. Guess I felt like nothing could ever be worse than what I'd already done."

I'd spent the first week of school still away at camp. Ruby told me stories of what happened. Nick was starting fights in the hallways over nothing. Standing up in the middle of tests and screaming. They determined early on he wouldn't be tried for what happened, so first they'd put him into extensive counseling. *He was just a kid, after all.* But with the outbursts and mayhem, they decided a different environment would be better, so they sent him several miles away to a small school for kids with various behavioral and adjustment challenges. He rode a bus that picked him up at six thirty in the morning and dropped him off at five thirty every night.

He started there the very day I came back to Cadence.

"I went to your house once," I admitted. I'd never said it aloud before. Even without knowing what Aidy had done, I recognized that telling her would only disappoint her. "You weren't home either. No one was. I sat in your backyard, waiting."

"I think this is why cell phones were invented," he said.

"I still had to share one with Aidy, then," I reminded him. Who knows how many times he'd tried to send me messages that she'd intercepted.

The years of silence between Nick and me had come from believing the people who didn't work the way we did, which felt like the cruelest hand of all. We had friends and family hiding us from one another. Therapists and counselors who made us interact with other traumatized kids. Kids who'd been through different bad things. We could understand their sadness, but we couldn't share it. It wasn't ours. We were the only two people who knew what it was like, and we didn't have each other.

Of all the things I thought I'd find in the fifth year, Nick was never on the list. But there he was, turning left when we needed to go right, buying more time to hang onto my every word.

"If she made me do this," he started, his voice shaking.

"Don't go there."

"Isn't that where we're going anyway?"

It felt funny to teach him a lesson he should already know. The first lesson I learned when the bullet hit Marley. The one I'd taught Aidy only hours before. "You know what I do when I'm stuck in a room with no exit? I rearrange the furniture," I told him.

"Well then, I think I'll take this chair," he said, not a second's worth of hesitation, miming one in front of him, "and smash it through the wall."

"I promise you the wall won't budge."

Nick stopped us. He turned to look at me. A heavy seriousness spread out over his face. "I promise you it will."

What was there to say? Nothing. There were no words to fix my heart hammering into my chest, shaking and shifting, spray-painting Nick's name over every internal piece of me, my whole body now leaning into his, frenzied by his face. His heart. His words. His promise. If I let him really see me, he would find all the falsities I leaned on to help me wobble through my life. And since he was the only person I shouldn't lie to, I lied to him the most. "I don't know about that," I said, fighting so hard, calling out for Marley, asking her to stop what I knew was going to happen next.

She didn't.

She couldn't.

Nick's lips touched mine: an answer, a silence, a stop to the start of everything. Mine pressed back: a question, a loudness, a start to stopping everything I'd done. I pulled him closer to me, felt as he became weightless in my arms, surrendered to this. To us.

This was why the battle had started. For everything to clatter and clang around us as we came together. "Shit," I said as I pulled back, my eyes on his shirt, not his face, knowing if I looked again, even for a second, he would see. And he would leave.

"What?" He tilted his head down so he was again at eye level. His mouth pressed into a sideways crescent moon. We kissed again.

And I didn't mind.

I had no mind.

"I promise," he whispered, our mouths still touching.

When I got home, I locked myself up in my room, pulling out Bigs's letter to distract myself from the impossibility of what had just happened.

XANDER CAMPBELL

Welcome to the Adventure. Eyes on your own paper, please.

Hi, Bigs! Hi, hi, hi! How are you? You're standing there, saying nothing, aren't you? Answer me! Not in your head. Out loud.

Did you feel weird doing that? What did you say? I bet you went, "C'mon," and you shrugged a little. But you smiled that beautiful smile, because you're a beautiful person. That's right. I called you beautiful. Now you're really blushing, aren't you?

Having you around is the greatest gift. You are kind and patient. You never get too upset. Just the right amount. An amount that makes people listen to you and respect what you have to say. I used to do annoying things to see how long you'd let me get away with it. It always went so far that it wasn't even fun for me anymore, because you never broke.

What was wrong with me? Why was that fun in the first place? And why did I want you to break anyway? I'm sorry. I hate that this is a world that wants to snap people in half and hide the pieces. I hate that I'm a part of that.

Say it out loud.

"I, Xander Bigs Campbell III, will not let the world take away what is so special about me, no matter how the world may try."

Are you doing any of this? Or are you reading this and rolling your eyes? Maybe this is the one true time in your life you've been annoyed. Have I done it? Leave it to me. I never know when to let something be.

It's because I love you so much. Don't tell anyone I told you this, but you've always been the one everyone loves the biggest. Bigs the biggest. Makes perfect sense, doesn't it? Your gentle heart grounds us. We lean on you when we're not strong enough to hold ourselves up. What I don't think you know, or you're afraid to see, is that you can lean back.

Together, we can hold you too.

Take a chance and let us try. Share something no one knows but you.

Love always,

Marley

JULY 11

Five Years Prior

MARLEY'S LAST WORDS BECAME A NURSERY RHYME THAT played against the tune of sirens in the distance. *Pull the trigger. Nothing's gonna happen.* Over and over the songs battled as the sirens grew closer. Sirens meant police. Police meant questions. Questions meant answers. Answers were Nick's to give.

The Brickets' screen door had a slab of concrete in front of it with a path that led to the pool and a path that led to a barn-style toolshed. The shed was an excellent hide-and-seek spot if you weren't worried about spiders, but Marley had declared it off limits the summer before with zero explanation. Like good soldiers, we didn't question our leader.

Nick's bloody footprints went toward the shed's entrance. I followed until I met the heavy rusted doors, and I tugged with all my might. Hard ground bruised my bottom as the left door awoke.

Nick was balled up in the corner of the cobwebbed shed, arms hugging his legs as he rocked back and forth. He hadn't been robbed of his When yet, even with spatters of blood decorating his bare skin and board shorts. "What did I do?" he asked, rising up and walking toward me as if we were going to hug.

"You killed her!" I screamed out. "You killed her!" I charged at him, shoving as hard as I could. Runt of the litter, but I made my mark. We fell together, breaking through a flimsy wooden crate to find solid ground.

The sirens laughed at us.

They'd start mocking Marley's last words.

Nick's eyes widened as he looked at me lying on top of him. He wiggled out from underneath and ran. By the time I stood again, he was out of sight, and I was helpless once more, his bloody imprint fossilized onto my skin.

14

With the melted peas held to my face, I sat atop a pile of clothes and stared at my bedroom wall. My eyes drifted to a soft focus that worked as a projector, letting my thoughts become what I actually saw. I rewound the kiss between Nick and me. I paused. Zoomed in. Sped up. I could do everything but rewrite it.

It was yet another turn on a path I once thought was straight.

Aidy came in every two hours to do our parental phone call song and dance. I did a song and dance for her too as I cradled the heavy secret of what she'd done to me. She performed right back. The two of us acted for our lives, struggling to one-up each other with subtext. I was too exhausted to figure out whatever she thought she knew about me. She, as always, was too scared to reveal it. Instead, we ate random snacks from the pantry and hatched a plan to get to the haunted house when our parents were asleep. She left me alone in our house as she snuck over to set up next door, taking with her the materials left in Marley's box.

I worked on hatching my own plan. I played out every possible scenario of the night, determined for my ideas to actually mirror reality for once, instead of spiraling into another mess I couldn't contain. Uncertainty thrummed against my bravado. I drowned it out with the movie I made about what could happen.

In it, all of the Albany kids were united. Bedsheets above us formed a tent we huddled under. String lights were our stars. We held flashlights to our faces and told stories to each other. As we spoke, sharing memories and hopes, each of us could see it. The true purpose of the Adventure.

It wasn't to understand why Marley wanted to die. It was to drag us to the crooks and corners of Cadence and dust off the cobwebs. Find what made our town so wondrous. What made *us* so wondrous.

We would all see that we'd already done it. We'd taken all of these simple things—letters, boxes, journals, phrases—and we'd made them into something memorable. We'd ridden our bikes across town. Snuck out of our houses. Met up at Cadence Park and conversed with all the seriousness of CEOs at a board meeting. We'd found the ending, because we'd rediscovered the magic we'd let die alongside Marley.

My Marley.

She would be so proud of me. Finally, I'd reminded everyone that she was not an idea, or a symbol, or a lesson, or a bargaining chip. Marley Bricket was a prism of a person, glinting from every surface.

I needed her to help me make my plan a reality. All the times I'd called out to her to give me the strength to get through something, I'd meant it. In her way, she'd always delivered. She'd given me her personality to hide behind. She'd kept me calm when I wanted to scream. She'd taken me to her house on the night of the memorial and kick-started the Adventure.

I needed her to guide all of us to the appropriate finish.

For once, I needed to willingly share her.

The movie in my mind turned to static when I heard our front door unbolt, followed by the unmistakable jangle of my mom's keys as she hung them on the hook in the kitchen.

I hurried to the mirror beside my dresser, rummaging through my makeup bag for the necessary products. My mom moved through the house in a series of formidable squeaks, each seeming to dance around my door like a threat. The face I wore would disappoint her. It held too much unwanted truth in it. My swollen nose and bruised eyes could not be covered completely, but with the right amount of concealer, foundation, and eye makeup, I could downplay the damage enough to make her wonder if she'd misremembered my appearance all this time. Or if puberty was turning yet another swift trick, evolving me further into the adult I'd one day become.

As I worked, Aidy crept down the stairs for a greeting. Her placid tone drifted up through the vents. She sounded like the automated voice you heard when you dialed a number no longer in service. Her indistinguishable murmur of pleasantries bought me time to finish my face and move to my hair. I curled the tangled pieces into soft waves that pushed away from my face, pulling the attention back. Back, back, back. Curtains opening for my great presentation. I changed into a sky-blue Marley hand-me-down romper, gave myself a spritz of perfume, and nodded with satisfaction at my ruse.

"Good grief, baby girl, you look like a doll," Mom said when I came downstairs. She kissed me on the forehead. "And you smell like a candy shop."

"I was telling Mom about our day," Aidy told me. She shifted her weight from side to side, unable to settle.

"Oh?" I questioned.

"I think donating some of your stuff is a great idea," Mom interjected. "Maybe we'll actually see your floor for once!"

I cut Aidy a sharp stare as I said, "Yeah."

Mom smiled at us. "Not sure I'll know what to do with myself when I see a clean bedroom in there."

"You and me both," I assured her.

"Should we do dinner?" Mom's bliss had a way of making her soft all over. "I can throw in a pizza before Dad gets back."

At the same time I said, "Perfect," Aidy said, "We already ate," so I had to add, "But I'm still hungry," as a courtesy cover. Aidy, having none of it, told Mom, "Oh, she's being dramatic. I fed her plenty."

"I'll throw one in, just in case." Mom read the interaction between Aidy and me as classic sibling banter.

I tried to read it back to front, searching for the ending.

Whatever Aidy thought she held over my head made her bolder than she'd ever been with me. I shuffled through all the things she might know, deciding she must've figured out that I'd broken into Marley's the night of the memorial. That would make her upset. And she was likely waiting for the right time to confront me. Why it gave her such a sense of power over me, I wasn't sure.

I decided to bet all my cards on this guess and told my mom, "Nah, don't worry about it, Aidy's probably right."

"Oh, I am," Aidy agreed.

My dad came home. He gave my mom a quick peck, and hugs to Aidy and me. "What've you girls been up to all day? Mom told me you made your calls like we asked." There was a hint of accusation in his tone.

"They're coming up with donation bags," Mom told him. She tried to sound dry, suspicious even, to temper her obvious happiness, but it was clear she felt pride. So much of it that regret started churning in my gut.

Dad examined Aidy first, then me. I took an instinctive step back, afraid he'd see beneath the makeup on my face. "Be sure to put them out *front*." The peculiar emphasis crawled out of his mouth as a threat.

"Hon, I was gonna throw a pizza in, if that works for you," Mom said to him. She leaned her head on his shoulder to spread more warmth our way. She seemed to believe she'd somehow law-of-attractioned this harmony into her life. "Unless you wanted to get dinner together? We haven't done that in a while."

He gave us a curious look. "Without the girls?"

"I was thinking all four of us."

"Let's do a date night instead." Dad turned to Aidy and me. "What's a few more hours without Mom and me here?"

Mom smiled. It wasn't belief. She saw all of this as *proof* that through sheer intention alone, all trouble within our family had been fixed. "Let me throw on something nicer!" she said as she flitted out of the kitchen.

Aidy and I moved to stand side by side. As plagued as we were by secrets, we still united against the unknown that was Dad's mood, which added more regret to the flooding pool at the bottom of my stomach.

Once Mom was out of earshot, Dad spoke. "I found something in the backyard." He stepped closer. "A bag of filthy clothes. Ring any bells?"

My jaw clenched so hard it felt like my teeth might break. I was waiting for Aidy to rat me out. This was my fault. Surely she wouldn't let our dad believe anything different.

"The shirt had blood on it," Dad continued. "Someone needs to explain to me why that is."

It never took more than a few threatening sentences for Aidy to toss me under the bus. When I caught sight of her in my peripheral vision, she looked as tight-lipped as me.

"We'll wash it," I blurted out. Aidy's solidarity surprised me so much I couldn't stop myself from redirecting the whole conversation. There was no telling how long I had before she changed her mind and admitted everything.

"You're not understanding me," Dad said. "Is anyone hurt?"

Ah. Bloody clothes. Our stubborn resistance. As if another one of our friends had dropped dead, and we'd decided the first go-round was such a mess, it was better to keep it to ourselves this time.

"No," I said, making hard eye contact, daring him to notice the bruises I'd concealed.

"I hope to God that's true. You two have your mother convinced you're actually playing by the rules this time. I'm going to take her out to a nice dinner, and you're going to take that time to do whatever it takes to make her keep believing that. And then you're going to tell me exactly what went on today and why there's a bag of bloody clothes out back." We didn't have a chance to speak before he added, "You both know exactly what will happen if you don't."

For me, it was Camp Califree. A longer stay there, or an earlier departure date.

For Aidy, whatever it was made her say "We understand" in a low, solemn voice.

"I'm sure you do," Dad agreed. "Please remember I love you." He left Aidy and me in the kitchen, the two of us conflicted by the ebb and flow we faced in our every shared breath.

"What do they have on you?" I asked when our parents drove off for their dinner.

"I don't want to talk about it." Aidy headed over to the house phone. She picked it up and started dialing, leaving me no choice but to go full drama, grabbing the receiver and slamming it back down. "I got caught plagiarizing," she said, bored with the staginess of our exchange. Before I could even form the necessary shocked response or ask the obvious questions, she kept going.

"That's the short version. It was actually Harrison who was caught, but he was the one writing papers for me."

I couldn't hold back my shock.

"I was going to flunk out if he didn't help me," she continued. "He, like the unbearably perfect boyfriend he is, couldn't let me learn from my own mistakes. I don't know how you don't know about it. The dean launched an investigation into Harrison and me." She seethed with contempt. "You know what the real problem is? It's not that I don't love him anymore. It's that I love him too much. There's never any room to breathe between us." She waved the topic off, batting her tears away like an unwanted fly. "I got expelled. Harrison was suspended for two quarters. Would've been expulsion too, but the dean showed some last-minute mercy when we went in and explained everything. Doesn't matter, though. Harrison probably can't go back. His mom can't afford it without his scholarships. And if I don't keep it together with Mom and Dad, I can't leave here either. I'll be another forever Cadence kid, married to my childhood sweetheart, living in the shithole haunted house next door, my admission letter some buried treasure my kids will find in the attic and toss aside while looking for something more interesting." She answered my rigid body language by saying, "So yeah, only you should go to camp. You're the only one of us with problems." She picked the phone up to dial. "I don't want to talk about it anymore."

Normal Ollie would've kept prodding anyway, but the regret kept flooding in, reaching higher and higher. The only fight inside me was for survival.

"Hey," Aidy said into the house phone's receiver. "You guys

can head over now. Our parents just left. When they're done with dinner, Olivia and I will have to go back to our house until they go to bed, but I think the earlier we start this, the better." She sounded clinical: a doctor giving her prescription. "Great. See you then." She hung up the phone and looked at me. "You're ready, right? I'm assuming, by all the…" She waved fingers at my face like I'd worked some wizardry on myself.

All there was to do was brace myself for what was to come. Hope—oh, pathetic hope—that whatever I was made of was strong enough to withstand it all. Every time I made a plan, I got thrown another wrench.

"Mm-hmm," I said. I retrieved the bag I packed earlier in the day.

Aidy turned on the TV. I hit a few more light switches. We did this so when we needed to rush back to our house, it looked lived in, in the recklessly negligent teenage way.

We left. We'd never used the Marley way to go anywhere but Marley's. The effort that went into the later parts of the path were what made it worthwhile. Aidy and I tried to remain dignified as we dusted ourselves clean, but bitterness punctuated our movements. There was no sense of accomplishment in crawling like dogs into our neighboring yard.

Aidy opened the haunted house's back door. The vacant building was aggressive in its many disappointments. It still hadn't become what it was meant to be: spooky and old, in muted grays, a chandelier swaying without any wind. If the walls whispered anything, it was, *This is what you'll become,* as they hacked a throaty laugh at me. Nothing but a rotting husk.

"Follow me," Aidy said. She led me past the kitchen and to the same stairs Marley once bounded up without fear. We inched up instead, soft darkness seeming to promise the aging architecture would fail us. In an upstairs room, Aidy had set up the party. She'd tacked a blackout curtain over the window, with streamers draped atop. String lights traipsed across the sheets she'd pinned from wall to wall. "The outlets were working," she told me in response to my gawking.

It looked exactly like my vision. My Marley had made it happen.

I could keep going.

Under the tent, my old sleeping bag waited for me, covered in rainbow tie-dye and reeking of attic mold. Earlier in the day, Aidy had carried over quite a few things from our attic, including an old coffee table and various drinks from our parents' long-forgotten liquor cabinet. Liquids I never imagined anyone, especially not myself, would ever drink. They were household artifacts. Aidy displayed them alongside a stack of white paper cups she'd found in the depths of our kitchen cabinets. "Harrison's bringing mixers," she told me, tracing the path of my eyes. "I thought the streamers looked best there. And the string lights look kind of like a sky."

"It's perfect," I said.

"And the flashlights? Any idea what I should do with them?" she asked, her brow furrowing.

"We'll know soon enough," I assured her.

We both perked at the sound of a downstairs creak. "Hello," Harrison called out. "You guys here yet?"

"Upstairs," Aidy told him. He came up with a bag of snacks and drinks in one hand, his sleeping bag in the other. "Put the food over there." Aidy pointed to the closet door she'd opened to turn into another little display area.

"Why are we in this room?" Harrison asked.

"Farthest room from my house," Aidy said. "The house where my parents are. You know, those people who grounded me."

His lips pressed into a flat line, eager to avoid trouble. He peeked under the tent to look around, making such a point of avoiding me that I had to say, "Hi, Harrison," to appease him.

"Oh, hey," he said back, like he'd just noticed I was there. "Do you have my letter?"

"It's at my house."

"I'd like to get it soon."

"Of course."

I hadn't brought it with me. I'd collected three letters, including my own, and I'd left them all at home. They were complicating the Adventure. We didn't need them for the sleepover.

Bigs and Teeny arrived next. I couldn't recall the last time it had been only the five of us somewhere. The room was alive with that unfamiliarity, giving the walls more to say. *Does this combination of people work? Can you even remember?*

When Ruby came, the six of us configured our sleeping bags into a pattern that made sense. Room was left for Nick's to go beside mine, which caught in my throat like a sweater on a hook. As we waited for him, we stayed tucked away under the bedsheet tent. I felt at once very small and very important, my favorite feeling in the world. I was with my secret society, reconvening in a secret hideout, for a secret party.

Secrets, secrets, secrets.

Teeny poked at the flashlights piled up in the middle of our formation. "If we're supposed to be telling ghost stories with those, I'm gone. It's already bad enough being in this house." She pulled her knees up to her chest. I couldn't decide if the Marley magic was growing, or if Teeny never once doubted the house was haunted. "If you wake up and I'm not here, don't leave thinking I went home. Walk this house up and down and make sure I haven't been dragged into the attic by some demon."

"Stop it! Now you're scaring me," Bigs said.

Everyone let out disjointed, apprehensive laughs, baited with anticipation. We were so close to what was going to happen. It was almost touchable.

Harrison stole away to make drinks for everyone. He brought them in one by one, each a different combination of liquids. "This is my specialty," he told us as he did it. "Call me Mr. Mixologist."

Aidy scoffed. "Yes, everyone please call him that. It's such a great gift he has. Let's make sure to celebrate his knowledge of mixed drinks as often as we can."

Teeny busted into a full throttle laugh. "You are *catty*." Harrison brought in her drink. "It is good, though," she told Bigs in whispered confidence, even though we all could hear.

Mine was the last drink Harrison made. As I pondered it, he told me, "Hey, I know what I know," and shrugged the same shrug I loved to shrug. The dismissive, know-it-all shrug.

We sipped away at the drinks in hand, skirting around telling stories of past memories. That kind of talk would surely be the catalyst, and everyone knew it.

A loud creak silenced us. Nick had arrived. He did not say hello downstairs or call out to ask where we were. He was all shuffles and swooshes, doors opening and closing. In our rational minds we knew it was him, but we sat stock-still with pursed lips, because that was what we kids of Albany did: created moments where there were none. Made the average into the entertaining.

How could they not see?

Eventually, Nick opened the door to our party room, and the rest of us dropped our charade. Nick crawled in without comment, making his way to the open space beside me. As he unfolded his old sleeping bag, black-and-blue stripes, the smell of soap and must and tree bark wafted over to my swollen nose. Once settled, Nick's bag overlapped with mine just enough for him to pretend to adjust it. Really, he gave my fingers a quick squeeze: a continuation of our earlier conversation. *I'm still here. Are you?*

I squeezed back. Oh, the thrill of our touch, in front of the others, but without them knowing. My drowning heart gasped. Wading through my regret was getting harder to do. Everything brewing inside of me was desperate to come out, if only to make room for the hugeness of the feeling between Nick and me.

"So, we're all here," Aidy said once Nick stopped fixing his sleeping bag. Her words had sharp edges, ready to cut details into what the night might become.

If I knew my sister, it wasn't an image that matched with mine.

If I knew myself, I could beat her.

Teeny gasped. "You're about to announce this is a séance."

Aidy replied bluntly, "It is *not* a séance."

Teeny reached across Ruby to grab my hand and hold it to her chest. "Feel my heart. It's pounding," she said to me. It was so flattering, I almost burst right then and there.

She knew I would care. She was starting to understand.

"I'd protect you," I told her as her heart beat into my palm. I'd always wanted her to toss me even the smallest of olive branches, so I could prove how that branch would root inside me and grow into an undying tree.

"Oh, because you know how to communicate with ghosts now?" Aidy probed.

"I do not do ghosts," Teeny snapped, breaking our connection. I pulled my hand back and shoved it under my sleeping bag, trying to stop the world around me from shrinking again. I was okay.

It was all okay.

"You're spending the night in the haunted house," Harrison taunted.

"If you think this story doesn't end with you being the first person here the demon kills, you haven't watched enough horror movies," Teeny taunted back.

"Why me?"

"Because your girlfriend hates you, and instead of dealing with it, you're acting like Mr. Mixologist, whoever the hell that is, and people are leaving you behind in tunnels and stuff. It's just, it's obvious, is all." To Bigs, she whispered, "And because I won't be a part of any situation where the well-meaning black people die first. I'll kill the demon with my bare hands before that happens."

Bigs laughed at her.

"What?" she asked. "You know I will."

Harrison folded his arms. "Who decided that was the person I was?"

"You did," Aidy said, holding his ego like a toy she might toss.

"Okay, I didn't say now was the time we deal with it," Teeny warned. No one wanted to pick at the scab covering Harrison and Aidy. "I guess I have to say this. I've been trying not to, but obviously the rest of you don't see it yet. This night is about ghosts."

The room went stiller than still. It was as if stillness itself tipped over and spilled out until it was dry, leaving us in suspended animation.

"Exactly," Teeny said in answer to the quiet. "You all know I'm right. We're here for a ghost, and I'm going to be the one to announce it, because then I can take the power out of what scares me. I'm about to leave for college, and I want to get out of this place for good. I'm not carrying her ghost around. Listen to what she told me." She removed her letter from the purse beside her sleeping bag. "You listen and try to tell me I'm wrong."

TENIYAH CAMPBELL

Welcome to the Adventure. Eyes on your own paper, please.

What do you think about when you're in dance class? All that time in front of a mirror, studying every inch of your body. Does it make you stop thinking of yourself as a person? You're a billion pieces, building and unbuilding, stacking and unstacking, hinging and unhinging, squeezing, pushing, pulling, leaning, standing, falling, all to create something bigger than you. I know when I watch you that you're more than a person. But do you? Is that what you think? It's got to be more than eight counts and technical corrections in your head. There's seriously no way you can do the things you do thinking like that. Or believing you're just a person. I've gotta think that you see yourself as so many things, like you're the sun and then the sky and then a ball and then fire and then a bird and then a tree, all in one step.

What happens to that when you're not dancing? Where does your sun and sky and ball and fire and all of it go? I feel like I see it in you, even when you're walking down the street. You're not just a body. That's only the most obvious part of you. How boring. We all have one of those. It's what's inside. Even if the body is gone, the rest of you would have to stay. It's so much bigger. I don't know how else to put it. It's the you when you aren't in the room. It leaves a beautiful mark over every place you've ever been. Maybe that's what you're thinking about. Maybe you're asking yourself *Is this the way people will remember me? When they hear this song, will I be woven into every beat?*

Sometimes when you dance, I swear you're actually fixing the sun and the sky and all the things that seem broken when people think they've been left behind. It makes me believe that we're always together, even when we're apart. We're all inside of each other, sometimes sneaking out in ways they can't be easily qualified. I am in your steps. You are in mine.

I really like believing that.

I wish I knew why I do the things I do. I wish I had a purpose for my body like you have a purpose for yours. I wish for so much. Like more words to say better things than this. More ways to tell you how important you are. How you stay with me, wherever I go.

Can you make it so I stay with you too?

Love always,

Marley

JULY 11

Five Years Prior

SQUAD CARS, FIRE TRUCKS, AND AMBULANCES arrived all at once. Fear gnawed at my stomach. Would I be in trouble? Was it my fault? What would they do to me? To Marley? I closed myself inside the shed as Nick had, letting the near total darkness devour me whole. Heavy air panted down my neck. Time became taffy, lapping and twisting over itself, stretching out in new ways, never once breaking.

The world outside whispered more questions into my ear.

"How did this happen?" and "She's just a kid," and "You know whose daughter that is, right?" and "She's fifteen," and "Fifteen? Christ," and "Where is Officer Bricket?" and "Why'd he have to take leave this week?" and "Did she do this to herself?" and "Has he been told?" and "Wife troubles, I think," and "No signs of life," and "It was with his gun," and "It makes me sick to my stomach," and "No adults around," and "They're all just kids."

A small sliver of light shone on my dirty toes. The concrete was cold. So cold. A perfect pillow for my heavy head.

"What are they saying?" and "Can we believe them?" and "Who left the scene?" and "A vibrator?" and "Just a kid," and "Blood everywhere," and "Vomit in the pool," and "For Chrissake, someone starting calling their parents," and "Put out an APB for Nick Cline," and "Now they're saying another kid left," and "What's your sister's name?"

Someone needed to rescue Aidy from questions for which she had no answers. That someone should've been Nick, but he was gone, so once again, that someone had to be me.

The floor was so cool. My head hurt so much. From my mouth escaped sounds that were meant to be words. The blackness of the shed swallowed their meaning, and they came out as mumbles. Now the dark was Marley's too. She'd taken everything.

The shed's temperamental left door fell open without complaint. Aidy carved her silhouette into the blinding light. "I found her," she said. Before anyone else could reach me, she scooped me up and pulled me into her lap.

"Olivia, listen," she whispered into my ear, calm as the sky before a storm. "I need you to be okay."

All my life, Aidy had done things like give me the best seat on our couch without argument. Let me go swim at Marley's instead of dragging me home with her like she should. She didn't wield the power older sisters were supposed to have over tagalong siblings. I saw then it was because she feared me. She thought I was too young. Too emotional. Too irrational.

She should've known me better than the rest, and she didn't. She thought the same things about me that everyone else did.

And she thought I killed her best friend, Marley.

Marley.

What would Marley Bricket do if she were me? The answer came as quick as the asking, because Marley herself was there with me in that shed. She wasn't an apparition. Marley would never be so boring. She was the primary colors. She was every loud noise. She was stars in the sky and the wind in the trees. She was the encouraging voice behind every apprehensive lie. Marley Bricket was who she'd always been, and we were going to cover her in a sheet and cart her off to the morgue. Bury her body in the ground and mourn her there. Forget her everywhere else.

Not me.

I could carry her.

I knew I could. Our friends always underestimated me, and there I was, the one who'd be doing all the work. The one who'd make sure Marley didn't get left behind.

So what would Marley do if she were me? She would pretend. And she would be so good at it that no one questioned her.

For Aidy, I put on my biggest voice and, for the first time in an infinite number of times I would utter this phrase in different iterations and not really mean it, I said, "I *am* okay." As soon as the words fell from my lips, I draped Marley around myself like fur, a coat I planned to wear for the rest of my life. She was mine.

The old Ollie was gone.

Aidy had to help me stand. I wasn't yet used to all the extra weight.

Uniformed bodies swarmed nearby, looking at me and then each other, using meaningful glances to decide who should ask me questions. A female officer nominated herself by pushing out of the chaos.

She greeted me with a smile made of cardboard. I looked around to see if anyone else was as offended by how fraudulent her expression was. All I saw were more flimsy smiles. Tongues pressing behind exposed teeth, biting back shock and fear, trying to trick the little girl in front of them into believing everything was okay. The lies lit up like tumors on a scan. Everything that was once dark to me was now bright, overexposed by a laser-focused beam.

"Are you hurt?" the officer asked.

A funny question. My outsides were fine. My insides were not, but not the insides that could be fixed. The insides of my insides, where all these new changes were ripping me up to build a stronger, better body. One that could carry dead girls and harbor secrets and keep the world bright and happy, all at the same time.

"I'm okay," I said again.

She looked at the blood on my tankini. "Let's have a medic check you out, just in case."

As a man examined me, the woman urged me to tell her everything. It amazed me that she didn't think I could tell she was not prepared for the death of a fellow officer's daughter. Anyone could see the little eyebrows of sweat under her chest and the hives forming above the collar of her uniform.

"Nick and I were swimming," I said. "Marley yelled for us. We came inside, and she had her dad's gun. She found it somewhere. She gave it to Nick. She said it wasn't loaded, but I guess it was. She asked him to pull the trigger. He did. I ran to get help. I don't know where Nick went."

"That's it?"

"I don't know."

"Where did you go after you got help?"

"Into the shed."

"Why?"

"I don't know."

"Are those your footprints?"

"I don't know."

"Did you get sick in the pool?"

"I don't know."

"How old are you?"

"Eleven."

"All right. Why don't you and your sister have a seat over there while we finish making sure you're okay. We'll bring you some water and some towels. Take some time to calm down, and try to remember everything you can about what happened."

I knew everything, of course. Every detail. I could have drawn a flip book, showing how the bullet flew, millimeter by millimeter, toward the golden pillow, entering the fibers, then Marley's body, pushing her back and in, turning off the light in her eyes forever.

But I'd never share all of that.

I would never share my Marley with anyone again.

15

WHEN TEENY FINISHED READING THE LAST SENTENCE OF HER letter, we tensed into an elevator silence—a group of people in an enclosed space, afraid to catch the potential conversations polluting the air. Unfortunately, no doors were going to burst open and free us of the unspoken obligation we'd all been avoiding.

There would have to be someone brave enough to speak.

It was going to be me.

It was always me.

Sentences curdled at the back of my throat, ready to spill. "Marley," I whispered.

Teeny jerked her head to see if the girl of the hour had manifested in the spot where my dizzy gaze rested. She hadn't. She wouldn't. But every sentence I spoke would have to start with her name, because everything that had happened in the past three days started with her name.

Everything in the past five years started with her name.

"Told me to do the Adventure," I finished.

I was greeted with "What?" and "What?" and "What do you mean?" and "Hold on," and "Ollie?" and "What?" again.

I measured the quiet into spoonfuls, swallowed them back, let them digest, and said again, "Marley told me to do the Adventure."

part three

UNBELIEVABLE REALITIES

16

A SMALL PART OF ME WISHED TO STEP AWAY FROM MYSELF for the rest of the night. Decide that I didn't owe anyone the rest of my truth. People got away with shutting down like that all the time.

But the great thing about the drink Harrison gave me was how it made my body slowly soften. Every few breaths, tension dripped off me, loosening years of knots I'd wound around myself to keep from giving away too much.

The others—eyes glued on me, waiting for my explanation—had not yet loosened. "Olivia, I'm not joking around; you need to explain yourself right this very second," and, "You can't just sit there," and, "So now she's some kind of statue. If this is some fake demon thing," and, "It's all right," and a squeeze of my hand.

Nick's palm nestled into mine.

Aidy and Harrison had hurt each other by linking up in every choice, good or bad, and saying through words or touch or actions, *I'm here. We face this together.* I knew this, but I wanted to take Nick with me. To keep holding his hand as the room filled up with the rest of what I would soon release. I wanted to ride the wave of it out onto Albany and away from our town. I'd warned myself not to pull him too close, but everything else I prepared got warped, so how was I to really know I shouldn't if I didn't at least try? My warnings never took proper account of my feelings.

Oh, feelings.

I squeezed back. Twice for get out of here.

Nick reacted in an instant. "Let me talk to her outside," he told the room. We stood together, pillars crashing into the cotton sky of bedsheets, dragging along the top until we broke free.

"Hold on." Aidy grabbed my other hand.

"I'll be back," I said to her.

Nick and I crept down the rickety stairs. The back of his hairline looked like a tiny tornado. The caramel brown swooped down and kissed his bare neck, a collision of chaos and calm. Nick's free hand patted the little swirl, warm from the pressure of my stare.

He pushed open the back door, and we stepped down into the yard. It was built from all the other fences connecting. We walked to the corner where Miss Sherry's chain-links met the strong metal stakes of someone else's backyard. I linked my fingers through the chain holes. Nick held a stake. We burrowed until our corners also connected, my shoulder and side pressed into his.

"Ollie," he said before anything else could be said, but that's not what he meant.

"Nick," I said right back. Our names were proclamations of something more.

"What's happening?" he asked, about me. And us. And Marley.

Me and us and Marley.

I said his name again, because I was still performing. I'd become the type to keep going long after the curtain came down. But the whole paper cup of mystery drink swishing around in me put a brand-new spin on my role. Even the order of my reveals was off, because I told him, "I did this," which under normal circumstances would've been the last thing I got direct about. "The stuff in her room. The letters."

"Olivia," he said back. First time he'd ever used my full name. He even said it with a wispy touch, making it sound like a promise and a regret. "That's why I don't have a letter," he realized. "I wasn't supposed to be a part of this. Was I?"

Yes. He was good.

But this was where it got complicated.

It was so complicated.

The impossibility of Nick's presence throughout all of this had no place in my logical mind, so I went to the place inside me where everything was whispered admissions and stolen touches. That place, full of changing landscapes and countless unbelievable realities, had always been the very heartbeat of who Nick and I were to each other.

"How is it that you see the things I see?" I asked him.

"Because it's real. And we're the only ones who know to look."

More words bubbled up. "But I can't tell what's real anymore." My eyes filled so fast, it seemed absurd, because tears weren't anywhere the moment before, and they were suddenly everywhere.

Nick looked at me. In his eyes, I saw my face filled with hope and terror and regret and mischief and sorrow and loss, so much loss, and still it was hard to recognize myself. Maybe because of the swollen nose and hidden bruises. Maybe because of the unfiltered honesty. My face hadn't worn it in years.

"I know what you mean," Nick said. He held me to him. His heart beat into my ear, steady and certain. I tried to set my breath to it. Eight beats to inhale. Eight beats to exhale.

"This was never supposed to be about her wanting to die," I told him. "It was about us. The Albany kids." Nick's white shirt was damp from my tears and discolored from my foundation. I tried to rub it away.

He ran his hand over the top of my hair. "You see her more than I do," he said.

"I told you before. I carry her everywhere."

He took the life out of her. He saw it disperse into everything around us. But he hadn't realized how much of it went into me.

And I hadn't realized how much went into him.

I'd been trying to rework the Adventure into something simpler. That night, looking at Nick, melting from alcohol, imagining eyes from upstairs moving rooms to peer down on us—I accepted another version of reality. The Adventure really did have a different purpose, like she'd said it would.

It was about a Marley I'd never met.

Because somebody somewhere decided that every five years, tragedies must be made extra important again. And without consulting me, Marley Bricket decided her tragedy would be reimagined entirely.

With so much to do, it was hard to choose what was next, especially since Nick Cline stood in front of me with a gaze that could break locks and shatter windows. I told him what I thought he couldn't know. And he was still there.

"I didn't even mean to be at the memorial," he said. "Every year, I wake up with the sound of the gun in my ears." He broke his endless stare to look at me, giving a *you know* with a raise of his eyebrows. "When it happens, it's like I'm wearing headphones with the volume turned all the way up. There's nothing else to hear. And then the sound becomes the feeling, and it's like I'm falling over, like I did when it fired, even though I'm only lying in my bed. That's when I get up and start moving."

In all my playbacks of the day she died, the moment belonged to Marley. As soon as the trigger was pulled, I saw no one other than her. I didn't even know Nick had fallen over.

Each word he spoke became a line drawn between stars, completing a constellation I hadn't noticed before.

"I walk for hours," he continued. "I go until my entire body can't feel anything anymore. I practically fall asleep standing up, that's how tired I try to make myself. This year was different, though. She started showing up in all those ways I told you, but there was more to it. I don't know. The morning of the eleventh

227

came, and the gun fired in my mind like it always does. When I opened my eyes, I felt as if she were behind me somehow, sitting me up. Pushing me out the door. As soon I started my walk, it felt like she was everywhere, and I couldn't catch her. I always avoid City Hall, because I know no one wants to see me at the memorial, but I was so caught up in trying to find her again that I ended up right in front of the building."

A soft breeze blew his hair across his forehead. I pushed it back into place for him.

"And there you were, getting out of the car," he said. He clutched a handful that wanted to fly away again. "So then I was walking in, and in my head I was asking myself, *What are you doing?* But I couldn't stop, because I knew you would never think I was making this up."

When Marley died, our lives to that point got put on permanent pause. It was up to Nick and me to figure out a new way to animate. We were not lucky to just be kids. We were cursed with big imaginations and open hearts. We felt everything. And then we felt nothing.

But even nothing was something.

"I realized it wasn't her I'd been looking for," Nick continued. "It was *you.*"

Heat rushed up to my cheeks. I had to look away. I still couldn't handle it.

"I get what you mean about the room with no exit," he said. "You and me, we're stuck inside July 11 forever. But I really do have to believe there's a way for us to get out. And I think we're finding it."

"You don't understand," I started. "There might not be any real answers to find, because *I* did all of this. Mr. Bricket didn't think it was weird when we were in his house because I'm always in his house. I've been going to his house, to her room, for years. I wrote the letters. I hid the journal and the map. I put things all over Cadence. I was even the one who put the lock on her nightstand, but I didn't have the key with me when we went there that night."

He raised his eyebrows.

"You and me, we feel her in everything we do, right?" I asked. "I felt like the Marley I carried with me wanted me to put this together. She'd told me on the day she died that the Adventure was going to have a different purpose that summer. And after five years, I felt like I knew what it was. I'd spent so much time watching our friends forget her. I mean, think about the day she died. We were all split up. She knew that would keep happening, and she wanted to create a way for us to stay together. That was all the Adventure had ever been in the first place. I don't think she'd realized until things started to fall apart. She was going to make it official, and she never got the chance. So I did it for her."

Nick soaked in my every word, nodding along.

"It wasn't supposed to start the night of the memorial," I continued. "I wasn't really ready. That's why it's all such a mess. I hadn't finished planning. But you showed up. And then everyone else saw this so much differently than I did. It was never supposed to be about her wanting to die," I repeated. "But that might be what it is. All the stuff I used came from real things she had. Like that map. Even the letters were all taken straight from things she wrote about us in her journal. And rereading some of it has made me see what Aidy sees, and I hate that I did this at all. I ruined her."

So much poured out of me that I was dizzy. The ground was the sky was the ground was Nick, standing in the tar that once filled me whole. A little under half-empty and incapable of deciding if it was good or bad, I took to blaming myself anyway. "It's turning me back into Little Ollie," I said. "I don't want to be her. I've spent every day of the last five years making sure I'd never be anything like her again. I thought I'd changed into something new. But the past is catching up to me."

"Olivia," Nick said, careful to use this name, passing it out as another anchor for me to grab. "There's no version of you I don't want to know."

He wanted this to mean everything to me, but he forgot the five years he didn't know me. The me before him was pasted together from all the mistakes I made in the time between, and the haphazard glue job was falling apart. The skin I'd shed when he showed up was the only layer of protection I had.

"Here's what I know," he said. "You're the person I always want to talk to. Whenever anything happens, I'm always wishing I could tell you. I can't count how many times I've wanted to walk over to your house and start a conversation. I used to imagine myself doing it. I'd talk to the you in my mind until I fell asleep. It was never enough. But I was too scared to do anything else. Then you were right in front of me at the memorial, and I started walking over to you. I was trying to psyche myself up by imagining a million greetings. Literally trying to imagine the moment into existence. I couldn't do it. I got too scared of all that would go wrong. I was gonna walk by you and hold on to the split second of time we shared. I figured it would have to be enough. I didn't deserve anything more. Then *you* said hi to *me*."

He wanted me to really hear this part, so he moved his hands down to my forearms, hoping the different touch further pulled me out. Or in. Wherever it was I was, he wanted me to be saved from it.

"You've always been the brave one, Olivia. You were the one who said we shouldn't play with the gun in the first place. You were the one who went and got help. At the memorial, you gave me that single word. *Hi*. You didn't owe me that and you gave it anyway. There's nothing you can do now that'll erase that. I will make the choice to stand beside you, over and over, for as long as you let me."

When he let himself, there was a way Nick Cline smiled at casual acquaintances. He did it like they were family. He smiled at family like they were the world. That night, he smiled at me like the world wasn't big enough.

All I could do was say his name.

Why was it that my sister thought I shouldn't have him around?

Yes, this was the Nick that left me. This was the Nick that pointed a gun at Marley and fired. I knew these things. I lived them.

I also knew forgiveness. And I knew change. He had hurt me. I had hurt him. We were hurt. We were fractures and splinters and gaps of time so long they rotted and replanted, over and over. And still, I hoped we had a chance. Hope worked like that. If it was odds I needed to beat, then I would beat them, betting my hope against the house, always.

He kissed me. "You can tell them what you told me," he said. "And everything you haven't. No matter what they say, I'll still be here. You and I can figure out the rest on our own, if we have to. Or we can have five other people along for the ride. It doesn't matter. This has always been about you and me and Marley, and it always will be."

17

THE HAUNTED HOUSE GRABBED ON TO US AS WE REENTERED. Each croak up the stairs became another story piece, wrought with suspense. We'd given the lonely space secrets to whisper and regrets to yawn out.

We'd given it an afterlife.

The tent had been taken down in our absence. Its colorful sheets sat crumpled in a sad pile in the corner. Our sleeping bags were whirlpools of fabric strewn across the floor. Our stars hung on by a single tack, the string of bulbs forming a triangle in the center of the room. Even though the atmosphere was deconstructed, drink cups had been refilled. Bodies swayed—in anticipation, frustration, fear, general disorientation—not at all synced to the music softly playing from someone's phone, but swaying nonetheless. Against all odds, it was a party indeed.

"Finally," Teeny said when I walked in. "Always disappearing when we need you most."

It should've hurt me, but I warmed instead. Teeny needed me. Not only that, but she needed me *most*. "I'm sorry," I said. And then, "No." I wanted to do my proper part for once, not just stamp my signature on the dotted line. Swimming against the current of myself, I searched for a how. How to be brave when I wanted to fall. How to get up again.

Before I could, Aidy stepped up to me. "Ollie, Ollie, Ollie," she said, using the rule of threes to its maximum effect, "Don't bother. I went ahead and explained to everyone exactly what you did. They were pretty mad at first, but I said, *What do you expect from Ollie anyway?* And they were all like, *Oh. Yeah.*" She pushed me, ever gently, like a tease. "Every knockoff has a tell. Something that makes it a little less valuable than the original." She hurried off to the corner and rummaged through her bag. "Did you already take it? Oh no, never mind, here it is." She pulled out her Marley letter. "I've read this over and over. Probably a thousand times. At first because I was like, whoa, more of Marley. Then because I was confused. Why would she have written us letters? Then, because I was scared. Had she wanted to die? And then, because I knew. She hadn't done this. *You* had."

Her index finger traced lines into the paper until she reached the part she wanted. "'Everyone respects you, and you keep it all to yourself, piecing it out into tiny servings. You don't want to give too much for fear of the pushback. But Aidy, you should try. Be the one to throw us a party. Do it somewhere cool and different. Get scandalous! Make it a sleepover! Bring some of that ancient liquor from your house. No one's touched it in years.

I guarantee your parents won't notice. Think of how much we steal from our houses, and we've never once been caught. I want you to sub in for me. Feel what it's like to hold the strings. I'll give you the other stuff you need to do it. I promise, it's not that much. All you really need to do is rearrange the furniture. Parties are just smoke and mirrors. That's all life is, I think.'"

The entire room was listening, far past the point of pretending to talk to one another.

"You get the point," Aidy said. She crumpled the letter into a ball and shoved it into her pocket, smart enough to know that in spite of it all, I'd still try to steal it. "Can you spot it?"

Again, I said nothing.

"I've read it enough that it's more than one thing now. The whole thing is so you, it's actually incredible no one else noticed, but there's one thing in particular. Do you know what it is?" Her words struck brass-knuckle blows. "Nick? How about you, since you and my sister are so in tune again? Do you know her well enough to know when she's pretending?"

What he knew was that no words could fix what had broken inside Aidy. It was Nick I was so afraid to hurt, and he turned out to be the only one who could stand what I'd done.

Aidy laughed at his silence and turned back to me. "I should be honest. Not that it matters. It's clearly not something you value." She swished around her cup. It was still the first drink Harrison gave her. And it was full. She was not drunk, I realized. She wasn't even buzzed.

She was angry.

"When I was in your room the other day, I saw a receipt on top of one of the piles on your floor. The product names were abbreviated, so I didn't really know what everything stood for," she said. "I didn't think anything of it until I opened up that box. Suddenly I knew what everything stood for. And here we are." Her face kept shutting down then surging back to life, a trick candle that kept on well past the point of being any fun.

Nick squeezed my hand three times, a new code I didn't know, but understood all the same. *Me and us and Marley.*

"Oh great, another thing I didn't miss, the little telepathy twins over here, not talking out loud because they're having a great little chat in their secret little world," Aidy said. Each time, the word *little* hit the hardest, like a cymbal clash. She meant Nick and me, but laughed when she realized there were actual twins in the room. "Sorry, Campbells. I'm sure you two are having some great conversation, but these two"—she glared at us—"have always been up to no good. Since I'm a nice sister, Olivia, I let you think it was all Thing Two's fault over here. But it's the both of you, always insisting on being so damn different every single second. A tree was never just a tree with you guys. It was a magical fortress. And yeah, that was cute for a while, but you two never stopped trying to make things more than what they are." She narrowed her eyes. "You made this into an adventure, as if that's what we all need to heal. Finally, the closure I've always wanted! I get to wonder if my best friend was so lost in her own life that she made you two shoot her point-blank in her parents' bedroom!"

The Olivia of days, even hours before, would've been able

to stop Aidy. Maybe with the perfect rebuttal or a well-timed redirection. But I didn't have her. I couldn't fight anymore.

"I should've been there," Aidy whispered. "I knew better than to take my eyes off you for a single second. But I let you convince me, like I always did." She took her first sip of her spilling drink, then spit it back into the cup, glaring at Harrison. "Everyone knows what you were doing that day, but do you have any idea what *we* were doing? The real reason we didn't stay?"

This broke the spell she'd cast over the room. Bigs and Teeny and Harrison all advanced on her, backing Nick and I into the corner closest to the closet. Ruby hung back, instead crawling onto the windowsill to sit on the blackout curtains, her arms wrapped around her knees.

"It's kind of perfect, actually. It's like you knew without having a single clue. We were writing a letter."

"Aidy," Teeny warned.

"We were never going to talk about this again," Harrison added, so aware that he was saying the wrong thing but so incapable of stopping himself. He grabbed at his throat as if battling against the words.

"And has it helped?" she asked him. "Every time you drink, you start slurring about it. Not in obvious ways, but I'm pretty sure all you'd need to do was blink, and I'd know what it is you're thinking, because I'm thinking it too." Aidy laughed like she'd finally gotten to the punchline of a joke years in the making. "We were kicking Marley out of the group. Calling her superficial and self-centered and clearly too good for the Albany kids. You'll be happy to know that your little Ruby wanted no part of it. She'd come with us that day to put up a fight over it. No one listened to her, so she closed herself up in your room to pout."

Ruby tucked her head into the space between her knees.

She'd never told me.

Aidy sneered. "If you're wondering why every one of us got our asses on our bikes and pedaled for our lives over to Cadence Park on the night of the memorial, now you know. No one cares about what you've done. Honestly. What they care about is whether any of it is true. If there really is anything left to hold on to. Some sort of forgiveness Marley can give us, even though she never even knew we did anything wrong."

Aidy's anger crashed into me with the volatility of a hurricane wave. For years I'd used Marley as my shield, pinging back everything I didn't want to touch me. But she couldn't protect me from what she never knew herself, and I was too weak on my own. The Marley I carried struggled to hang on to my fragile frame. She wrapped around my throat, pressing into my trachea. The room shrank, everyone becoming miniature while I remained life-size.

No one could see that I was suffocating. They were too small. Too far away. I had no way to breathe them back to their regular size.

Soon enough, the entire room went black.

18

"She's been asleep since you left! What was I supposed to do?"

"Wake her up!"

"I tried! You know how she gets sometimes."

"So, she was sleeping and you couldn't do what I asked all by yourself?"

"I forgot."

"You forgot?"

"She fell asleep so fast I thought maybe she was sick."

"That doesn't make any sense."

"I don't know what to tell you, Dad. It's the truth."

"You really don't seem to care about what's going to happen to you."

"Of course I do."

"Are you sure? Because I can't think of a single thing I've asked you to do this summer that you've actually done, and I can think of quite a few things I've asked you not to do that you've had no trouble accomplishing."

I started to shift around, figuring this was as good a time as any to announce I was awake, but in her continued whisper-fight tone, Aidy said, "Dad, I've been trying to look out for her this entire summer," and I turned myself toward our couch's pillow cushions, burying my head in the crease between two, trying to keep my breath as steady as it was in sleep. "That's pretty much a full-time job. She's—she's acting like she did the first—" Her volume dropped so low my dad couldn't even hear the rest of her sentence.

"What?" he said, matching her urgency.

Murmur, murmur, murmur.

The kitchen had never seemed farther away. I must've slept for at least an hour. Probably more. My parents were already back from dinner. My last dose of ibuprofen had worn off. The pain in my nose radiated out from the center of my face and into my cheeks and eyes. And the mystery drink from Harrison. Oh, the mystery drink. It felt like I'd never be right again.

Aidy was too quiet, as if she knew my ears were trained on the conversation.

My dad, unaware or unconcerned, remained loud enough for me to understand. "Earliest we can get her there is the end of the week. We can't afford to take off any workdays. Your mom and I gave up all our PTO when we came down to your school. And this camp's not cheap. We're not made of money, you know."

My parents had left me home alone for a week toward the end of May. Told me they'd decided to visit my great-aunt, who'd been sick with cancer for years. It only furthered my headache to realize how oblivious I'd been. They'd left me an expanse of unsupervised free time, perfect for organizing the Adventure. It did not occur to me then that they never once said exactly why they were visiting her, or what they were planning on doing there for a whole week, or upon their return, how it had gone.

"We're gonna tell your mom we have a feeling," Dad said. "Not that anything more has happened since the memorial."

How the alliances had once more shifted. Aidy and my dad were now on a team that didn't even involve my mom. I comforted myself by appreciating my own loyalty. People could accuse me of a lot of things, but being a traitor was not on that list.

"Mom's already up in bed," Dad said. "Bring the clothes to that dumpster on Arbor. If there's stuff in Olivia's room that you need to get rid of, maybe now's a good time for that too."

Aidy's volume returned to normal. "Okay," she said confidently, always appreciating a clear task.

"Is there anything else I need to know?"

"No," she said with equal confidence.

The floorboards creaked. He must've moved to hug her. Their conversation was lost in the closeness. The squeaks moved closer, until my dad's breath hung over me, full as a rain cloud. "Good night, Ollie girl," he said. "You'll be okay."

The people in my life decided for me I was okay. And I decided right back I was whatever I wanted to be, at least on the inside. But time made the inside sneak outside, until every part of me became Marley's death, and no one, not even me, wanted to admit it out loud.

Dad went off to his room. Once his door closed, my eyes opened. Aidy stood nearby, as if she knew it would happen that way. "As always, your timing is perfect." She pulled me up from the couch to look me over. "You seem to be okay," she said (of course), and started walking to the back door, expecting me to follow.

The pain and the liquor made for a perfect storm of disorientation. Aidy took the bag from the shrubs by our garage. I did my best to keep pace. We walked along the side of our house and out onto Albany Lane. We made it all the way to the intersection of Albany and Arbor, past the haunted house and Marley's, before Aidy spoke. "What part of this is the act?" she asked me as we turned.

She didn't want me to answer.

It was another seventeen steps before she spoke again. "Because I believe you when you tell me you're okay, and I believe everyone else when they tell me you're not." The garbage bag thumped against her legs as she walked, catching between her thighs and tripping her up. She tossed it over her shoulder instead. Thirteen steps more. "You collapsed," she said. "It was so scary. Then you stood and announced to everyone that you were gonna take a 'little nap.' Not even Nick could convince you to stay or drink some water. Or do anything to actually help you. You were all, *I'm fine, I'm fine,* and the part I don't understand is that you actually looked like you were. You were smiling, Olivia. I couldn't even follow you right away because we all had to help Teeny, who was about three seconds away from passing out too. That's where I'm like, ugh, you wanted her to think there was a demon, because that's the kind of person you are. Always looking for the best story. Trying to stop me from going in on you. But then I think about all that's happened." She hesitated. "I don't know."

We made it to the end of the block, to the very dumpster eleven-year-old Nick hid behind after he left me in the Brickets' shed. Aidy tossed our dirty clothes inside it. The lid closed with a pronounced *thump*, punctuating Aidy's sharp turn. "I get home, and you're already asleep on the couch. I shook you over and over, whispering your name, then screaming it. You wouldn't wake up. I don't get it. And I don't know what to do anymore." Tears welled in her eyes as she looked on expectantly, knowing full well this was the moment I had to come clean.

Explaining my Marley to her could not go like it had with Nick. Aidy worked in literals. Marley transcended them. Still I tried unraveling it as best I could, hoping she'd know these truths were more truthful than other things I'd advertised as truths before.

She leaned herself against the dumpster to listen.

"Olivia," she said through heaves, barely letting me get more than a few sentences out. "It doesn't help you to see her in every-thing. Because you know what you're not seeing at all?" Tension traveled up from the base of her and out through her mouth. "She was mean! Marley Bricket was mean, and unfair, and liked to pick on you because you were the youngest and you thought you were somebody special. She ripped you apart every chance she got, and

I let her, because I looked up to her too. But now, if I could go back, I'd shut her down every time, because she died and you rewrote history to make her into someone worthy of the power we gave her."

The moon was majestic, a large glowing semisphere of yellowish gray. It illuminated the fresh gloss on Aidy's cheeks.

"You're the one who's rewritten who she was to us!" I screamed. "You made her into someone who could disappear, and we'd all get to keep living our lives as if she was never there in the first place!" This was the last of my murk inside me. The stuff at the very bottom, grimy and toxic. "I left Cadence and went to the camp. Put in the work at therapy. All of it. For you!" I slumped down beside her, leaning against the dumpster to catch my breath. "You told me I had to be okay. So I was." Long, solitary seconds turned into drawn-out minutes. I fawned over the smudge covering the pallor on my knees, rubbing back and forth with excessive attention to detail, hoping for something to strike us both: inspiration, courage. Anything at all.

Aidy whispered my name as a start to a sentence she didn't know how to say. More of my toxic sludge bubbled up like an adverse reaction to her. "The memorial was coming, and I knew people would make it a bigger deal than it usually is. Year five and all," I said. "You'd all come in your nicest clothes and tell your nicest stories. But that would be it. You'd forget her again, maybe until year ten, when we'd all stand around as Mayor Bayor unveiled a bronzed statue of Marley in the park or something ridiculous."

It was a future we could both see, as absurd as it sounded. Cadence would never be done with Marley. I hammered down that imagined distance, trying instead to build an explanation Aidy could see just as well. "No, she wasn't perfect. She could be mean and unfair. But so can you. So can I. It's not right to box her into only one way of being. That's not all she was. And it doesn't make her worthy of forgetting." I shook off the chill chasing my words. "I wanted you to say her name, out loud, in public, on a day other than July 11. I tried to remake what happened into something everyone would look at. One final adventure for the kids of Albany Lane. And it worked. Every single one of you started talking about her. Started remembering what we used to be."

Aidy buried her face in her hands.

"Everything I used came from real things Marley had," I said. "When I put it all together, I thought what we gathered up and all the places we went to would make you guys realize how much you missed her. How much we all missed each other. But you..." I stopped to wipe away my spit. I was talking faster than I could manage. "You made this whole into something else. You changed her."

Aidy pulled her hands away from her eyes, using them to instead cover her nose and mouth like a mask. "You don't know where you end and she begins, do you?" Her phrasing took me by surprise. As I contemplated, she took my silence as confirmation. Her entire disposition morphed. "Olivia," she said, treating my name like it was to be my North Star. "For *you*, we will finish this adventure, or whatever we want to call it now. For *you*, we will gather up the rest of this stuff, and we will decide for once and for all what we think happened to her. Okay?"

All my life, I wanted to be seen as someone other than Aidy's little sister. Ollie Stanton, the knock-kneed brat with mud on her clothes and a bad attitude on her tongue, always needing other people to clean up her messes. Yet I never stopped finding myself in that role. No matter how I staged the scene. What lines I fed to my costars. That was the part I kept playing.

"When we do that, will it be enough?" Aidy asked, and I couldn't help myself, I knew what I had to say, even if I wasn't at all sure I meant it.

"Yes."

Aidy's arms extended toward me. I grabbed on and let her pull me back up. As our hands connected, the rest of our lives seemed buried in the connected imprint of our palms. We would die Big Aidy and Little Ollie, regardless of how I tried to swallow secrets to age myself faster.

We walked down Arbor Street, window-shopping for signs of life inside the houses along the way, drinking in the small glimpses of the multitudes held in each. There were so many stories to know. I could reach and reach and never have all of them.

We opened the haunted house's gate. The front door was ajar. When we entered, we learned it was because the group had moved out of the upstairs bedroom. They were shadows scattered around the first floor, quiet as the night. Everything except the string lights and the sleeping bags had been brought downstairs and placed wherever must've been easiest for the carrier, creating trails of thought impossible to follow.

I walked past the entryway and into the living room. Nick sat in the corner. When I got close enough to be sure it was him—not that it could be anyone else, but faces were just dark enough to be a bit unclear on everything—he stood and pulled me into his chest. My nose, barely functioning, could smell the sweat on him.

"Is everything okay?" he asked.

"No," I admitted for the first time in years.

He squeezed me tighter. "I know." He kissed my hair. "It's not." He pressed his lips to my ear. "Do you want to go somewhere?"

"We can't leave," I whispered back.

"We won't." He lifted me up until my feet were no longer on the floor. "Quick! Be anywhere but here!"

He spun us in circles. The room swirled until the walls of the haunted house fell down. With each revolution, we flattened another building in Cadence until the entire town had been ironed out, and it was only Nick and me holding each other in the middle of an empty desert, our hearts beating faster and faster and faster, Marley smiling through the countless stars above us.

At once, he stopped.

Everything crashed back into place, exactly as we'd left it.

"Did you see it?" he asked, holding me as we swayed into the wall.

"Always," I breathed out.

"Me too."

I looked past him to the room around me. The other faces clicked into focus. Ruby. Aidy. Teeny. Bigs. I scanned again, slower, coming up with same four. "Where's Harrison?"

"Right after you left, he took the map to go to all the other spots marked on it. He wanted to collect everything else you'd buried."

"Was I wrong to do this?" I asked.

"I'm the last person who gets to decide what's right or wrong." He brushed his finger across my cheek. "But if you hadn't started this, you and I wouldn't be here. We'd still be lost."

Lost.

Not Marley.

But Nick. And me.

We were the ones who were lost.

Harrison dashed into the house with a full backpack on his shoulders. "Let's go upstairs; it's way too dark down here," he said, out of breath. Shadows pushed out of corners to surround him. He looked around until he saw the one that made Aidy. "Unless we have the all clear to bring some lights downstairs?"

She considered, then said, "Not a good idea. My dad actually knows we're out right now, but there are other people that live on Albany who might be suspicious."

Harrison jogged the stairs two at a time.

Before following him, Teeny snapped her fingers in my direction and said, "I swear on my life, if you do one more thing like you did earlier, I will run out that door and all the way home, and I will never ever look your direction again."

"That's fair," I told her.

"Then let's see what you and Marley made for us," she said, taking her time walking up each step.

Me and Marley. Both of us.

I smiled at that.

This was the cusp, a flicker, the edge of it all. And we were finally ready to tip. It only took everyone saying it many times for it to be true. That, I discovered, was the difference between plan and execution. There's always a delay that can't be accounted for, even when you plan and plan. The delay is the nuance of reality, as fine as the fabric on the pillow Marley held in front of her the day she died. Each fiber was important, different from the next. Each changed the impact of the bullet. Each was an essential part of the story.

A hand pressed into the small of my back. "I'm right behind you," Ruby told me.

As I ascended, I tried to guess whose footprints were whose, despite sufficient disturbance to the dust on the staircase. The tracks were untraceable, yet they all led to the same place.

Harrison emptied his backpack in the triangle of space between the string lights. "I think this is everything. I went everywhere on the map that we hadn't been yet," he said. He looked down at the pile, first smiling, his dimples pricking both sides of his face, making me ever so fond of him. Then he was crying, two perfect streams flowing right into the divots on his cheeks. "I tried to be as quick as I could. I used your bike, Ruby. I wasn't in the right mind to drive. I hope that's okay. I mean it's done now, so I guess it has to be, huh? I'm sorry. It's a nice bike. I can see why you like it so much." His thoughts exploded out of him. "I wish you all had been there with me. I kept thinking that. Even though we know Olivia hid all of it, and it's not the same kind of real we thought it was, I still wished you all were there." His Adam's apple disappeared and bulged, on and on, as he fought back tears. He looked at me and nodded. "But anyway, this is everything," he repeated, then nodded again, remembering he already said that. His dimples danced across his flushed cheeks for one more embarrassed smile. "This is hard. Someone else take over."

There was a hesitation. Each body leaned, contemplating stepping forward. *A room full of leaders*, I thought, first as a throw-away observation, then as a revelation. Each person in the room did not just go along with the flow. Together, we created a flow in which we all decided to follow. When one person faltered, there was always someone else to step up and keep us charging forward. Each person was the lead character in their version of the story, the stakes highest for them, always guided by choice, above all. Even the feeling of obligation was a choice.

They felt obligated to figure out what Marley had done—or what I had done, depending on how they saw it—but chose to pursue it. And these people, the kids I'd known my entire life, chose to stay long past knowing it was a bad, or at least a very complicated, idea. They chose me and my version of the story. Even chose to let me lead us to its ending, knowing any choice would've been correct, but I needed it most.

I did. That was the truth. I needed to see I could be the young-est and still go toe-to-toe with the rest of them.

I stepped beneath the triangle of lights. All around me, our Marley was in pieces. While I'd slept, Aidy must've given Harrison everything we'd already found, because at the bottom of the pile there was the trophy head, and Marley's school picture, and the red notebook, and the wooden box. All three parts of Marley's leather journal. The two I hadn't yet rediscovered were stained with dirt, dug up from where I'd buried them. Everything else was illuminated by the resting firefly bulbs: a broken tiara, Officer Bricket's old badge, Ms. DeVeau's pearl necklace, a family photo from Marley's eighth grade graduation. One dead iPod. All the letters I'd hidden in my bedroom.

I was Houdini, standing before a rapt audience awaiting my final trick. But it was always Marley who told me how to perform. The last version of me that existed without her was Little Ollie, shrieking and crying for someone to fix the terrible mess she'd made. She flashed in front of me, examining the wreckage on her—Marley's blood, already dried. Little Ollie held a wet towel, rubbing the blood into her skin. Painting herself with it until her mother called her name, telling her the shower was ready. I needed to accept that she would have to be where I began again.

So I took Little Ollie's hand and washed her skin clean of the blood.

She was me.

She always would be.

The middle section of Marley's journal sat highest on the pile. Holding it stopped my hands from shaking. The pages were familiar and still surprising, like remembering details of a movie I hadn't seen in years. They told the story of a girl with a mother who expected a beauty queen at all times. A father who expected a level of respect no one could achieve. Sometimes Marley tried.

251

Sometimes she rebelled. The real problem was, her father loved her, but he did not love her mother, at least not in the way married mothers and fathers were expected to love one another. But Ms. DeVeau loved images.

And Marley loved adventures.

She took her father to their shed every night and worked on a blueprint of Cadence, telling him it was a map for the Albany kids. She told Bigs it was a secret project.

It wasn't either of those things, I began to realize.

One by one, the other Albany kids came closer to me. Where my arms were useless and weighted, incapable of letting go of the middle section of Marley's journal, theirs picked up the letters and other parts of the journal, investigating and comparing, constructing a symphony of solving around me.

Harrison held his Marley letter like the prize he wished it was. His hands trembled but his eyes held no malice. In spite of himself, he wanted for it all to be directly from Marley herself. "Did she ever actually say any of this?"

Ruby held the last third of Marley's journal. "She talks about all of us in this," she told Harrison. "But it bounces around a lot. It's like Olivia took the suggestion of what Marley said and turned it into something more concrete."

Harrison came near her to read over her shoulder. Ruby turned back a few pages to find the excerpt she wanted. "'I wish I could be as still as Harrison,'" she read. "'He's there, doing his thing, living his life. Minding his business. Everyone notices everything I do. I can't walk to the park without it being a whole event. Dad telling me my shorts are too short and I shouldn't wear them because I'm better than that. As if that's a thing. As if my clothing determines my worth. Mom telling me I shouldn't wear them because they show off my cellulite. Little does she know, I like my cellulite.'"

"Can I see?" I interrupted, so eager to figure out if the last section had the most answers that I couldn't endure a single second more of not knowing. I'd read it before, but not since Aidy had planted the idea that Marley knew what she was doing the day she died. Ruby handed the journal over, another choice to let me have the moment.

The first few pages were drafts of riddles and rhymes. *The town holds the answers,* Marley wrote over and over, testing out fonts, hunting for the pressure and size that best conveyed her intentions.

Lists of potential items to hide, crossed out and written over so much the ink had turned smudgy. *What if I give them a picture of myself and one of my trophies? Like I'm a human, not a trophy. Does that make sense? Everything is Something.*

I was her and she was me, trying to make sense of the important and the mundane, wondering how it all threaded together.

Then it hit me. The purpose of the Adventure had nothing to do with the Albany kids at all. It was a plan to bring her parents back together. A plan as ambitious and outrageous as Marley herself. A plan she made in secret, without the other eyes and ears she'd always had as backup.

It was so crystal clear now, reading it with our group. I found myself imagining the suggestions we would've given her. The thoughts helped steady me. Ruby would've reminded Marley, "Who you love is never the problem. It's how you love them that matters."

Marley's father did not love her mother like she asked of him. Still she loved him back.

But Marley was a dreamer. She dreamed of a life where her parents' fundamental differences could be fixed by a grand adventure down memory lane. She'd been running practice tests on us Albany kids for years. It was time for the real show.

I'd taken her story for her parents and made it a story for our friends, but I, like she, could not find a way to make it work as planned. This was a girl who wrote, *Everything is Something,* then told Nick, "Nothing's gonna happen," knowing full well that even Nothing is Something, because Everything is Something, and oh how the world made no sense at all, and up was always down was always up again, and who could right it? Who could straighten it all out?

Toward the end of the journal, her words became frantic, scattered, sprawling pages and crisscrossing thoughts, jumping from the Albany kids to her parents to her fears for herself. She did not want to be the person she was. She hated all the people who judged her. It came down to a simple truth I'd always known— Marley Bricket hated all the things she could not control. Which was everything but us, her loyal friends: leaders choosing to let her lead. Giving her that power because she needed it most.

She wished, like Ruby read, that she could be as still as Harrison.

As the entry went on, she wished to be as trustworthy as Ruby.

As kind-hearted as Bigs.

As assured as Teeny.

As level-headed as Aidy.

As selfless as Nick.

As cunning as me.

As her writing came to an abrupt end, about thirty empty pages between her words and the back of the journal, the last line read, *I wish to stop wishing at all.*

She'd split my reality into so many parts, all ground into a fine powder by what seemed to be true. I passed the journal to Aidy and tucked myself into a tight ball, squeezing for relief. For a definite. For anything.

My Marley was all the things I always thought she was. And yet so foreign. She seemed so young. She *was* so young. And so was I, I knew, no matter what I'd seen, or how I felt, or how I'd tried to bend time forward for myself and backward to keep her around. I'd never stop being the youngest in our group. But Marley would never stop being fifteen.

How could that be right?

Aidy finished reading the third part of the journal, stoic. "Regardless of everything Olivia did, it really might be true, after all," she said, her voice a brushstroke, barely filled with paint, daring to add her words to the untouchable canvas that was Marley Bricket's death.

19

THERE WAS THE MARLEY WE ALBANY KIDS KNEW. AND THE
one her mom knew. The one her dad knew. The one both of
them knew when together. Every version of Marley had different intentions. Different forms altogether. There was the Marley
I saw in every primary color. The Marley I heard in the trees. The
Marley in the stars, smiling at me. The Marley that came to Nick
through music and sound.

Somewhere in my quest to make everyone else remember
the Marley we knew as children, I stumbled upon a Marley who
needed help and didn't know how to ask for it, too afraid to fail
us by being seen as weak. As Aidy passed the journal around the
circle, each person met this Marley, in all her wavering contem-
plations and self-loathing thoughts, tired of being what she was,
and tired of thinking it at all, for she knew her life was a gift, but
it was one she hadn't asked for, and one she thought her parents
wanted a return on, because their product wasn't perfect.

"She never says it," Bigs whispered. He wouldn't say the word. No one could. Her eyes that day, so full of mischief, sparkling with countless plans yet to be carried out. Those eyes told me her own death was never one of her plans. But her words seemed to scream it. Which one was right?

"I can't accept it unless she says it somewhere," Bigs said, much louder.

"But Biggy, she was so lost," Teeny countered, tucking her arm under her brother's and leaning against their titanium connection. Tears fell out from beneath her fanned lashes, so long they grazed her cheekbone when she closed her eyes.

"Are you sure this is everything?" Aidy asked Harrison.

"We can definitely go back to check all the places," he said. "I mean, I found something in every spot. So unless there's more than one thing hidden in each place, this is everything."

Aidy tapped my shoulder. "What about in your room, Olivia? Is there more I didn't find?"

"I don't think so."

"What do you mean you don't think so?"

"Exactly that."

"Did you write this journal for her?"

"No."

"But you wrote our letters?" Aidy asked.

"I typed them."

"You know what I mean."

"I do. But I've said all there is to say." I was being frustrating. But it was the truth, in all its imperfect glory.

"When you're stuck in a room with no exit…" Nick started.

Harrison did a three-sixty. "What do you mean? The door's right there."

Aidy, Nick, and I exchanged knowing glances, a substitute for the smiles we would've shared if the mood was lighter. I always knew we'd be forever stuck in the room of Marley's death, but it was a surprise to find new ways of surviving it, like the three of us landing on the same side of something. The moment flickered by, folding back into the shadows as quickly as it came.

There was so much to see, even in places I'd searched through for years and years.

Marley's journal gave us no out. No matter how much he wanted to, Nick could not break down a wall with the weight of the words she wrote.

Marley had left it up to us to decide. Did she know the gun was loaded? Why wouldn't she tell us she was hurting? Why would she ruin Nick's life by asking him to do what she couldn't? They were ugly thoughts. The ugliest of Marleys lived inside them. They were the reason the room had no exit. Uncertainty was a trap we could not work around.

I neared a full panic, clutching my knees tight, trying to find my breath before I lost it again. If I wanted to know everything, I had to deal with what it took.

Ruby placed her hand on my knee. "I have an idea," she said, redirecting my focus. "If this is all we have, and it's not enough to know for sure, we have to make our own kind of peace with it." She gently shook the journal out of my balled fists. "I could look at all of this for hours and come up with a million points for either column, but in these past few days alone, I've barely eaten. I haven't slept. I'm so sick over this every second I'm awake." She started neatening the pile of hidden objects. "We should hold our own memorial."

Ruby streamlined the thoughts clanging into me. Cadence did not know how to remember our Marley, because Cadence didn't know our Marley. Cadence's Marley was yet another of her infinite iterations, and we'd been memorializing that version for five years. She was dead and gone. Buried under our constant attention to her foam-board stare.

Ruby started fitting all the hidden objects into the wooden box. Aidy took a permanent marker and wrote *MARLEY.* on the top. A period for a girl who did not deal in sort-ofs or maybes, yet left her whole life as a question mark for us to forever ponder.

Our whole group traveled down the center of Albany Lane. The sky had fallen into a deep slumber, so dark the streetlights could only touch the edges of each intersection, waiting for us like mile markers.

I took a spot next to Ruby at the back of our *V*. I didn't need to be up front anymore. It made no difference. We'd all get there, whether or not I was the one to lead us. Instead, I snapshotted each person, determined to preserve the memory of the night.

Because there would be no next time. I felt it like I felt Marley. Impossible to explain, but real all the same. If there was an acceptable way to move that was slower than walking, like getting on my stomach and slithering toward Cadence Park, I would've done it, if only to hold on longer.

Teeny wore jean shorts and a navy-blue crop top that sat right above her navel, showing a hint of the tattoo that traced her ribs—her brother's time of birth. Her braids were so long they almost covered the ink. She stretched her fingers out like the air was water to wade in, and she was testing the temperature.

The night was hers.

Bigs, in a maroon shirt and black mesh shorts, looked across the street to his twin as she did this, her motions a language he spoke fluently. He joined her in touching the night by looking up to the stars.

The night was his.

Harrison had on his old tennis team shirt. It said SHIN on the back, with MVP written below. He walked a few paces behind Aidy, following her as he always had. And maybe always would.

It seemed then that they were each other's compasses, sometimes flitting too quickly between directions, but ultimately headed the same way. It was yet another Marley who had wedged between them, desperate to be acknowledged, the two of them not letting it happen, afraid of what it meant. I could see her there, sideways like Harrison and Aidy were connected rocks she'd hammered into, and she'd gotten stuck in the middle, so immobile she could do nothing but wait for them to notice. If they would let her pass all the way through, the jagged line she'd cut into each of them would sit flush, leaving only a hairline fracture in place of what was once a gaping hole. Then Aidy wouldn't have to lead with anger all the time. She could heal.

Harrison sped up to reach for Aidy's hand. She grabbed on,

lifting their tightly balled palms to her mouth for a gentle kiss, creating a little more space for their Marley to one day sneak out.

Harrison smiled the widest smile I'd ever seen, his teeth glowing against the dark.

The night was his.

Aidy walked proudly at the tip of the *V*, wearing a striped bow-neck shirt and her favorite high-waisted black shorts. Her hair was pulled into a neat ponytail that was high enough to create a waving waterfall down the sides of her head. With her unlinked hand, she held the box of Marley like she sometimes held me, willing it to be okay.

The night was hers.

Ruby leaned into my side, her hand in mine like always, ready to go wherever I needed her. Even in the dark, her wine-tipped hair was distinct against her warm skin and painted lips. A long, black tank swished against her leggings. Her eyes were all around us, taking in every moment as I tried to, another memento we both wished to keep. She picked up a rock instead, twirling it between her fingers. It was an item to tuck away in our box of trinkets, looking mundane but so full of significance, something physical to remember the untouchable. She pressed it to her chest.

The night was hers.

And on the other side of the street, diagonal from Ruby and me, filling in the Nick-shaped space that had shadowed my life for five whole years, walked the impossible boy himself, towering over his old outline. He twisted time in his white tee and jeans, changed and unchanging, his cheeks as bashful but his eyes no longer cheerful; instead, weary and cautious and still somehow hopeful, the curse of the life of people such as us. He looked over his shoulder, passing me a glance that burst into flames.

The night was his.

Then there was me, of course, little Olivia Stanton in Marley's sky-blue denim romper, a cardigan tied around my waist. Dirty tennis shoes on my feet. Always dressed for possibility. Maybe I'd need to run. Maybe it would be cold. Maybe I'd need to look nice. Maybe Everything was Something.

The night was mine.

Once we passed the first intersection, we entered the block that belonged to Ruby and the Campbells. Ruby stopped inside her house to grab something, slinking in and out without turning on a single light, no comment toward what she'd taken, only that it was necessary.

"Anything else?" Aidy asked when Ruby came back, the first words spoken aloud since we'd left.

"Shovels," Bigs said. When we got to his house, he opened the garage and grabbed two. He held one in each hand, waiting to hear what else we needed.

There were many things we each wanted, but we had all we needed. We continued along Albany, trudging up the steep incline, a leg-scorching task that always signified the last hurdle before relief.

A warm glow from the streetlamps surrounded the swing sets and wood chips of Cadence Park. Pushing on, our pace accelerated, somewhere between walking and jogging. Every few steps became a long sliding skip, each person ready to reach this sacred space of ours. The hot breath of night blew on our backs, egging us on, conspiring with us. Our *V* turned single file as Aidy led us through the playground and down into the bowl. We coiled around until we formed a circle in the center of the dry grass.

"We made it," Aidy said, a bit breathless. No car had seen us walking. No cell phone had rung to tell one of us to go home. We were intact.

"Let's dig the hole," Bigs said, already breaking ground in the bone-dry soil. The tip of his shovel dug down and flipped back up, more force than he anticipated, creating a firework of grass and dirt, sparks landing on Teeny.

"Xander!" she yelled. She picked up a handful of loosened soil and threw it back at him.

"Sorry, T," he said. He didn't even brush her revenge dirt off his shirt. He kept digging, much more carefully.

Harrison picked up the other shovel and joined him. "How deep are we going?"

"Not very," Bigs told him.

It still took longer than expected to carve out a satisfactory shape. As the rest of us waited for Bigs and Harrison to finish, we huddled together. The closeness was a hug, so tight my busted nose could smell perfumes and body sweat and a trace of all the drinks Harrison had made. Nothing hurt much then, not my head or my nose or my heart.

Bigs and Harrison set down their shovels to wipe their

foreheads at the exact same time, which gave me the bizarre thought that maybe twins were twins with everyone, just by nature. As if they couldn't help but link right up to someone else's movements because they were so in tune with what it was to share space with someone.

Maybe everyone was a twin, in some way. I leaned closer to Teeny to test it out, just enough for the pressure of my shoulder to seem accidental. She matched me right away, the two of us conjoined at nearly identical heights. Maybe it meant nothing, but even nothing was something, and I liked the idea of her and me as twins of some sort. Twins of circumstance, forever connected.

Aidy opened her purse and took out the flashlights. She passed them out to us, ignoring questions about their purpose. Once we each had one, she sat down a way back from the discarded dirt. "Ruby, do you know how you want to start this?"

"I do."

We unpacked ourselves to let Ruby through, then coiled back around into our circle, sitting legs crossed with our hands in our laps. Aidy turned on her flashlight and pointed it toward the discarded dirt. We copied. All our beams looked like rays, the hole in the ground our sun.

Ruby stayed standing. The wooden box was beneath her feet. She considered it, then picked it up to hold, her fingers tracing Marley's name. "When she left us, we were supposed to forever ask, *How did this happen?*" she said; a question I'd repeated more times than I could count. "How did she get her hands on such an ugly thing? How did she not know it was loaded? Who turned off the safety? Why would she play with it? We had to think in consequence and in regret, but we didn't think of any answers. Looking at her life before that moment was a no-no. But you guys, we've always been the kids who dug around where we shouldn't. And not one of us touched it after she died." She stopped moving her fingers. "Except for Olivia."

It was like all the lights in the ground turned to face me. I shifted to find a position that would make me more comfortable, not that such a thing existed. Ruby had created a moment designed for squirming.

"Asking questions without looking for answers is an easy way to live. I know I liked it. I bet all of you did too. Olivia did the heavy lifting for us. She was keeping tabs on everything so the rest of us didn't have to: speaking at the memorials, helping the committee set up scholarships. Younger than all of us and doing all the work. For five years, I watched her. I could see how it wore her down, but for some reason, I didn't think I should help. It felt like an invasion of privacy or something. This was her thing now. Best to stay out of her way."

The lights brightened.

"Why did I think that was what I was supposed to do? Why was I doing what I thought I was supposed to, anyway? When have we ever done that? We ignored Olivia. Let people who didn't know her try to help her. When we were younger, we treated figuring things out like it was our job. It should have been us that did this with her."

Now everyone had to share in the squirm of the exposure.

"The reality is, the answers don't make sense. Yeah, there's some evidence that suggests Marley might have made Nick… take her life. It's way more likely it was a terrible accident that can't be erased, no matter what we do, or say, or create to try. There is no easy out. Why did we try to make one? Why did we automatically think the easy way was the best way? Are you noticing how many more questions we've created because we ignored the first ones?"

She held the box closer to her. "I look at this, and I can imagine Marley climbing up a tree behind City Hall and tucking the map into some little nook no one would ever think to see. I don't care what Olivia did. I know in my heart that this all came from Marley. We all do. That's why we're here, regardless of whatever other reasons you all made up to explain to yourself why we're all basically adults and we're at the playground with flashlights and a box of pretend. We're here because we love Marley, and we love Olivia, and we know the two are not that different."

The grass under me bristled. I tugged at it, holding a handful, rubbing the dirt into my palms.

Ruby knelt. "Marley, the girl I loved so desperately. My first crush. My *worst* crush." She laughed. "My biggest enemy and my favorite friend. A villain and a hero. All of the things any girl could ever want to be. Smart and tough and proud, staying friends with us younger Albany kids because she liked us better than the people in high school. She loved us, and we loved her, as imperfect as she was. But we missed how much she needed our help. We were too busy looking at other things to see it. The thing is, we all see Olivia. I know we do. I watched everyone's faces when she came up with that broken nose. I felt the room sink away when she fainted."

I closed my eyes.

There was an activity we did a lot at Camp Califree. In front of a small group, two people would stand and get a suggestion from the group leader. Something random, like *hat*. From there, they had to make up a scene using the suggestion. The only rule was that they had to agree with everything the other person did and said. The small idea was to help us see it's okay to fail, and to trust the other people in our lives. The big idea was to help learn how to navigate conversations that might turn toward whatever sent us to Camp Califree in the first place. To help free us of the fear of talking about it. Or talking at all.

From the periphery of myself, I could see how it was helpful. I'd already faced constant scenarios where I had to talk about what happened to Marley. I didn't just talk, I relived, climbing right back inside that hot July afternoon, the metallic smell of her fresh blood curdling up under my nostrils as I did. I was constantly swept away by the rushing tide that was the loss of her.

The activity reaffirmed that I didn't have to make it so hard on myself. Life was a performance. Like Marley had always taught me. As long as I could read what the other person wanted, I truly had the power, even if I was going along with their idea. I learned to write myself the best role that way. To swiftly pivot and swirl and turn and climb until I hovered above the reality of my life, crafting myself into someone everyone liked better.

What I never took into account was how my kind of story ended. Living so high above everyone else meant I either floated away or they climbed up to meet me in the clouds. And there they were, a ladder leaning right onto the teetering edge I'd constructed above them, extending their arms, ready to help me back down. I could not catch my tears. The dirt in my hands started turning to mud.

"Marley's mom and dad needed to be better people, and they weren't," Ruby continued. "Let that be a lesson to us. We can be better. We should think of her every time we hop a fence instead of opening the gate. Or peek under the bed at a new friend's house to see what interesting things we might find. That's what we owe her. So, we're going to get up here and cry our eyes out. Tell the stories we thought we forgot. Put this box in the ground not to bury it, but to keep it as a secret monument. This is who we were. We owned this place. The kids of Albany Lane." Ruby placed the wooden box into the hole. "Let's make it so that we never again have to ask ourselves, *How did this happen?*"

It wasn't exactly as I imagined, but the night was becoming everything I wanted. It took my best friend to make it happen. Even though I'd tried to hide, she saw me anyway.

One by one, the others got up and shared stories of us as we used to be.

Harrison told of the weeklong saga that was Marley attempting to build a tree house out of wood scraps we found near City Hall.

Teeny reminded us of all the times she and Marley hosted runway shows down Albany. We'd all go into our houses and wrap ourselves up in anything we could find, then parade down the yellow catwalk painted onto the center of our street.

Bigs brought up the time we fell asleep watching a scary movie, and Marley woke us up in the middle of the night with an air horn. She informed us we'd be sleeping outside. In her backyard, our sleeping bags filled the space between the shed and the pool. Marley proceeded to tell us ghost stories until we couldn't keep our eyes open. Everyone crashed. Except for Bigs, we learned. Marley woke up not long after the rest of us had gone to sleep. She realized Bigs was still awake too, so she stayed with him, leaning her head on his shoulder as they kept an eye on the rest of us.

With each story, the teller tossed a handful of dirt and closed with, "I love you, Marley. I love you, Olivia. I love all of you."

Aidy used her time to apologize for writing a letter trying to kick Marley out of the group. Harrison stood back up to echo the sentiment. Bigs and Teeny joined them. "We never really wanted you to leave. We just didn't know better." They each tossed in an extra handful.

Nick got up. He took a handful of dirt and passed it from hand to hand. "Marley," he started. "There's so much we didn't understand about you. We weren't paying attention, I guess. Or we were too afraid to ask. I'm sorry we didn't. I would've at least tried to make you laugh. You didn't like to admit it, but I know you thought I was funny. I used to be, at least." Soft dirt fell through his fingers. "We could've helped make it better. That's what we were best at. Every memory tonight proves it." He stopped. The rest of the dirt fell from his shaking hands. "Marley, I wish I knew to be stronger that day. I wish I had listened to Olivia. I'm sorry you wished to stop wishing, because it's a powerful thing. My wishes are the only things keeping that day from swallowing me up. I hate thinking you knew. That you would do that to me. It makes me wish I could hug you and tell you not that it will all be okay, but that it will be easier with our help."

He leaned over to cup a fresh handful of dirt. His palms clasped together like the soil held power. "Olivia, you don't have to carry her all on your own. This has always been as much mine as it is yours, and I pushed it away. Turned it into wishes. Right now, I have the power to do what I didn't that day five years ago. I can say to you not that it will be okay, but that it will be easier—for both of us—with help." His palms parted. "I love you, Marley." He looked to me. "I love you, Olivia." He looked around. "I love all of you."

From the second I saw him at the memorial, the mark of Marley's work was clear in Nick's presence. As he stood there, trembling, it was clear as a Marley blue sky in July.

Marley wanted to release Nick. Give him back to us.

The night was as much for me as it was for her. I'd never shared that kind of responsibility before. Never shared anything at all. It made me so light, I was glad for the hands that helped me back down, because without them, I would've sailed up forever, never to return again.

Finally, it was my turn to speak. The grand finale. It was a familiar place for me to be, in front of a crowd, preparing to tell a story about Marley. But for the first time, I was going to tell the stories I'd swallowed.

Word by word, I handed my Marley over to my friends. I told them about the melatonin cookies and the Marquez family's car.

Ruby gasped. "That was *you?*"

I told them about all the afternoons in Marley's mom's closet.

I told them about the California quail. How it was alive, even though it was dead.

I told them everything.

When I finished, everyone stood and wrapped their arms around me. I was patched up and damaged and a little off center, but all myself, amazed to learn my friends were willing to hold the excess I could no longer carry.

I was just Olivia Stanton, sixteen years old. Older than Marley would ever be. Younger than everyone else. Both a cannonball from the sky, arcing back to the ground, and a cannonball in the water, rushing back to the surface.

I was back.

That was the point.

Night became night that was actually morning. It was convex, pushing up from all surfaces, preparing for the next sunrise. I threw my handful dirt atop the box.

Finally, we'd remembered her right.

"I took this from our other box," Ruby said.

In her hands was a picture of the eight of us in Marley's pool. Teeny's eyes were closed. Harrison was midjump, his whole torso a blur. Aidy was looking at him, stern. Bigs and I were photo ready, smiles wider than our faces, arms wrapped around each other like sorority sisters. Nick was solemn. Ruby was fixing her swim top. Marley was looking up.

It was a self-timed photo Marley thought she'd deleted from her camera roll. Ruby had secretly sent it to herself then printed it out for us to keep. It had always been our favorite, forever sitting at the top of our box of trinkets.

Ruby held the photo to her heart. "No stops," we said to each other, not because we needed the reminder, but because we knew we'd done it. We'd crossed our finish line. The secret picture fell from Ruby's hands and fluttered into place atop the rest of Marley's belongings.

Bigs and Harrison picked up the shovels and start tossing back large piles of dirt. When they were done, we stomped the loose soil back into place.

The seven of us went back how we came until we arrived in the upstairs bedroom of the haunted house. We unfurled our mangled sleeping bags and tucked ourselves underneath, leaving the string lights as our constellations.

Nick wrapped his arms around me, and I pressed against his torso, no longer needing the light of an imagined sky to find sleep.

20

THANKS TO THE BLACKOUT CURTAINS AND NICK'S BODY, morning did not get to intrude upon me. One last little gift from our best Marley.

Nick was stuck on me. Literally stuck. Our skin had congealed in the growing afternoon heat. I peeled myself away, leaving his white shirt drenched with the impression of me.

"It's hot," I noted.

"I don't mind," he said.

I curled back into him once more.

A few other sleeping bags were rolled into tight bundles, same as the lights. Only Harrison was still upstairs with us. He said, "Breakfast," and headed out of the room.

Nick and I followed the promise of food all the way out the front door and over to my house, where the rest of the previous night's remnants had already been returned.

"Afternoon," Bigs said once we entered the kitchen. He and

Teeny sat where Aidy and I had the day before. They were eating pancakes, just as we'd done twenty-four hours prior. Twins of circumstance, I remembered with a smile.

"Dad made those," Aidy told me. "I found a huge stack on the kitchen counter, along with instructions on how to best reheat them, as well as a very long, extremely detailed list of things we have to get done today if we expect to ever survive life again."

"Joy," I said, still taking in the confusion of the morning, marred by a blaring headache.

"We need to hurry. We have work in an hour," Bigs reminded Teeny. They shoveled down their last bites. When they stood and hugged me goodbye in what felt like the same motion, my foggy brain could barely process what leaving meant.

"Thank you," I mouthed as they walked out. The Campbell twins were the first to be removed from me after Marley's death, carted off to a world outside of Cadence, where they built promises for bright futures. And still they returned.

Still they remembered.

Still they loved me back.

We didn't require a long goodbye. Our history did it for us. Time and space could never touch what we kids of Albany had been to each other, and now that we knew our legacy was safe, memorialized in secrecy at Cadence Park, we didn't need words to reaffirm it.

Only Aidy, Harrison, Nick, and I remained. "Where's Ruby?" I asked.

"You didn't hear her phone blowing up this morning? She was

supposed to be babysitting her brothers. She ran out super early," Harrison said.

Aidy's eyes narrowed on Nick. "Do you have anywhere you need to be?"

One last remaining swig of my murk swished around the very base of me. Why did she keep us apart? There was no reason I could find, even still.

"No," he told her.

"Would you mind helping Harrison do some of the things on the list? Olivia and I have somewhere we need to go."

"We do?"

"It won't take us very long. We'll be back to help soon," she assured Nick.

"Of course," he said without hesitation.

The four of us finished eating the chocolate chip pancakes. It was so strange and so normal, like the continuation of a well-loved story that had been interrupted by unconscious hibernation. The normalness of strange—or the strangeness of normal—begged to be noticed. What a world this was, the Stanton girls with their boys, communing at noon for a meal in the family kitchen. Every pot, pan, and plate took on a different, brighter sheen. What a world, indeed.

I went to change. The piles on my floor had been rearranged into an unfamiliar landscape. Aidy had unearthed all my buried secrets. Even my own journal was open and lying atop my bed, with all my plans for the Adventure reading like Marley's had, bold and nonsensical, lacking nuance.

I snapped the journal shut and sat beside it. My dresser

drawers had been spilled out, long-neglected bottom contents flipped up to the top. I rummaged through everything and put on clothes I forgot I owned. Went to the bathroom and washed my face of yesterday's disguise. The yellow in my bruises matched the golden flecks in my hazel eyes; flickers of Marley I'd never before noticed.

I was new.

I was ready.

"Your nose looks better," Aidy said when I came back into the kitchen. "It definitely isn't broken." She walked from the sink to the door. "We'll be back soon," she told the boys again.

"See you later, Olivia," Nick said with a grin.

"Okay, Nick," I said back, about to burst.

Aidy looked at Harrison like she didn't understand what was so amusing, and said, "Grab the sleeping bags from next door, please." She tugged my arm and pulled me outside.

We walked around to the front and hit the sidewalk. "Where are we going?" I asked.

"Ms. DeVeau's."

"Why?"

"We owe it to her to at least tell her what we found."

Normal or strange, Aidy was Aidy, her morals skewered but persevering. An Aidy who cared about rules but kept secrets from her sister. An Aidy who hated to cheat but let her boyfriend try and save her academic career.

My last drops of murk slipped out. "Why did you think Nick would hurt me most?"

No longer capable of tripping her up, she maintained our synchronicity as she said, "I've figured out that I like to rewrite rules when it comes to the people I love."

We made a precise turn, like scissors cutting edges.

"I thought changing what you two were to each other was going to fix what happened to you. There was no line between Nick and what he did to Marley. You used to wake up yelling, *He killed her!* Over and over." Swift and graceful, she leapt over the uncountable cracks in the concrete. "But you've changed. Or I may have been wrong. Maybe both. Maybe neither. But I can see that it's better for you now. And I'm sorry I did that. I was doing what I thought was best for you."

"I love you," I said, surprising her.

I thought for a long time that I didn't love anything. But I loved my Marley so desperately and fully, I couldn't see life outside of her. I chose her death as the moment that would forever define me, in spite of my therapists and counselors and neighbors and family and friends telling me I was just a kid, and I could bounce back. I could change it.

Marley's love pulled me up into the clouds. Other love pulled me back. It was all a balance, so fragile, always ready to tip one way or the other. I could never love people like they asked of me. Not exactly. I could only love them the best I knew how. Chances were, they'd still love me back.

"I love you too," Aidy said back.

"And Harrison?" I baited her to lighten the mood. Some habits would never fade.

"I know. What am I doing? I make no sense."

"You make perfect sense to me."

We didn't hug. That wasn't our style. We kept walking, understanding our rhythms would always be different and somehow forever match.

Ms. DeVeau's orange house stood in protest at the edge of the road. Ms. DeVeau herself was out in her front garden, squatted down, her arms gesticulating wildly, fussing over the hole Harrison had dug there the night before. I saw myself in her place, cloaked by night and guided by Marley, pulling out yellow flowers and putting a third of the journal beneath them, then tamping the bright red flowers back into place.

Grabbing the reins before I'd even formulated a plan, Aidy called out to her. "Ms. DeVeau!"

Marley's mother tilted her head up and over her shoulder to see us, her taut face a grand reveal from beneath the brim of her straw hat. "Girls," she said.

"Can we talk?" Aidy asked.

Ms. DeVeau gestured to the hole that had her so dismayed. "This was you?" she guessed.

"Can we talk?" Aidy repeated as a confirmation.

Finger by finger, Ms. DeVeau plucked the gloves off her hands. "Come on in." She tossed them onto the dirt and sauntered up her two-step staircase. "To what do I owe this pleasure?" she asked as she opened her front door. We followed her into the warm orange house with the cold interior, straight back until we were in her sterile kitchen. Ms. DeVeau opened the refrigerator and took out a pitcher of lavender lemonade, pouring out a cup for each of us.

"We found some things of Marley's." Aidy looked into her cup like she wasn't sure what she was about to ingest. "We thought you should know about them. It's kind of a long story, but Olivia got her hands on Marley's journal, and in it she says a lot of stuff—"

"Are you coming to tell me you think Marley might've known her father's gun had ammunition?" Ms. DeVeau interrupted.

Aidy coughed up the small sip of lemonade she'd started to swallow.

"We read those journals a long time ago," she told Aidy. "Gave over all of Marley's stuff to the police for a thorough investigation. If you think her father didn't have every hair on her hairbrush examined for clues, then you really don't know that man. He loved Marley some kind of fierce."

She took a long dragging gulp from her lemonade.

"Trust me when I tell you, we looked into every avenue. The official verdict was that she was a teenager coping with her parents' divorce and their quote 'unrealistic expectations' as most teenagers do. By acting out. Stealing important things like her father's gun, oblivious to the true consequence of such an action." She set down her glass. "Did you ever find the money she'd been storing in one of her broken trophies?"

It was my turn to stumble on a sip of lemonade.

"She was saving up to leave as soon as she turned eighteen. She loved to tell me that every chance she got." Ms. DeVeau stared into her counter. "Marley's death was an accident," she said softly.

Aidy thought she'd found a last unfinished thread; unaware it was in fact the very first thread to be tied up. Ms. DeVeau's certainty swiftly answered our biggest question.

Suddenly, Ms. DeVeau started crying. "I'm sorry, I'm sorry," she poured out, hugging me as if I were her own daughter, kissing and petting my head. "I didn't want her stuck in the same life I was." Ms. DeVeau clung onto me. "This place is all I have left of her." Her nails formed half-moons along the side of my arm.

"She loved you," I assured her. Even though Ms. DeVeau had been cruel at times, Marley wanted her mother to have a happiness that didn't exist. Marley tried to build it anyway. Much like the rest of us. Skewering rules and logic for love.

"She loved you too," Ms. DeVeau said.

A truce of sorts unfolded between us. We recognized our shared ability to play grand roles. Knew it was a way to remember Marley. We didn't agree with each other's interpretations, but we accepted the talent. The whole exchange seemed to be the only way Ms. DeVeau knew how to admit she'd gone too far. She told it to me through her tight grasp and genuine tears; another secret hidden in plain sight.

"I'm sorry about your garden," I told her.

She laughed. She knew a good transition when she saw one. "What were you trying to do out there?"

"Finish one of Marley's adventures."

"The one with the buried treasure and the map?"

"How'd you know?"

"I read the journals. And I know everything you kids used to get into." She pasted on her most knowing smirk, so reminiscent of Marley, I had to do a double take. "Wasn't it supposed to be some plan to get me back together with her father? If so, I can tell you that certainly won't be happening."

"I didn't realize that's what it was supposed to be, so I made it about the Albany kids," I said.

"Trust me, no hard feelings there." Ms. DeVeau swirled her finger around the edge of her cup. "You know what's funny about that map she and her dad made? That's how I chose this house. She'd marked it on there. It was vacant when she was alive, of course. Up for sale for years and years. I bought it because I knew it meant something to her, whatever that something was."

Ms. DeVeau's Marley was a house. And the idea of a town. Broader than the Marleys I knew, but still the same girl. Facets of the prism I'd never examined. There was still so much to know about Marley Bricket.

"Anyway," Ms. DeVeau said, pulled back from the edge of her memory. "Did you?"

"Did I what?"

"Finish the adventure."

I shrugged. "Kind of hard to tell."

"If it's my daughter's plan, it's never done."

A phone started ringing. It went on for three long, shrill shrieks before Aidy realized it was hers. "Dad left it for me on the counter," she said, fumbling around in her purse. "I totally forgot." Harrison's name flashed up on the screen. "I'm going to grab this, if that's all right," she told Ms. DeVeau.

Marley's mother flicked her wrist, happy to gain an unexpected moment to gather herself. "Go ahead." She blotted her eyes with the edge of a napkin.

"Hello?... What do you mean?... Where at?... We're still here, but I think we're done... Okay... Yeah, we'll come right over." Aidy hung up and looked at me, her eyes so wide that pink veins were visible.

"What did I tell you?" Ms. DeVeau said with the ghost of a laugh.

We thanked her for the lemonade. I promised to come by and help with the garden. Aidy complimented her hat. Ms. DeVeau stood in repose, lips pressed into teeth, barring her from saying any more. When I turned around to steal one last glimpse, she was standing in her door frame, a hand across her chest, clutching at her heart.

I couldn't keep up with Aidy. She glided, using the many inches she had on me to her full advantage. She went fast, but she wouldn't run. Every time her pace came close, she did a little hop to slow up.

"What is it?" I begged. She wouldn't answer.

Into the mouth of the haunted house we went. We hurried up the stairs and down the hall to the bedroom.

Nick and Harrison stood over a floorboard that had been wedged loose. In his hands, Nick held a yellowed piece of loose-leaf paper.

"On the map," Harrison panted out. "Was this place marked?"

"Of course," I said.

"What did you put here?"

I pulled open cabinets in my brain. Shuffled through piles of memories. Had I forgotten this place? I hoped Aidy would hold her party here. That's what I planned around its marking on the map.

"Nothing," I said, touching my lips as the syllables released, taking shape in front of me. I didn't do this. Marley did. Marley did. Marley did.

Nothing was happening.

It was real.

Nick cleared his throat and began to read.

Dearest Nicky Cline,

Do you hate it when I call you Nicky? I should stop, but I can't help it. Adults break hearts. I want you to stay a boy forever. You can't, though. You have to grow up. If it's not me that makes you, someone else will. That's how it works, my friend. Somebody somewhere decided that long before you or I ever came around. It's like heartbreak was designed into the fabric of the universe. It gets us all eventually.

I always make you stand guard. That doesn't mean you should stop being an investigator, though. If you watch and you search at the same time, you'll already know what it is you're going to find, because you've been paying closer attention. Know what I mean?

I'm sure you don't. I'm making zero sense.

Anyway, I've hidden this letter for you. It's the end of the Adventure, and it's perfect, because you will never find it. You have absolutely no reason to come up here. Our visit to this house was less than exciting. I really hoped you guys would like it, but you didn't get it at all. That's how it goes sometimes when it comes to our group.

That's okay. I still like it. I can sit here and think without being distracted. For as long as I can remember, I've been sneaking into vacant houses to clear my head. This place has become one of my favorites. Sometimes I can hear the Stantons next door. Otherwise, it's perfectly still. Nothing but me and my thoughts.

Wow. How perfect. Right at this moment, I can hear Ollie screaming at Aidy. They must be outside. She's yelling something about it not being her turn to vacuum. It's kind of hilarious.

Okay. They went back inside.

It's quiet again.

I'm writing these words to you because then they are permanent, even if you never read them. Maybe that's all it takes to make sure they come true. My thoughts will crumble through the floorboards and seep into the ground, out and back into the universe again. They'll reach you wherever you are. They'll stop you from being broken by someone else.

I choose to write to you because you're different. You look in ways other people don't. Ollie does too, but a lot of the times, she's wasting that by looking too much at me. I'm not anyone she needs to copy. Trust me.

Okay. I can't lie. It's flattering. I don't hate it. I think she's about five trillion times smarter than me, and I'm afraid of what that means. Heartbreak might soften her. It honestly might help. Not that you should be the one to do it. Don't go getting ideas.

I know one day it'll happen with you two. You guys are practically babies, and it's so obvious even my mom's noticed, and she's never paying attention to anyone but me and my magnificent shortcomings. But I mean it when I say you shouldn't be the one to break Ollie. Let me handle it. I'll figure out a way to do it better. Everyone has their eyes on you when she's the one to watch.

So watch. Do your job. But don't forget to search.

See what I mean? It's a complicated thing.

Promise me you'll consider your choices before you make them. One second could create the moment that breaks you forever. I'm trying to stop it, and I already know I'll fail. So when it happens, I hope someone can find a way to mend you. I'd like to believe we canŌt be broken beyond repair.

And since this is the end, I'll tell you the truth about the Adventure. It isn't actually supposed to have an end. If I gave you guys a prize and said it was over, we wouldn't have anything to chase. So I make sure you guys never reach it.

Right now you're thinking: Marley, what are you talking about? You just told me this was the end.

Well, Nick, I'm a woman of my word. Every year I promise that there's a prize, so I created one, but I've hidden it so well you won't ever find it. Muahaha.

May you search for years and years.

Our whole lives, I hope. We, the kids of Albany Lane, will always search. And we will always have each other. That's way more than most people can say.

Nothing is ever gonna happen to change that.

Love always,

Marley Bricket

21

USING THE LONG, LOOPED CURSIVE I COULD NEVER SUCCESS-fully replicate, Marley Bricket left a letter for the one person I hadn't. The girl who wished to stop wishing put one wish into the world. Her words did in fact seep into the ground. They spread to the house next door, where a little girl with big ideas waited with her ear pressed to the soil.

I took the wish and made it my own.

"I found it," Harrison told me as soon as I finished reading Nick's letter. "I didn't even mean to. I was doing exactly what I'm doing right now"—he was kicking—"and a floorboard wiggled." He stopped moving. "I get it," he said to me. "Why you did every-thing you did."

Aidy cranked her neck so fast, her ponytail lashed her own face.

"Okay, not everything," Harrison clarified. "But why you'd go in her room and look at her stuff and all that? It's kind of like sitting in silence. Like in the tunnel. Once you do it for long enough, you can hear the noise you didn't notice before. That's what it was like being with her stuff too. Even being near it. When I was out last night trying to find where you hid all of it, I just stopped and listened. I could imagine where Marley would put it. I don't want to say I heard her, but yeah, like I said, I get it." He gave me a cautious half smile, raising the side of his face that was turned away from Aidy. "Earlier, I was up here by myself, looking around and thinking about her. Boom, the floorboard comes loose."

My mouth wiggled, trying to decide if he got a smile back. My lips folded inward and spread anyway. He did understand, in his own way, and because of that, he found a piece of the real Marley no one ever knew about.

He found the end of the Adventure.

The four of us sat up in that room for a while, taking turns passing the letter back and forth, not saying anything. I think we were all imagining ourselves as Marley, trying to hear the world around us as she once had.

Eventually, Aidy put an end to it. "We have to finish Dad's to-do list," she whispered.

We left the haunted house and went back to our own, spending the rest of the afternoon ticking off items on my dad's list, as uneventful as it was productive. Nick kept his letter in the back pocket of his jeans. Seeing it sticking out, a tiny triangle of our Marley meant just for him, filled me with hope.

Everything was something.

I'd been right all along.

My dad came home early. First, he inspected my lightly bruised face, accepting my half-truth about falling while outside; then, he inspected our house, most impressed at the sight of my bedroom carpet, marred only by the small cigarette mark Ruby had burned into it all those years ago.

Mom came home sometime after, trailing happy tears from top to bottom. A clean garage! My neat bedroom! Even my bruises did not deter her. She was so pleased, she invited Harrison and Nick to stay for dinner.

Despite my best efforts to stay grounded, I drifted up one last time, so high above reality I could do nothing but watch us all as we sat around the dinner table making small talk. It was a perfect window into the life we might have had. A world where Marley would be eating dinner three doors down from us, home from college for a few weeks. Her great-great-grandfather's birdhouse clock would chirp out its hourly greeting, that California quail celebrating his temporary freedom right as Marley would back her chair away from the table.

"I'm going over to the Stantons'," she'd tell her dad.

"Be home before midnight," he'd tell her.

"Dad, please. I'm an adult now."

"I know, but you're still my baby girl."

I never had to close my eyes to see it, but I needed to close them to erase it. Squeezing tight, I releasing that imagined life like a balloon, letting it float off without me attached to it. When I opened my eyes again, Nick placed his hand atop my leg and squeezed three times.

I put my hand atop his and squeezed back.

We finished our meal. Nick offered to wash the plates. Harrison offered to take out the trash.

"Time for the boys to be on their way," Dad said when their voluntary chores had been completed.

Aidy and I escorted them to our front door.

"Thanks," Harrison whispered to me. "I needed this."

"You're welcome," I said. "Bro."

"Nah," he responded with a laugh. He gave me a quick, committed hug, then kissed Aidy on the cheek. "Love you," he told her. He ducked his head and took a left, off to his spot along Albany Lane.

"Love you too," she replied.

The three of us watched his shadow disappear into the night. Aidy turned to Nick and me. Her lips squeezed tight as she swallowed back what looked like tears. "I'm sorry," she said. "I know it's not enough, but I am." She left before she got any more emotional, bounding up the stairs and into her bedroom.

Nick and I stepped outside. We craned our heads to see the sky above us. No matter how I squinted, my Marley was indecipherable among the blur of stars.

"Do you feel her anymore?" I asked him.

"Not like I did before."

"Me neither. But I know she's still there."

"I do too."

Nick and I stayed like that, standing side by side, gazing at the stars, until my dad came out to say Nick needed to go home.

Nick kissed my cheek. "Goodbye, Olivia," he said.

"Goodbye, Nick." He turned left, crossing Arbor Street and jogging into his house along Albany Lane, the last of Marley's chess pieces to be returned to position.

When I went back inside, I learned Dad didn't buy the last-minute Hail Mary save I'd pulled off. He put more stock in Aidy's words from the night prior, and explained to me that I needed to pack a bag for camp. Aidy came downstairs to stand beside my dad, her eyes pained but certain. Plans had been made, and there was no room for changes in execution.

"You need to be there, Olivia," she said. "You need to find yourself again."

So, I've been going through the same motions I did five years ago. Taking the classes, speaking with new therapists and counselors and support groups. Swimming. Eating a thousand of the little yogurt parfait cups they make. The new ropes course is nice, my dad was right about that.

It's not the same as it was five years ago when I balled my fists and shouted, "You don't understand," every time they tried to tell me my Marley was a coping mechanism. A response to the trauma I'd suffered. Everything but a person.

Now I'm using my time here to find my own interests again. Make the most of the next few weeks posted up in cabin four. The other people here, as young as seven and as old as seventeen, are all the strange kind of normal, which is to say they're the kind of people I appreciate. I don't mind Camp Califree. In fact, I quite like it.

It's never been about hating it.

It's always been about leaving home.

But I have to remember who I am without Marley on my shoulders. Even though I don't carry her anymore, I still keep her with me in different ways. And I want my family and friends to see that it's okay for me to do that. I want to iron out all the kinks in my truth and present them with something that's completely mine.

I want to show my sister, who held me so tightly when I left and whispered to me, calm as the sky before a tornado, "Let yourself heal."

I want to show my parents, who kissed my forehead and waved me off, then leaned into one another like bookends without a book to hold.

I want to show the other kids on Albany, who write me letters and send me gifts. The rock from Ruby sits beside me now. She drew a star on it for me. And a tiny letter *M*.

I want to show everyone, from the other residents of Cadence to complete strangers, that things that are lost are not gone.

I'd never been on an airplane before I came here for the first time. When I'd watch one fly overhead, I didn't consider a person inside it, pressing their forehead against the window, seeing the towns below as nothing more than colors and shapes: beige square, green circle, jagged brown triangle.

On my way here for the second time, I realized that below me, someone must be standing there watching like I used to, full of hopes and dreams and wishes and wants, pains and truths so large they could reach up and touch my plane. No matter how hard I looked, I never saw that person. They never saw me.

Both of us were there.

It's up to every one of us to realize that a white sliver in the sky is not only an airplane, and the earth below it is not only colors and shapes. It is people inside of people inside of people, all of us filled with pieces of the ones who came before us. We hold on to their strengths and their weaknesses. Their memories. Their laugh. Their scent. Their spirit.

Believe me.

Just *believe* at all, because it always takes more than one person to strengthen the power of something. If ever someone stops believing—gives up hope and accepts that someone is lost forever—there is another person who has to try harder. Hold on tighter. Sometimes too tight.

The beautiful thing is, if the person who gave up finds the courage to return, to pick back up what they've tried to leave behind, the load is lighter for all.

I want everyone to remember that.

There's so much to remember, isn't there? How can we ever keep track of it all?

With the help of others, of course.

In the endless stream of things to keep track of, my name and my story might get misplaced as years pass. But by being here now, I will remain somewhere inside of everyone I've ever met. I will be remembered through them in ways they might not notice. They will pass me on to their family and friends. I'll go out and out until I've touched all corners of the earth, just by stepping outside of my small town and into the bigger world. I will not look the same as I do to myself or those that know me. But I will be in every beige square and green circle, waving my arms at the people inside the planes overhead.

Marley's wishes are now my wishes are now my friend's wishes are now the next person's, and so on and so on.

That's how I will send Marley out of Cadence and into the world she never got to meet. That's how I will set her free, remembered as she was, not by what happened to her. She existed in every corner of this story, and now she exists in new shapes yet to come, reaching further than she ever could've imagined on her own, finally cashing in the pennies and dimes she saved inside her trophy.

From now until forever, the world will never be without Marley Bricket.

ACKNOWLEDGMENTS

For a while, this story wanted to press on all my bruises and pour salt in all my wounds. But I'm writing my thank-yous, which means this book and I finally set aside our differences and started working together. It also means you, dear reader, are in possession of a very specific, jagged, tender, emotional, imperfect piece of my heart. It will never stop being a surreal, gratifying thrill to know you are here.

My agent, Taylor Haggerty, you handle my freak-outs and my celebrations with poise and care. I am forever grateful you plucked me out of your slush pile all those years ago. You are the best teammate in this publishing adventure.

My editor, Annie Berger, you helped me see this story in a different light, pushing me to make it stronger. Thank you so much for believing in this book and in my ability to complete it. Immense gratitude to the entire Sourcebooks Fire crew: editorial assistant Sarah Kasman; production editor Cassie Gutman; copy editor Christa Desir; art director Nicole Hower, for my striking cover; and everyone else involved in the production and distribution of this book.

Mom, while I was growing up, you gave me space to find my voice and embrace my passions. The older I get, the more grateful I am for that freedom. Thank you for your art and your unending love. Dad, you are the perfect calm to my storm. You listen without judgment and you remember everything that matters. You keep me going, #40. My siblings, you've made me the luckiest youngest child ever. I got everything. A hilarious, protective older brother in John. A second mom in Liz. A cool, confident inspiration in Raina. And a mortal enemy turned best friend in Rose. I love you all so much. I am also the proudest aunt in the world. Major embarrassing auntie hugs to Deklin, Brielle, Caleb, Brannon, Lily, Emma, and Sophie.

My writerly people: Bree Barton, Dana Davis, Jilly Gagnon, Britta Lundin, Maura Milan, Farrah Penn, Lana Popovic, Aminah Mae Safi (a.k.a. the friend I dreamed up in *What You Left Me* come to life), Chelsea Sedoti, Austin Siegemund-Broka, Lisa Super, Emily Wibberley, and all the other Electric Eighteens I know and love—not only are all of you extreme talents, you're all unfathomably generous. I'd be lost without the support, feedback, critiques, advice, laughs, joys, and woes we've shared. And the snacks. I love when we share snacks.

My sweet, nonwriterly friends: bless you all for the pictures, reading updates, and general cheerleading I've received. Seeing all of you interact with my work really touches my heart. Major hugs to Ryan S., Brittany, Jake, Brian, my mom, and my sisters Liz and Rose for the very early reads on this story. Full-volume shout-out to Oak Forest, Illinois, for the enduring support. To the *Grease* Ten-Year Reunion cast, that iconic performance brings a full-wattage smile to my face every single day. The Class of '08 is forever. My extended Morrissey clan, few people do it as large, loud, and loyal as the South Side Irish. I am four-leaf-clover lucky to call all of you family. To the 2018 Chicago Cubs, I watched your games nearly every time I sat down to edit this book. Play by play and page by page, we both got through it. You'll get 'em next year.

Mrs. Donna Tyrka, my third-grade teacher, you surprised me at my hometown book event, showing up with an old class picture in hand. We cried as we hugged each other. You taught me everything from cursive to creative writing to being a good person. I've said it before, I'll say it again—educators are superheroes, and you, Mrs. Tyrka, are one of the best.

My gymnasts, who always manage to make me believe again, right when I'm at my lowest—over and over, you girls prove to me that courage defeats fear. That is a greater lesson than any gymnastics skill I could ever teach you. May you never lose your heart and determination.

My childhood friends, from the neighborhood group to the Arbor Park kids—this story is not *our* story, but it exists because of all of you. I carry deep affection for every person I've befriended along the way. Bianca Reyes, specifically, asking you to be my friend during kindergarten nap time might be the best proposition I've ever made. Distance and time can do nothing to tarnish your impact on my life. I will always love you as much as we inexplicably loved CoverGirl makeup our freshman year of high school. Thank you for the secret languages, the late nights telling ghost stories, the way your whole family always welcomed me with open arms, and all the other memories we know by heart.

And finally, Elizabeth O'Connor, the kindest, gentlest, smartest girl in any room—since you left this world, not a day has passed that I don't marvel at the picture of you and me on my wall. You're smiling, looking off in the distance at something I can't see. It so perfectly captures your essence. Bright. Mysterious. Curious. Beautiful. Warm. Unforgettable. Lizzy, you are forever loved and missed beyond measure. I wrote this book years before you passed, but revising it after you were gone taught me something invaluable: the light you gave the world will never go out.

DON'T MISS BRIDGET MORRISSEY'S

★ "A tragic, suspenseful, and inspiring novel."
—*Publisher's Weekly*, Starred Review

1

FRIDAY, JUNE 8

Right here in the middle, with 867 other sweaty kids herded like cattle around me, I want to die. End it all on the football field. Burn up into ash and leave behind this hideous robe. There's no way I'm spending my afterlife wearing yellow polyester.

The first thing I did when I walked out here today was make an official announcement to everyone in my general vicinity. "In this gown, I am a disgrace to the McGee family name," I said.

I can't have my classmates thinking I don't know how ridiculous I look. I know, okay?

I know.

I'm not the most ridiculous person here though. That award goes to our valedictorian, Steve Taggart. There's no refund on the six minutes of my life I'm currently donating to his speech about how we're all birds taking flight. Dude, I'm not a bird. I'm

Martin McGee. I'm hot, I'm bored, and I don't have anyone to talk to right now. Forgive me while my eyes glaze over as I drift off into oblivion.

If I counted, and I mean if I got really specific, I'd say I know about four hundred of the people graduating today. That's including, like, the drug dealer who sits at my study hall table, that super tall blond who has a cross-country picture on the wall by the main entrance, and the girl who threw up before picture day in first grade. I don't see any of them right now. Based on the amount of random people around me, this could straight up be my first day of school.

Okay, maybe I don't want to die, but I could go for teleportation. I'd find Spits and talk him out of our bet. When this is all over, I'll need my ten bucks for a celebratory meal. It's the only money I have to my name, and, well, high school will be done.

That calls for a sandwich.

......

Oh, Steve Taggart. Sweat has painted circles through his yellow robe. The random smattering of claps that follow his final sentence must be more for his underarm artwork than his terrible speech. My personal applause is for the end of Steve Taggart's reign as smartest kid in school. See you in hell, Steve Taggart! Or at Notre Dame, but maybe the universe will grant me one kindness and make it so we never cross paths there.

At the rate I'm going, it won't be a problem.

Steve walks back to his spot, smug and sweat-drenched, and settles into the innermost aisle seat of the front row. The rest of the top ten sit alongside him in order of class rank. The chosen ones.

I'm in the miserable middle, plain old Petra McGowan of the M section, sandwiched between my alphabetical neighbors. Three different middle schools merged into our high school, and while there are faces nearby that I've known my whole life, there are also faces I swear I've never seen before. Like the two complete strangers on either side of me. For four years, we've coexisted, sharing walls and desks and hall passes and gossip without ever managing to cross paths. When you try hard to be good at this whole school thing, you end up with the same group of people in every class. As the years tick by, the numbers dwindle. No one ever randomly decides to take an AP course. This is the first and only time we've all been united; a bunch of squirming and vibrating cells being observed by the microscope that is the high-noon sun, waiting for this pomp and circumstance to end.

Steve Taggart's speech marks the end of one part of the ceremony and the beginning of the next—the ever-important receipt of the diploma. It begins with the parade of our most intelligent: Valedictorian Steve, Salutatorian Marissa Huang, third in the class Jay Cattaro, and then, my favorite mouthful of a name, Cameron Catherine Elizabeth Hannafin-Bower.

Cameron's wiry auburn hair engulfs her profile until she becomes nothing but a moving ball of energy, all warm colors and excited twitches. She turns to face the crowd and flashes her most vibrant gap-toothed smile at me. Or in my general vicinity. I'm not sure she can see this far back. Rank eleventh like me, and there is no fanfare. You're deep among the plebeians, permanently imprinting your lower half into a foldout plastic chair while waiting for your spot in the alphabet.

At least I was blessed with McGowan for a last name, not Prabhu or Stetson. Poor Aminah and Daniel. It'll be hours before they get to graduate. *P* and *S* may not seem very far from me, but I'm almost positive a third of our graduating glass has an *M* last name.

Mister tenth in the class—the last of the spots that could have been mine if things had been different—walks across the stage, ending the stream of academic overachievers getting their only moment of priority over the athletes.

How nice it would've been to get that single candle flicker of justice.

The march of the mundane begins with Alex Abraham. His mom breaks the rules and uses a blow horn when his name is called, sending a much-needed jolt of energy through our class. The boy next to me jumps out of his seat.

......

Alex Abraham's mom uses a blow horn. I jump out of my seat.

"Aw, c'mon," I say to myself. And kind of to the girl next to me. She turns a little, brushing a piece of her hair out of her eyes to see me, so I keep going. "Alex Abraham's gotta be angling for some kind of last-ditch recognition as a rebel or something. I swear I've never heard that kid say more than five words in my whole life. Now he's got the family bringing out blow horns? Let it go, kid. It's over."

The girl does something halfway between laughing and shrugging. We aren't supposed to talk, but it's a rule without consequence. It's not like they'll take away our diplomas now.

I pass time by trying to list every Cubs manager I can recall, in reverse chronological order. I'm all the way back to Leo Durocher (1966–1972), when I catch sight of Spits shuffling into his seat. He's arrived right in between the graduations of Bryant Carpenter and Eduardo Carrera, and he's causing a tiny commotion while making his way down his row. The other graduates yelp as he trips over their feet. Spits just laughs.

"He's such a loser," I mutter, half laughing to myself.

"I'll say," the girl next to me quips back.

I'm stunned. I shoot her a look, but she's got her eyes right back on her hands, the smallest trace of a smile hanging on her lips.

A paper airplane crashes into the lap of the dude on my other side, who has somehow managed to stay asleep through the horn blowing. Good for him. I look around for a culprit—it's Spits of course, his metal mouth on full display, grinning like he took a hit seconds before and is riding the high. Classic. He points to the airplane.

bet you can't get that girl next to you to come tonight.
also get my ten bucks ready.

—spitty

"Wanna hear something funny?" I ask the girl. Might as well make one last friend before I dance across the stage, grab my damn diploma, and keg stand my way into a victorious summer. "My buddy, uh, Spencer, bet me ten bucks that my mom will yell out Marty McFly when they call my name."

"Why would she do that?"

"Because my name's Martin McGee."

"Then who is Marty McFly?"

"You have to know who Marty McFly is."

"A sports guy?"

My laugh is the blow horn now. It scares her. "Come to my party tonight," I say. "I'll lend you *Back to the Future*."

"Where's it at?" she asks. It looks like one of her cheeks gets red, but it's hard to tell when she's facing the other direction. Her hair's curled in that way all girls seem to do for special occasions, pieces of it twisted like coiled ribbons around her head. She wraps one strand around her finger until it becomes a perfect brown spiral.

"My place," I tell the girl. "Mama Dorothy lets me use our basement for parties. Everyone has to put their car keys in a bowl and promise to spend the night if they drink. I live right behind the school." I point toward the trees beyond the field. "Ugly orange house with a basketball hoop in the driveway. You can't miss it."

"Cool," she says. She puts her hands in her lap and starts chipping off the sparkly stuff on her nails.

......

This whole ordeal is supposed to be my last punishment, closing up shop on the era that will someday be known as *the time Petra just graduated*. Emphasis on the word *just*, as if plain graduation is a disease to be contracted, because there isn't anything to follow it with, such as *in the top ten*, like my sister Jessica, or even better, *as the valedictorian*, like my sister Caroline.

Just graduated.

But here's Martin McGee. Interrupting me.

"Gotta kill the time," he says, "or this thing is gonna kill me." He has the delivery of a stand-up comedian, every word crackling with extra flair so that no sentence sounds ordinary.

"I hear you," I respond, wiping away the newest beads of sweat forming along my hairline. I spent half an hour curling my hair just right, and the heat has been trying its hardest to undo all my work.

Our principal cuts in front of the man reciting the names. "In the interest of time, we ask that everyone refrain from making any noises for the remainder of the ceremony. Thank you."

Someone boos in an act of defiance.

"Wow. Gotta love this town," Martin mutters under his breath.

I've never understood why you're supposed to feel this unfounded disdain for where you come from, as if it is the unclassiest, most smothering place that ever existed. "I like it just fine," I say to him.

"You might be the first."

We go quiet again.

......

Spits makes faces at me. *You failed*, he mouths, smiling of course, and pointing to the girl, who's kind of pretending to ignore me by leaning forward and staring at the grass. I wad up the note and try to throw it at Spits, but it bounces off the head of someone who doesn't even react.

"My friend over there told me to invite you to my party. He thinks I failed," I say to the girl.

"How? You already invited me."

"Failing would be you not showing up."

"How does he know that I won't go?"

"Exactly. Orange house. Basketball hoop. Ten o'clock."

"We'll see."

"Who are you?"

"The name next to yours in the yearbook," she says.

I try to get a good look at her, but the sun's so bright she becomes her own kind of light. Her eyes are all I can make out. They're brown, but a shiny kind, like maple syrup glistening on a pancake.

Man, I'm hungry.

"Guess I need to pay better attention to the yearbook," I say.

"Same," she whispers.

......

When I open my mouth to speak, my voice crackles with Martin's style of speech, one so easy to fall into, I do it without even realizing. My dress may as well be made of concrete. It blocks my exasperated air from releasing, shoving it into space around my rib cage.

"We've got a whole list of things to do," he says. "Number one, watch *Back to the Future*. I can't sleep until you've met the real Marty McFly."

"You know I can stream it, right?"

"You can?" His tone isn't mocking, just playful. "My copy is special though. It's the Marty 'Fly' McGee platinum edition. Extremely rare. Actually, one of a kind."

"Wow. What an honor."

"Please, please. It's not a big deal. I don't like to make a fuss. At the end of the day, I'm just a regular guy."

We share a laugh. As it tapers out, there's a pause, like in the space between words, something has shifted. It's almost awkward.

Martin swoops back in to save the moment. "All right, back to my list. Number two, look at our yearbook. If I've missed you, my alphabetical neighbor I've never been put next to at any other school thing, who knows what else might be in there?" He pauses to smile at me. Mouth open, molars visible, so lacking in self-consciousness that I have to bite the inside of my cheek to keep myself from smiling too big in return. "Number three, I'm gonna need you to show me what there is to love about this place." He takes out his phone. "So, Graduation Girl, how about a phone number for your new friend Marty McGee?"

I shake my head no, because if there is one lesson I will take away from my four years here, one definitive thing I have learned, the hard way, it is to beware the smiling sweet talker.

Stop while you're ahead, Petra.

You have more important things to accomplish this weekend.

......

Graduation Girl's got her own set of tricks. No name. Won't give me her number. Smells like that fancy soap store in the mall where all the girls get their bath bombs. "Seriously though, how have we never met?" I ask her.

Ms. Hornsby, resident terrifying math teacher, walks by to shush us. Graduation Girl gets all flustered, which makes me laugh. "What can she do to us for talking?" GG doesn't answer. "I've got a lot of bucket list items to cross off with you," I say, trying to puff out my voice so it sounds bigger. More confident.

"Martin!" Ms. Hornsby scolds. "Be quiet!"

"Yeah, Martin," GG jokes, "be quiet." She plays it like she's kidding, but I can tell she means it. Her chipped-off nail polish is all over the lap of her gown, and she's going to town on the little that is left on her nails.

My mind runs through all the ways I could get her to notice me again. There's always flicking her arm. Eh. Being annoying doesn't seem like the right move. I look around for another idea and accidentally make hard eye contact with Hornsby, which makes me sweat, which makes me overcompensate, which makes me start humming, which is actually the perfect solution. It's not talking. It's fair game.

After a big throat clear and a good neck crack, I push air through my teeth to recreate the synthesized greatness of Van Halen. No human being can resist the musical mastery that is "Jump."

I check in on Graduation Girl. The ridiculousness of my humming should be at least a half smile's worth of points from her.

Nope. She is stone-faced. Royal guards would be jealous.

I amp up my effort, hammering the song's rhythm into my leg and humming louder. I did choir in grade school, so I know I'm nailing my pitches (boy sopranos represent!), but the end of the introduction is nearing, and the magic of the music doesn't seem to be affecting her. Still, I hit the final majestic synth high notes, burying my head into my neck to give the kind of commitment the song deserves, and *sweet-holy-patron-saint-of-Cubs-baseball-Ernie-Banks,* I catch sight of movement on the ground.

It's her foot. Tapping along.

Like David Lee Roth and Sammy Hagar and every other

random lead singer they've had, she comes in for the first line. "*Dog it off,*" she sings under her breath. The rest comes out as an incoherent mumble.

The lyrics are so wrong I almost keel over and die laughing. I decide to bring my other hand in for a better drum section instead. This is too good to stop. GG takes over the humming, and I pick up the next line of the song (with the correct lyrics, of course) as if we planned it this way all along. We look at each other, her pounding the beat into the grass and me into my legs, and we sing together until we get to the chorus's lead-in. Graduation Girl hits me with the most ridiculously wrong lyrics of all time, but she is one hundred percent committed to the feeling. When it comes time to speak the line before the chorus, I say it all cool, and then she echoes back the title with perfect timing, shouting it with the exact amount of power and feeling required. She throws her head back and laughs at herself. It's like an ad for shampoo the way her hair falls over the edge of her chair, all long and curly and flowing.

"Shut up!" the no-longer-sleeping guy on the other side of me whisper-yells.

Graduation Girl and I laugh louder. "My dad loves that song," she whispers, catching her volume. "We always just make up the words as we go."

"I can tell," I say. "My dad loves it too. Official postseason anthem for the 1984 Cubs, baby. Big ups to two of the all-time greats, Rick Sutcliffe and Ryne Sandberg. Love you, Rick and Ryno." I pat my chest and then blow a kiss to the Rick and Ryne in my head.

Ms. Hornsby pulls her finger to her mouth and gives the loudest shush ever known to man. Graduation Girl straightens up.

......

This is outrageous. Four years of high school have come and gone without a single sighting of Martin McGee, now here we are singing our respective fathers' favorite eighties rock anthem together on the football field. Ms. Hornsby has threatened to remove Martin from the ceremony if he speaks again. He's mostly obeying. Just nudging me and tapping my foot with his.

I can feel my head getting lighter, pulling me out of my seat and into the clouds, loosening the anchor at the bottom of my stomach. I'm fighting for gravity. Fighting to stop my mind from wandering and wondering about this kid that's been one name away from me all this time.

Come on, Petra. Stay ahead.

You cannot piss off Ms. Hornsby now.

......

I play games on my phone to get Hornsby to leave me alone. I'd love to see her try and kick me out of here, but it's more entertaining to sit next to Graduation Girl. We communicate through elbow nudges and impatient foot shaking. Sometimes you don't need to speak to have a conversation.

After a long while, my fingers get so hot from the sun beating down and my phone's battery working overtime that I put it back in my pocket. Graduation Girl eyes me. It'll be worth it to get kicked out if I can just get her number. Hell, even her name. "Hey," I say.

She glares at me.

"I know. I know." I knock it down to a whisper. "What if we played a game? You give me three letters of the alphabet to guess from, one of which is the first letter of your name. If I get it right in less than thirty tries, you have to come to my party."

"That sounds like a terrible game." This girl cuts no corners.

"You're right. It does." I nudge her shoulder. "At least I'm not our valedictorian, out here talking about how we're all baby birds ready to leave the nest."

"Did you watch his nose when he spoke?" She sounds kind of mischievous when she asks. Clearly, I've chosen a solid topic.

"Can't say I was paying much attention to his nose, no. Why?"

"His nostrils always do this flapping thing every time he breathes."

It's not what I'm expecting her to say. I belly laugh. She wraps her hand around my forearm in a vice grip to silence me. "I'm sorry," I whisper, almost breaking. "How did you even notice that?"

"Steve Taggart is my archnemesis," she answers in the most deadpan whisper I've ever heard. "Knowing everything about him used to be my life's mission."

She's so close I can smell her again; this flowery, honey scent is wafting right up into my nostrils. I'm glad she seems to refuse to ever look at me because I might be doing the Steve Taggart thing too without even knowing it. "I think I need to make it my life's mission to know more about you."

ABOUT THE AUTHOR

Bridget Morrissey lives in Los Angeles, but proudly hails from Oak Forest, Illinois, a small yet mighty suburb just southwest of Chicago. When she's not writing, she can be found coaching gymnastics, reading in the corner of a coffee shop, or headlining concerts in her living room. Visit her online at bridgetjmorrissey.com.

FIREreads

#getbooklit

Your hub for the hottest young adult books!

Visit us online and sign up for our
newsletter at FIREreads.com

 @sourcebooksfire

 sourcebooksfire

 firereads.tumblr.com